Praise for Joseph Na

By the Blood of Heroes: The Great

"Relentless pacing, nonstop action, and improbable but nifty-sounding military gadgetry . . . power an unremittingly entertaining story line that [will have] . . . broad appeal for history buffs, horror aficionados, and fans of steampunk."

—*Publishers Weekly*

"*By the Blood of Heroes* is a genre-twisting madhouse of horror, Steampunk SF and zombie madness that is too damn much fun to miss! Buckle up . . . this is a wild ride!"

—JONATHAN MABERRY, *New York Times* bestseller of *Rot & Ruin* and *Flesh & Bone*

"Urban fantasy and sf author Nassise raises the alternate history genre to brilliant new heights. This is a treat for zombie and horror fans, military fiction aficionados, history buffs, and steampunk lovers alike, all of whom will be clamoring for the next installment."

—*Library Journal*

"Joseph Nassise's *By the Blood of Heroes* is that rarest of books, a genuine game-changer. This book . . . is a vital leap forward for the zombie genre. . . . I would argue [that] Joseph Nassise [is] the most important thing to happen to zombies since Max Brooks, and that's no hyperbole. He's really that good. . . . Madman Burke and his crew are about to take you to Hell and back."

—JOE MCKINNEY, author of *Dead City* and *Flesh Eaters*

"The pacing is fierce and as unrelenting as the undead themselves and Nassise is firing on full-auto—a tour-de-force of adrenaline-drenched mayhem. . . . Don't miss it!"

—JOE MERZ, author of *Shadow Warrior* and the Lawson Vampire series

ALSO BY JOSEPH NASSISE

The Great Undead War

By the Blood of Heroes

The Jeremiah Hunt Chronicle

Eyes to See
King of the Dead
Watcher of the Dark

The Templar Chronicles

The Heretic
A Scream of Angels
A Tear in the Sky
Infernal Games
Judgment Day

ON HER MAJESTY'S BEHALF

✪ ✪ ✪

THE GREAT UNDEAD WAR: BOOK II

JOSEPH NASSISE

HARPER Voyager
An Imprint of HarperCollinsPublishers

Harper Voyager and design is a trademark of HCP LLC.

ON HER MAJESTY'S BEHALF. Copyright © 2014 by Joseph Nassise.
All rights reserved. Printed in the United States of America. No
part of this book may be used or reproduced in any manner whatsoever without written permission except in the case of brief quo-
tations embodied in critical articles and reviews. For information
address HarperCollins Publishers, 195 Broadway, New York, NY
10007.

HarperCollins books may be purchased for educational, business,
or sales promotional use. For information please e-mail the Special
Markets Department at SPsales@harpercollins.com.

FIRST EDITION

Designed by Paula Szafranski

Library of Congress Cataloging-in-Publication Data

Nassise, Joseph.
   On her majesty's behalf / Joseph Nassise. —First edition.
     pages cm — (The great undead war ; book 2)
     ISBN 978-0-06-204878-3 (paperback)
   1. World War, 1914–1918—Fiction. 2. World War, 1914–1918—
England—London—Fiction. 3. Great Britain—Kings and
rulers—Fiction. 4. Zombies—Fiction. I. Title.
   PS3614.A785O54 2014
   813'.6—dc23
                                                   2014007994

14 15 16 17 18   OV/RRD   10 9 8 7 6 5 4 3 2 1

To all those who gave their lives
in the midst of the Great War

ON HER MAJESTY'S BEHALF

CHAPTER ONE

✪

MAJOR MICHAEL "MADMAN" Burke stood with his back to the sea and stared out into the semidarkness, watching for movement. Twenty feet behind the recently promoted major the waves lapped gently against the gunwale of the fishing boat that had carried him across the Channel, the same boat that, God willing, would take him back again when the mission was over.

What in heaven's name had possessed him to volunteer for this?

It had been nearly a week since the Germans had launched a surprise attack against the cities of London and New York. Tens of thousands of canisters of a new strain of corpse gas, one that affected the living rather than the dead, had been dropped onto the streets of the metropolises, turning those who came in contact into one of the ravaging undead now known as shredders.

News reports from the States indicated that New York had been cut off from the mainland, the bridges and tunnels blown to rubble. Armed units now patrolled the shoreline adjacent to the island of Manhattan, and two reinforced companies stood guard at the egress to the ruined tunnels that connected them, determined to keep those who had been infected by the gas from getting out into the rest of the country. There was talk of firebombing the city into oblivion in the hope of eliminating the threat in one fell swoop, though how much of that was rumor and how much was reality Burke didn't know.

London was a different issue entirely. The nature of the surrounding terrain made it nearly impossible to isolate the city and its infected inhabitants. To make matters worse, the municipal units that might have been called in to maintain order within the quarantine zone were unavailable. Practically every able-bodied male was on the other side of the Channel fighting to keep the German menace at bay. To add to the chaos, communication had been lost with those few military units, such as the King's Guard, that were stationed inside the city.

Allied Command outright refused to write off the city's population without making some kind of effort to save anyone who might have survived the bombardment. Burke had seen the effect of the gas and didn't have much hope that anyone was still alive within range of the bombing. There were some, however, much higher in the chain of command than he, who held to the theory that some people had to have been inside during the attack, people who had seen what was happening to those exposed to the gas and had then taken appropriate measures to protect themselves. Burke, however, didn't believe it—if the gas hadn't gotten them, the shredders would. What he believed didn't matter, especially in the wake of the destruction of one of the world's foremost cities. People simply refused to believe that there was nothing to be done and perhaps that was for the best. In the wake of the attack, a makeshift rescue operation had sprung up almost overnight. Aircraft had dropped millions of hastily printed leaflets onto the city streets, directing those who survived to make their way east along the Thames estuary where they could be picked up and transported out of the danger zone.

Every available boat was then pressed into service, from fishing trawlers to four-man dinghies. Night after night they crossed the Channel like some kind of ragtag fleet, determined to save whoever they could from the ravages of the undead. Burke had been helping with the evacuation effort for the last several days, searching for survivors along the coastline, until he'd been tapped for tonight's jaunt.

He shrugged his shoulders, trying to get the heavy pack resting on them to settle more comfortably. The pack was part of a new weapon straight out of Professor Graves's lab, a weapon Burke had agreed to field-test. It had sounded reasonable when the process had been explained to him back at headquarters, but now, with the sea at his back and the possibility of an unknown number of shredders in the darkness ahead of him, he was starting to second-guess the whole venture.

He glanced down at the shockgun, as Graves was calling it, and wondered briefly if it was going to work.

From a distance it looked like an ordinary rifle; it wasn't until you got close to it that you began to notice just how much it had been modified. The barrel was much wider, closer to the circumference of a shotgun than a rifle, and at least three inches longer than one might expect. A pair of capacitors sat on either side of a vacuum tube, which in turn rested atop the barrel in just about the spot where the breach normally would have been. The shoulder stock had been replaced by a large metallic canister wrapped in rubber. A power cord ran from the bottom of the canister to a small hand crank at his belt and from there around his waist and into the bottom of the rucksack on his back. It might not be the strangest thing he'd seen come out of Professor Graves's underground lair but it was certainly up there with the best of them.

As long as it worked, he didn't care how ugly it was. Just to be safe, he had his usual Colt 1911 automatic in a holster slung gunfighter style on his right thigh. Neither of them were a satisfactory replacement for the Tommy gun he'd been carrying around for the last few weeks, but carrying both the shockgun and the Tommy gun had been too awkward and he'd been forced to leave the latter behind.

Burke glanced over to where his two companions were climbing the short ladder from the deck of the fishing trawler onto the pier where he waited, noting, not for the first time, just how different the two men were.

Private Nicholas "Nick" Montagna was a twenty-two-year-old Italian American kid from Philadelphia, with a thick, burly frame and dark hair. Nick's father had been a watchmaker and his talent had clearly rubbed off on the next generation. Nick was a virtuoso with anything mechanical, be it an internal combustion motor or a tiny set of brass clockworks. He was loud, boisterous, and far too overeager, but Burke knew they'd drum the latter out of him pretty quickly.

Private Levi Cohen, on the other hand, was a quiet, shy kid a few years younger than Montagna. He hailed from a Jewish neighborhood in Brooklyn and had been some kind of scholar before enlisting. So far Burke had discovered that the man spoke English, Hebrew, French, and Italian. He wouldn't be surprised in the slightest if that was just the tip of the iceberg. Even though the kid was quiet, Burke got a sense of courage and unyielding determination from him. Burke had a hunch he'd be as steady as a rock in the thick of things and that was just the kind of man he wanted on his squad.

He waited for the two men to join him, saw the nervous look on both their faces, and decided a little pep talk might be in order.

"All right, look. We're here to do a job; the sooner we get it done, the sooner we go home. Stick close, keep your eyes open, and remember—as little noise as possible."

It wasn't much as pep talks go, but Burke had learned that dwelling too much on the details just made the new men more nervous than they already were. Short and sweet was best.

The mission planners had chosen Southend-on-Sea, a seaside community at the mouth of the Thames, as their designated test area. The residents had been evacuated in the early days of the rescue operation, leaving a ghost town behind that provided plenty of room for Burke and his team to operate in. Southend-on-Sea was roughly forty miles east of London, making it close enough for some of the more ambitious shredders to have wandered onto its streets but not so close that the entire town would be overrun with the undead.

Or so they hoped.

Uncertainty over just what they would encounter once they came ashore was the primary reason they had docked halfway along the Southend Pier.

That, and the mudflats.

Southend-on-Sea might technically be on the sea, but at low tide it was isolated by over a mile of water too shallow to even row a skiff through. As seaside vacations became more popular at the end of the last century, the town fathers had recognized that their beloved mudflats would keep them isolated and send seaborne traffic farther south to Margate and other deeper-water ports. Unwilling to see the probability of a prosperous future for the town falter, they'd pushed to have the Southend Pier built in order to allow boats, both large and small, to have a convenient place to dock. The pier was an immediate success and it was extended several times over the years until it reached its current length of nearly a mile and a half.

The pier was roughly twenty feet wide, with two rows of electric lamps bisecting its length equidistant from each side. The men's boots struck up a steady rhythm against the wooden floorboards as they made their way along its length, the sound sending an eerie chill up Burke's spine. It was so quiet that their footsteps felt like an intrusion, and he was worried that the sound would bring the shredders out like flies to a corpse, but he and his men managed to traverse the distance without incident.

The smell of the sea was sharp in Burke's nostrils as he started down the length of the pier, the ocean brine a welcome respite from the stench of the unburied dead and the corpse fires that hung about the battlefield like a noose around the neck. The sun had been up for a couple of hours, but the sky was filled with smoke from the fires that burned out of control in parts of London. It filtered out much of the light, and Burke felt like he could taste the ash on his tongue as easily as he could taste the sea.

A two-story brick pavilion with a sloping roof squatted like a spider at the end of the pier, guarding the entrance into the town, and Burke and his men approached it cautiously. So far they hadn't seen anyone, living or dead, but a building the size of the one in front of them could hide any number of horrors and Burke was determined to not walk into them blindly.

Three sets of double doors provided entrance to the pavilion. All the doors were closed, though the glass in two of them had been broken out. Burke headed for the nearest one after signaling for his two companions to wait where they were. He crept forward in a crouch, not wanting to be seen by anyone through the broken window. When he reached the door he flattened himself against the jamb beside it and then slowly rose up until he could get a glimpse of the interior.

Vendor carts knocked over, storefronts left open, the gleam of broken glass; plenty of signs that the building had been deserted in a hurry, but he didn't catch the telltale flash of movement.

"Follow me," he said. "And stay close."

He reached out with his mechanical hand and eased the door open, praying all the while that it wouldn't squeak, and then slipped inside. A moment later Montagna and Cohen followed suit.

They found themselves standing inside a large, open space. Two rows of thick, round support columns that were designed to hold the weight of the ceiling ran down the middle of the space. Between each column were three rows of iron benches, seating for those waiting to embark on a particular vessel. The walls around the interior space were lined with vendor stalls and small shops: a pastry shop, a butcher shop, a pub, a barbershop, and various shops that sold curios and souvenirs and the like.

Burke and the others had entered through the right-most door, putting them on one side of the open space. They began making their way along the length of the building toward the exit doors at the far end. Even from there they could see through the windows in the doors to the road beyond that led up a short hill to the town.

That was their destination.

They had crossed about half the length of the room when they heard a clatter come from inside one of the shops.

Burke immediately stopped, holding up a clenched fist in a signal for those behind him to stop as he settled into a crouch. The soft rustle he heard from behind him told him the others had understood.

He swept his gaze along the stalls on the side of the building where he'd heard the noise, searching for the source of the sound. Most of the shops and stalls were in shadow, and the dim light filtering in through the windows wasn't making things easy. Thankfully, whatever was making the noise wasn't trying to be quiet about it; the clatter came again and Burke was able to pinpoint it coming from the inside of a barbershop about twenty yards away.

Burke looked back at his companions who were crouched a few feet behind him, pointed at his eyes and then at the barbershop, indicating that he was going to take a look. Both men nodded that they understood.

One of the large columns providing support to the ceiling was a few yards in front of him. It would give him both an unobstructed view of the entrance as well as a bit of cover should he need it, so Burke chose that as his destination and headed for it as quietly as he could. He slipped in behind the column and peered cautiously around the edge just in time to see a shredder lurch unsteadily out the door of the shop and into the main room.

It had been just a boy when the gas fell; Burke guessed twelve, maybe fourteen years old. Tall and thin with a mop of dark, unruly hair that probably hadn't wanted to cooperate much even when the boy had been alive. Burke couldn't see the creature's gray-black skin in the building's dim light, but the way it stumbled about, seemingly disoriented, was proof enough that it was no longer one of the living.

Looks like we won't have to go into town after all, Burke thought.

He reached down and began to rapidly wind the hand crank on his belt at his hip. He winced at the high-pitched whine the crank made as he spun it in its seat, but that couldn't be helped—without the charge, the weapon was about as useful as a peashooter.

Across the room, the shredder began searching for the source of the sound, no doubt eager to rip and tear the flesh from Burke's bones in the characteristic way that had earned those infected by the gas their nickname.

The whine became a steady tone, indicating the gun was ready to be fired. Burke made a mental note to tell Graves that he had to find some way of reducing all the noise.

Nothing like having your weapon give away your position!

Graves had warned him that the gun delivered quite a kick so Burke held it the same way he would a room sweeper, with the stock tight against his waist and the barrel braced in his artificial hand. Satisfied, he stepped out from behind cover.

The shredder spun in his direction the moment he revealed himself, but it did not yet begin its inevitable charge.

Burke didn't intend to wait; he lined up the shot as best he could, braced himself, and pulled the trigger.

The gun roared, the sound echoing in the enclosed space, as a metal spike about the size of a tent peg shot from the barrel of the gun, sparking with the electrical charge he'd just given to it. It flew through the air with a whistling sound, headed directly for the shredder, and Burke was already starting to grin in victory when the shredder twitched to one side and the projectile shot harmlessly past and ricocheted off the wall of the barbershop behind it with the crackle of a sudden electrical discharge.

For a moment, the soldier and the shredder stared at each other with almost identical expressions of surprise.

Then the shredder screamed, a hideous shrieking sound, and launched itself forward in a frenzied rush.

CHAPTER TWO

HOLD YOUR FIRE!" Burke yelled to his companions, even as he snatched another spike off the row on his belt and jammed it into the muzzle of his weapon. Without taking his gaze off the oncoming shredder, his fingers found the crank on his belt and he began turning it as fast as he could to charge the projectile.

It was going to be close. The shredder was surging across the distance that separated them, tossing aside anything in his way that wasn't bolted down. When it reached the first of four rows of iron benches, it vaulted clear over them, leaving only three to go.

Come on, come on, Burke thought to himself. *Faster!*

The slowly rising whine from the crank seemed to mock him as the shredder vaulted another row of benches.

"Major?" asked a nervous voice behind him.

"Hold, I said!" Burke replied. He didn't know if it was Cohen or Montagna who had spoken, nor did he really care. All he wanted was to keep the shredder alive long enough to get off another shot. If they opened fire before he told them to, they could screw up the entire mission . . .

The shredder shrieked again as it vaulted the third row of benches, leaving only one bench between itself and Burke. Its attention was fixed on Burke and Burke alone; it was as if the shredder didn't even notice Montagna and Cohen crouched only a few feet behind.

Burke braced the gun, ready for another shot.

Come on, you ugly sonofabitch . . .

The shredder leaped up over the fourth and final row of benches.

Wanting to limit its ability to dodge, Burke fired while it was still in the air.

The spike roared out of the barrel of the gun and slammed straight into the shredder's chest. The instant the tip of the spike penetrated the shredder's flesh, the charge inside the projectile vented itself, sending a wave of electricity crashing through the creature's body. Sparks flew out of its ears, nose, and mouth as the charge sought the easiest escape route and the shredder crashed to the floor and slid to a halt practically at Burke's feet.

"Holy shit . . ." Montagna said from behind him.

Burke was inclined to agree; *holy shit* was right.

He grabbed another spike, shoved it into the barrel of the gun, and cranked the handle, waiting for the chime. Only when it came did he take a step forward for a closer look at the shredder, keeping the muzzle of the weapon trained on his opponent all the while.

The creature's eyes tracked his every move, indicating that it was still conscious. Its body, however, seemed to be locked in a rigid pose, bent backward at the waist so that the back of its head was pointing at the heels of its feet. Sparks were still emanating off the metal of the thing's belt buckle and the now blackened cross it wore about its neck.

Burke kicked the exposed sole of the creature's foot. Its eyes tracked his movement, but no other part of the creature's body moved. It was paralyzed, it seemed.

But for how long?

Burke didn't know. He'd asked Graves that very same question before leaving for the mission and the lanky professor had shrugged his shoulders and said something about the entire body being driven by various types of electrical impulses and how the shockgun's charge would affect those impulses at different rates in different individuals.

When Burke had pressed him, his friend had shrugged his shoulders and said, "Damned if I know."

It hadn't been the most reassuring of replies.

Burke would just have to make sure he was prepared if the shredder regained mobility before they were ready. Burke called out to the others. "Get those ropes over here. I want this thing trussed up tight before it wakes up."

Burke kept the shockgun trained on the shredder as Montagna and Cohen approached, but aside from rolling its eyes in their general direction, it didn't make a move as they stepped up beside it.

They had no idea how strong a shredder actually was and Burke wasn't taking any chances on that topic either. Under his supervision, the men bound the shredder around its ankles, calves, knees, thighs and then secured its arms flat alongside its chest with multiple turns of the rope. At first the men were hesitant, afraid it was suddenly going to regain its ability to attack, but after a few minutes of inactivity on the shredder's part, their confidence increased and they were able to get the job done with little delay. A leather hood was slipped over its head and cinched tight at the neck, to keep it from biting anyone when it finally began to regain its ability to move. Air holes had been punched in the hood just in case the thing still breathed in some bizarre fashion. No one really knew one way or the other; which was the reason Burke had agreed to undertake this crazy mission in the first place. They needed more firsthand knowledge of this new threat and they needed it quickly if they were going to be able to do anything to help the former residents of London and New York. Never mind the rest of the British and American populations.

This wasn't going to stay confined to the bombed-out metropolises; Burke knew that much already.

"All right, boys, let's get this thing back home to Professor Graves and let him worry about it from here on out," Burke said.

The two men argued about who was going to take what until

Burke ordered Montagna to pick up the creature's feet and Cohen to take it by the shoulders. Thankfully, the shredder had been a teenager before the change and wasn't too heavy to carry.

They retraced their steps across the pavilion floor and exited through the same door through which they had entered. Burke was struck by the sudden fear that they had been abandoned, that the grizzled old fishing captain had thought better of tying up to a dock in what was effectively shredder country and had sailed for open waters, and he breathed a sigh of relief when he stepped out into the meager sunlight and saw the trawler bobbing in the waves alongside the pier right where they had left it.

The trio moved as quickly as they could given the burden they carried, with Burke periodically turning about to look behind them and make certain that they weren't being snuck up on by a shredder they might have overlooked.

At one point, about halfway back to the boat, Burke thought he heard something. He stopped and turned back toward the pavilion, his ears straining to catch the sound a second time.

All he heard was the lapping of the water around the posts of the pier down beneath his feet and the footfalls of his men.

Must have been the wind.

Deciding it had to be either that or his imagination, he spun about and hustled to catch up with the others.

He had just reached them when the sound came again. This time it was recognizable as a human voice.

Could someone have remained behind after the evacuation?

As far as Burke knew, shredders couldn't speak. The change they underwent did something to their vocal cords, robbing them of the ability to articulate words or make anything beyond the most primitive of sounds. Still, that was no guarantee that what he'd heard had been a survivor; the sound had been too garbled and faint for him to be positive of anything.

Cohen and Montagna must have heard it also, for they lowered the shredder to the deck in front of them and turned to look back the way they had come, their rifles in hand.

"What the hell was that?" Montagna wanted to know.

Burke was about to tell the other man that he didn't know, but the sound of the pavilion doors crashing open behind him drowned out his reply.

Burke spun around, the shockgun in his hand at the ready. The sight that met his eyes was certainly not what he was expecting to see.

A man stumbled out of the now-open doors to the pavilion. His clothing was ripped and torn, covered with ash and mud, but it was still clear that he was dressed in the uniform of a British infantryman, or Tommy as they were known to the Americans. He came forward a few more steps and then tripped and fell to his knees, only to scramble to his feet as quickly as he'd gone down. The man was clearly exhausted but still found the energy to reach out a hand in their direction and shout, "Wait!," in a quavering voice.

As if in reply, a fearsome cacophony of shrieks sounded from within the depths of the pavilion.

Company coming.

Burke was already shrugging out of the shockgun's charging pack as he turned and addressed his companions. "Get the shredder in the boat and use the chains to secure it, just as we planned," he said sharply, forcing their attention away from the noise at the other end of the pier and on to him. "Tell the captain to fire her up and get her headed out for deeper water."

Cohen stared at him, his eyes wide. "What about you?"

"We'll meet you at the end of the pier," Burke said, even as he shrugged the rest of the way out of the backpack and snatched the man's rifle out of his hands. "Get that shredder on the boat. Now!"

Burke turned and ran toward the newcomer.

CHAPTER THREE

Running toward the injured British soldier, Burke was able to get a good look at the shredders as they burst out of the pavilion behind the man. There were five in all—three men and two women. Unlike their shambler cousins, who moved in a stumbling, barely functional walk, the shredders scurried forward with a strange, spiderlike quickness that Burke was coming to recognize as a hallmark of this new breed of undead. The exposed skin of their arms and legs had the same grayish-black coloration as the shredders Burke had seen previously, and the clothing in which they were dressed had clearly seen better days.

Two of the shredders, a man and a woman, put on a burst of speed the moment they laid eyes on their quarry and rushed out ahead of the rest of the pack. Within seconds they had closed to within a dozen yards of the British soldier and Burke knew the shredders would reach the man before he did.

Skidding to a halt, he shouted "Down!" and brought the Enfield up to his shoulder in one fluid move.

To his credit, the Tommy didn't hesitate, he just threw himself face forward onto the deck. There were men Burke had known for years, men with whom he'd fought side by side in the trenches of

Cambrai and Ypres who wouldn't have obeyed his command so quickly and certainly not with a group of shredders charging up from behind.

Burke didn't hesitate either, firing the rifle in his hands the split second that the other man passed out of his sight picture.

Crack! Crack! Crack!

Burke wasn't the world's best marksman, but then again he wasn't half bad, either; it took only three shots to put both shredders down with a bullet through the brain. He didn't waste any time admiring his handiwork, however, but rushed forward to where the other man was just pushing himself up. Burke reached down and hauled the Tommy to his feet.

"Are you hurt? Bitten?" he asked.

The other man shook his head.

Burke quickly looked him over just to be safe. He didn't see any obvious injuries or bloodstains on the man's clothing that might indicate otherwise, so he had little choice but to take the man at his word.

"Head for the trawler at the end of the dock," Burke told him, pointing in that direction. "I'll cover your retreat."

"Righto, mate," the man said wearily, his voice heavy with a Scottish accent. He staggered away from Burke and headed toward the boat as fast as he could.

Burke turned his attention back to the oncoming shredders.

There were three of them left, two men and a woman; from the looks of them, all were somewhere on the early side of middle-aged when infected. The man in the lead was completely naked; every inch of his gray-black skin was on display for all to see. Burke might have laughed at the sight if the situation hadn't been so damned tragic. In front of him was a man who would never laugh or cry or return to his family. The gas must have reached him in the shower or in the midst of changing and now he was charging around the countryside *in flagrante* searching for the living to consume. He was already filthy, his skin covered with grime and dirt and what looked to be fleshy remains of some kind or other, though whether animal or human Burke didn't know.

He and his two companions were closing the distance to Burke quickly. Burke tried not to let it fluster him as he brought the gun back up to his shoulder and centered the sights on the lead shredder.

His first shot struck the shredder in the shoulder, knocking it off balance and slowing it down. As it stumbled to regain its footing he fired twice more, putting the last bullet through the creature's temple when it turned its head.

One down, two to go.

Burke expected the two remaining shredders to come charging right for him just like the others had and he shifted position to line up his next shot only to nearly drop the rifle in surprise when the creatures broke in opposite directions, putting a row of lampposts between them in the process.

Shit!

It only took a few moments of glancing back and forth, trying to keep his eye on both of them, for Burke to realize that he was facing the impossible. He was going to have to concentrate on one and hope that he had enough time to deal with the other.

Cursing beneath his breath, he took up a position to the right of the nearest lamppost and focused his attention on the shredder to his right.

Burke's first shot missed; the shredder slipped behind a lamppost right as he pulled the trigger.

The second shot didn't fare any better as the shredder slipped its head to the side at the last second, allowing the bullet to pass harmlessly over its shoulder.

Burke could have sworn it grinned at him.

Fuck you, you sonofabitch! he thought with a snarling smile of his own as he steadied the barrel of the gun with his mechanical arm, lining up for another shot. He pulled the trigger the moment he had the shredder in his sights once again, but this time he bracketed his first shot with two more, one to either side, just in case the shredder tried the same stunt a second time.

Burke's third shot missed, as expected, but as the shredder

slipped to the side and opened its mouth to howl at him, the fourth shot entered its mouth and tore right through the back of its skull, sending the shredder crashing to the ground in a twisted tangle of flailing limbs.

Burke didn't waste any time celebrating his victory. He spun around to the other side of the post, his heart hammering with adrenaline as he sighted along his weapon, seeking a target.

The third and final shredder was less than twenty feet away and coming on fast. This close he could see the bits of vegetation and other trash that had gotten caught up in the tangled tresses of her hair as well as the gaping wound in the middle of her face where something had chewed off her nose.

His mind caught on the image and began to worry at it, like a dog with a bone—*Did other shredders do that? Before or after she was one herself, I wonder?*—even as he centered the barrel of his gun right on that very spot.

With less than a dozen feet between them, Burke pulled the trigger one final time.

Click.

There was no mistaking what that sound meant.

"Sonofa—"

The shredder closed the remaining distance and lunged forward.

Burke reacted instinctively, reversing his grip on the now-empty Enfield and shoving its stock into the creature's face as hard as he could. His blow struck it right along the bridge of the nose and knocked it clear off its feet.

He wasn't about to give it time to recover, either. The minute the shredder hit the ground he moved in, rifle in hand, screaming in fear and rage as he slammed the stock of the rifle down on the shredder's skull, once, twice, three times until it shattered under the impact, sending black blood and brains splattering in every direction.

The shredder went still.

With his chest heaving from the exertion, Burke staggered

back away from the twice-dead corpse. A quick check told him that the immediate threat had been taken care of, but he could hear incoherent shrieks and howls in the distance and knew that they had overstayed their welcome. This place was going to be crawling with shredders any minute now; it was time to take their prize and get the hell out.

Casting a final glance at the remains of the shredder on the ground before him, Burke turned and hurried after the man he'd just rescued.

The soldier was staggering about, barely on his feet, when Burke caught up to him. Whatever he'd been through, it had clearly sapped his strength and there was no way he was going to make it on his own if Burke didn't do something to help. Casting the now-empty Enfield aside, Burke slowed down just enough to slip the other man's arm over his own shoulders in support and then got them moving.

A loud crash came from somewhere behind them and it didn't take much for Burke to guess what was behind the sound. A glance over his shoulder confirmed his suspicions.

Another, larger group of shredders had just burst through the pavilion doors in pursuit of them. Burke gave a half-second thought to pulling his sidearm and sending a volley in their direction, but then dismissed the idea; the range was just too great for him to realistically expect to hit anything, and shredders would probably scramble for cover at the first sound of gunfire the way humans might. Instead, Burke concentrated on moving the wounded man next to him along a bit faster.

Looking ahead of them, he could see the trawler nearing the end of the pier. He expected it to heave to at any moment and some quick mental calculations assured him that they would have enough time to scramble aboard before the horde caught up. From there it would be a straight shot across the Channel to the safety of the Allied camp at Calais.

But as they drew closer to the end of the pier, it became clear that the captain of the trawler had other plans. The boat reached the end of the pier . . . and then continued past it, headed for the open water beyond.

The captain wasn't going to wait for them!

Anger flooded Burke's system, giving him a burst of energy, and he hustled the two of them forward, shouting as he went.

"Hey! Hey, wait!"

At the sound of his voice the howling behind him grew louder, the shredders filling the air with their eager cries.

"I said wait, you sonofabitch!"

Burke could see Cohen and Montagna staring at him from the stern of the boat, frozen in indecision by this turn of events. He needed to do something to break the paralysis that gripped them or it was going to be all over right here, right now.

"Stop the boat!" Burke hollered, waving his mechanical arm at them in frustration. "I don't care if you have to shoot him, stop the boat!"

His orders seemed to do the trick. Both men started, as if shaken out of sleep, and staggered into action. Montagna drew his pistol and headed for the wheelhouse while Cohen began casting about the deck, looking for something.

Please, God, let it be a rope!

He could see that he was twenty feet from the end of the dock and closing, but that was still twenty feet too far. Even as he hurried forward, Burke knew they were never going to make it. By the time the boat turned around and came back, the shredders would have already fallen upon them from behind. They were done for, unless . . .

"Can you swim?" he asked the other man suddenly.

His companion mumbled something incoherent in reply.

Burke chose to take that as a yes.

A gunshot sounded from the wheelhouse, followed immediately by the rumble of the boat's engines as they were thrown in reverse.

A glimmer of hope.

Thank you, Montagna!

It still might not be enough to save them, he knew, but at least now they had a fighting chance.

Burke glanced back over his shoulder and saw that the snarling mob of shredders was only a half-dozen yards behind them now.

It was going to be close.

He reached deep down and pulled on the last of his reserves, speeding them up just a fraction as they charged pell-mell for the end of the pier.

The gray water of the Atlantic looked cold and uninviting and Burke mentally braced himself for the shock that was about to be delivered to his system.

Cold or not, I'd rather drown than be eaten, he thought as he and his companion ran right off the end of the dock, splashing into the cold Atlantic ten feet below.

Following close behind, the horde of shredders did the same.

CHAPTER FOUR

✪

Silence.

Darkness.

There was even a sense of peace as Burke sank down through the cold, dark waters.

For just a moment he was tempted to let it all go, to let the water take him down, down deep, away from the mud and the muck and the sheer terror of the battlefield, sinking deeper toward the ocean floor so far below, sinking, sinking . . .

That was when a hand grabbed his ankle.

The sudden, unexpected feeling of that viselike grip wrapping around his flesh shocked him out of his torpor, banishing his lethargy as he suddenly found his will to live and began fighting for the surface. He couldn't see anything in the dark water but knew instinctively that a grip that strong didn't belong to anything living. The realization flooded his system with adrenaline, and he kicked wildly with both legs, trying to free himself from the shredder's grip as they sank deeper with every passing second.

He imagined the shredder staring up at him hungrily from below, its eyes piercing the darkness without difficulty, its mouth opening in a silent scream of hunger . . .

Burke nearly screamed himself at the thought.

With air already starting to dribble out between clenched lips, he knew he didn't have time to fool with this thing. If he waited too long, he wouldn't have enough air to get back to the surface and then it all would have been for naught. He kicked and thrashed but still it did no good.

The shredder held on, dragging him deeper.

Since it didn't need to breathe, the water wasn't affecting it much. Burke hated to think of what it would do to him if they reached the bottom before he could get free.

He had to do something quickly . . .

I take it back; I don't want to drown!

The weight of his mechanical arm, now filled with seawater, gave him an idea.

He jackknifed his body forward, bending at the waist and reaching downward with both hands until he could grab his own leg. He felt around with his good hand until he came in contact with the shredder's hand on his ankle, then guided the mechanical one downward along the shredder's fingers until he came to its wrist.

His chest was burning with the need to take a breath, but he fought it off as he wrapped his mechanical fingers around the shredder's wrist and squeezed as hard as he was able.

Bones snapped like brittle twigs and suddenly the grip on his ankle was free as the creature's fingers stopped working.

Burke felt it flailing at him with its other arm, trying to grab hold of something new, but he didn't hang around to give it the chance. He kicked frantically for the surface, reaching upward with long strokes of his arms, his chest screaming for air, his mind fighting a war with his body to hold on a few seconds longer as his vision began to tunnel and the black haze at the edges began to close in from all sides even as he surged upward . . .

He broke the surface of the water with a shocking gasp and saw that he was not twenty feet from the gunwale of the trawler.

"Here! He's over here!" he heard a voice cry as he sucked in great lungfuls of life-giving air and shook his head to clear the fuzziness. Something splashed into the water in front of him and he reached for it instinctively, discovering only once he had it in hand that it was a rope.

"Hold on," the voice shouted and this time he recognized it as Montagna's.

For once, Burke did as he was told and in a matter of moments he found himself bumping up against the wooden hull of the fishing trawler. Hands reached down to pull him up and he dropped down over the side and into the boat, wet and bedraggled but alive.

The British soldier...

The fuzzy form bending over him solidified into that of the private who had just dragged him out of the drink and Burke knew he startled the younger man by grabbing him and gasping out, "The Tommy! Where's the Tommy?"

"Take it easy, Major," Montagna said, grabbing Burke's shoulders as he struggled to get up. "We fished the Tommy out of the drink a few minutes before you popped up like a cork from a bottle. Cohen's doing what he can."

Doing what he can?

That didn't sound encouraging to Burke, and when he looked in the direction Montagna was pointing, he understood why.

The Tommy was lying flat on his back on the deck, unmoving. Private Cohen knelt beside him, pumping up and down on the other man's chest with both hands. With each compression a thin stream of water bubbled out of the man's mouth and onto the deck. Burke had seen men revived with the same process so for a moment he was hopeful that it would turn out all right, but after a long moment where the Tommy failed to respond, he began to have his doubts.

Then Cohen did a strange thing.

He bent over the wounded man and kissed him!

Burke's jaw dropped open and he stared at the two soldiers

in shock. The young American's lips were pressed completely over the drowned man's, his fingers were pinching the other man's nostrils shut, and he seemed to be blowing deep into his throat.

If that's a kiss, it's the strangest one I've ever seen . . .

Burke was about to say something—he wasn't sure what, maybe order the younger man away perhaps—when the Tommy suddenly coughed up a lungful of seawater right into Cohen's face and began thrashing his arms about in a panic, no doubt thinking he was still in danger of drowning.

Cohen looked up and caught Burke's stare. "A hand here, please, Major," he asked calmly, as he struggled to hold the other man down.

Burke scrambled to his side and grabbed hold of the British soldier's arms, keeping them from flailing wildly about, while Cohen gently turned the man's head to one side. He was just in time, too; the Tommy suddenly convulsed and vomited up a puddle of seawater.

"Easy now," Cohen said to the man, in a surprisingly gentle voice. "Easy. You're safe now; we left the shredders behind."

The Tommy looked wildly about, his face drawn with tension, but that began to ease up a bit as he took in the scene around him and seemed to recognize them as fellow soldiers. His gaze focused on Burke and he tried to say something, but all that came out was a low mumble.

Frowning, Burke leaned closer.

"What was that?"

Another mumble.

The man's head drooped down against his chest, the demands the day's events had placed on his body having finally surpassed his limits.

Yet whatever it was that the soldier was trying to say must have been important, for he visibly fought back against the encroaching darkness, grabbed the front of Burke's uniform blouse with one hand, and dragged him closer.

With his ear half an inch away from the man's lips, Burke finally heard what the other man had been trying to say.

"I have a message from the King."

Startled, Burke pulled back far enough to look the other man in the eye. The Tommy nodded at him, as if to assure him that what he'd just said was true, and then the last of his strength deserted him and he slipped away into unconsciousness.

CHAPTER FIVE

AN HOUR LATER Burke stood in the bow of the trawler as it made its way into the harbor at Calais and did his best to ignore the anxious looks that he was getting from the crews of the other boats as they passed by. He knew it wasn't his presence that was making the other men nervous, but rather the shredder wrapped in chains and thrashing about while hanging off the transom at the back of the boat. As shouts passed from boat to boat like the flames of a wildfire amid the dry tinder of an Arizona forest, Burke began to realize that he might have a problem on his hands.

After the Tommy had lapsed into unconsciousness, Burke had ordered Cohen and Montagna to make the man as comfortable as possible while he stepped into the wheelhouse to have a few words with the captain. His anger at being left behind as shredder bait must have come through loud and clear, for Burke found the man to be far less boisterous and demanding than he'd been on the journey out earlier that morning. A few quick questions revealed that there wasn't a convenient room or even an empty storage tank in which to lock away their prized captive, so Burke decided to hang the shredder upside down off the transom at the back of the boat for the journey across the Channel to the mainland. He figured it was the safest option available; if they needed to cut it loose for any reason, it would sink to the bottom of the Channel under the weight of its chains and that would be that.

What he hadn't counted on was how inflammatory the sight of the shredder might be to those stationed in Calais.

Word spread quickly, and a crowd of soldiers and dockworkers had gathered on the wharf by the time the captain began his docking approach. Burke eyed the crowd for a moment, not liking the looks of them, and then turned to his two subordinates waiting on the deck behind him.

"I don't care who they are; no one gets close to that shredder without my express permission, understood?"

The two men nodded.

"Good. Let's hope they aren't that eager to cause trouble for us, but just in case, if I raise my left hand, I want you both to put a bullet into the dock in front of where I'm standing."

"Sir?" Cohen asked.

"You heard me, Private. If I give the signal, fire at the dock a few feet in front of the crowd. Can you do that?"

"Sir, yes sir!"

"All right then." Burke gave them a long look, decided they'd stand up if and when the time came, and then turned back to face the crowd.

With a shock he saw that they had nearly doubled in number in just those few short moments and his stomach did a slow roll at the sight.

Where the hell was Graves?

Burke looked out over the heads of the crowd, but he didn't see any sign of the professor or the truck he was supposed to be arriving in. Without that truck, and the specially prepared cage it carried, he was going to have to find some other way to transport the shredder back to Graves's lab at MID headquarters. That, of course, would take time, and time was something they didn't seem to have a lot of at the moment. The longer the shredder was in view, the more agitated this crowd would get, he knew.

All it would take was one overzealous idiot . . .

He pushed the thought out of mind and put on his game face, determined not to let all their hard work up to this point go for nothing. As the captain brought the boat up against the dock, Burke drew his sidearm and jumped out of the boat to stand about fifteen feet in front of the crowd.

When in doubt, go on the offensive, he thought to himself.

"I want this dock cleared and I want it cleared now!" he shouted at the mob, making no effort to hide either his mechanical arm or the Colt automatic that he held in his good hand. "If you're still here thirty seconds from now, I'll have your asses hauled down to the brig where you can spend the next week digging latrines and contemplating what it means to disobey a direct order!"

An undercurrent of angry murmurs ran through the crowd at his statement, but except for a few stragglers out along the edges, no one moved.

If your first bluff fails, bluff again, but make it bigger and bolder this time around, Burke told himself.

He searched the row of men directly in front of him for a second, settling his gaze on a large, hulking man with master sergeant stripes on his sleeve who appeared to be leading one of the larger groups. Burke stepped up and got right into the man's face.

"Do you know who I am?" he demanded.

Caught off-guard by the combination of Burke's command voice and being called out in front of all the others, the master sergeant responded just the way Burke had hoped. The man's bald head nodded vigorously. "You're Madman B . . . ah, Major Burke, sir."

Normally Burke would have objected to the ridiculous nickname he'd been tagged with after the battle of Cambrai, but in this case it worked to his advantage. Madman Burke had a reputation for taking on overwhelming odds with the single-minded determination of a rabid bulldog and right now that reputation might be the very thing that got him and his men out of this mess.

"That's right, Master Sergeant. Major *Madman* Burke," he replied, emphasizing his nickname so the others around them would hear it, betting that it would spread through the crowd in seconds and figuring that he might as well put his notoriety to good use. He could see that those in the front row had stopped paying attention to the shredder and were now watching his interaction with the man, which was exactly what he wanted.

"I don't know what this bunch of rabble is doing away from their posts, but they're interfering with an authorized military intelligence mission and I'm ordering you and all the rest of them to get the hell out of my way. Do I make myself clear?"

Years of habit of accepting the commands of senior officers had the master sergeant practically snapping to attention by the time Burke had finished speaking. "Yes, sir!" he replied before turning to face the crowd.

"You heard the major!" he yelled. "Show's over! Back to your posts or he'll have you up on charges faster than you can blink!"

Burke began backing away from the assembled mob, and for a moment he thought it was going to be all right. He'd apparently chosen the right man; the master sergeant was a known entity to these men, and many of them were listening to him. They were grumbling and clearly unhappy, but at least they were moving away from the boat and that was precisely what Burke had been hoping for. A few minutes to unload the shredder and secure it for transport to MID headquarters and they'd be on their way.

But then some jackass in the back of the crowd shouted, "I don't care if he's in charge of the entire war effort! If that thing gets loose, we're all dead. I say we kill it now and be done with it!"

There was a moment of silence as the crowd teetered on the edge, trying to decide what to do, and then an answering shout rose up from somewhere to Burke's left—"I'm not waiting around for that thing to get loose and bite me! Kill it now while we still can, I say!"—and Burke lost them completely.

The crowd surged forward, more than a handful of them shouting, "Kill the shredder!" as they came.

Burke stood his ground and calmly raised his left hand in the air.

The bullets thudded into the dock a few feet in front of the surging crowd a half second before the sound of the shots echoed over their heads.

The crowd came to a stop as suddenly as if they'd run into an invisible wall. Silence fell in the wake of the gunshots, thick and heavy.

Satisfied that he had their attention, Burke calmly raised his sidearm and pointed it at the crowd in front of him.

"I'll shoot the next man who takes another step," he said.

He was bluffing, but they didn't know that. At least not yet. All it would take was a single step for the truth to be revealed, though. Burke was hoping they wouldn't risk life and limb just to take out a single captive shredder.

The two groups stared at each other, waiting to see who would blink first.

Into the silence a truck horn began blaring from behind them. Glancing over the master sergeant's shoulder, Burke could see a four-ton lorry driving slowly down the dock in his direction, the crowd parting reluctantly before it. The driver kept leaning on the horn, the grating sound clearing the way before him almost as effectively as the bulk of the vehicle itself.

As the crowd pulled back, Burke got his first look into the cab and breathed a sigh of relief at the sight of the thin, hawk-faced man behind the wheel.

Once one of Nicola Tesla's most-skilled protégés, Professor Dan Graves was now MID's resident scientific genius and in-house expert on all things supernatural. He was also a tried-and-tested member of Burke's Marauders, having accompanied the team on their recent mission behind enemy lines to rescue the president's illegitimate son, Julius "Jack" Freeman.

Burke would be the first to admit that he hadn't liked Graves all that much when he'd first met him; the man's obsession with the undead was creepy as hell. But Burke had grown to not only like the man but trust him with his life, and he'd had to do just that during their hair-raising escape less than two weeks ago from the secret base outside Verdun of Germany's top ace, Baron Manfred von Richthofen.

Given it was because of Graves that he was here at all, Burke was very happy to see him.

A younger man with gold-rimmed spectacles sat in the passenger seat beside Graves, a leather medical bag clutched tightly against his chest. Burke stared at him for a moment but was pretty sure he didn't know the man.

Graves brought the truck up parallel with the boat and parked. He sat in the cab for a moment, staring in what appeared to be fascination at the chain-wrapped shredder twisting from its hook at the rear of the boat, then he shook himself and said something over his shoulder to someone in the cargo area, out of Burke's view. Seconds later the canvas flaps at the back of the truck were thrown back and a squad of military police poured out over the sides, forming up around the vehicle, weapons at the ready.

Reinforcements had arrived.

The lieutenant in charge of the MP squad stepped forward and raised his voice over the angry talk of the crowd.

"All right, show's over. Back off and get back to work or you'll be spending the night in the brig. Don't make me tell you twice!"

There were a few shouts from the crowd that questioned the legitimacy of the lieutenant's parentage and a whole lot of grumbling to go along with them, but faced with the implacable stare of the lieutenant and the increased firepower his men added to the equation, the crowd finally began to break up and turn away.

Once the dock was secured, Graves stepped out of the truck and hurried along the edge of the dock to stand opposite the shredder, his gaze locked firmly upon it.

"So it worked?" he called over his shoulder at Burke, who was watching him with a mixture of amusement and revulsion. *How the man could be so enrapt by such creatures . . .*

"More or less," Burke replied. "I've got a list of suggestions that I think might help make it a bit more useful in the field."

Graves nodded, but Burke could tell he wasn't really listening, his attention completely captured by the undead creature hanging off the end of the transom.

Knowing they could talk it all over later in the debriefing, Burke turned back to find the newcomer standing in front of the truck, watching them both. When the man realized that Burke was watching him, he stepped forward and saluted.

"Private Bankowski reporting for duty, sir."

The newcomer was in his midtwenties, with blond hair and blue eyes that hinted at either German or Polish ancestry. Burke eyed the leather bag the man carried. "You a doctor, Bankowski?"

"Medic, sir. I was a doctor's assistant before the war."

"Good enough. I've got an exhausted and potentially injured man inside the wheelhouse. I'm turning him over to your care for the time being. If he wakes up, I want you to notify me right away, clear?"

"Yes, sir."

Burke gave him a hand up onto the boat and then turned his attention to the job before him, namely, getting the shredder unloaded and on its way to Graves's lab for further study.

Along with the squad of MPs, the truck also contained a large iron cage, similar to those used by zookeepers to transport dangerous animals. Burke had once seen a lion being taken by train from New York to Los Angeles and it had made the journey in just such a device. The bars were round and very thick, the cage itself large enough for Burke to have lain down in.

Unlike most cages, however, this one opened from the top, rather than from one of the four sides. Burke puzzled about it for a moment, until he realized that having it open in such a fashion would make it much easier to unload the shredder from the fishing trawler; all they would have to do is swivel the boom out over the cage and then use the winch to lower the creature inside.

Simple and effective, just the way Burke liked it.

Graves came hustling back down the dock at that point, and they got to work transferring the shredder to its temporary home.

It was considerably more active now than it had been on the trip across the Channel, and Burke was at a loss with figuring how to subdue it when Graves suggested using the shockgun. Burke had been thinking of the weapon as purely an offensive one and it simply hadn't occurred to him that it might have other uses. Shaking his head at his own nearsightedness, Burke picked up the weapon and used it to shock the shredder into immobility again, thereby reducing the chance that someone might get accidentally scratched or bitten by the creature as they maneuvered it into the cage.

Everything went smoothly from that point forward. Forty minutes later the shredder was in its cage and the men were settled in the rear of the truck with Burke riding shotgun up front, ready for the long ride back to Camp Whitmore, the casualty clearing station and regional headquarters where the Military Intelligence Division was based.

With his mission all but accomplished, Burke sat back to enjoy the ride.

CHAPTER SIX

★

IT WAS MORE than two hundred kilometers from Calais to Provins, a trip that, even under the best of conditions, would normally take a few hours. These were not the best of conditions, of course, not even close, and so the journey took considerably longer. The road ran close to the front, and on several occasions the troops had to climb out of the cargo area while Graves carefully maneuvered the vehicle around shell craters and the occasional piece of unexploded ordnance. There was also the ever-present threat of being dive-bombed by a squadron of enemy aircraft patrolling behind the lines, all of which contributed to making the trip a less-than-ideal one.

Not that any of that bothered Burke. There weren't any shamblers, shredders, or other assorted undead creatures trying to eat him at the moment and that was a considerable improvement over his usual circumstances. From a tactical standpoint the mission had been a resounding success; they'd captured a shredder, rescued a fellow soldier, and made it back alive in one piece. As the gates to Camp Whitmore came into view through the windshield before him, Burke couldn't help but smile.

Score one for the good guys, he thought.

The Tommy they'd rescued was still unconscious, a condition that had Burke more than a little concerned, but Doc Bankowski assured him that the Tommy's condition was simply a result of the dehydration and sheer exhaustion that he was experiencing. Some decent food and a night's rest should have him back on his feet in no time. Knowing Colonel Nichols would want to question the man when he awoke, Burke ordered Bankowski to escort the injured soldier to the casualty clearing station and stay with him until he regained consciousness, at which point he was to notify Colonel Nichols.

Satisfied that he'd done all he could in that regard, Burke retired to his tent and immediately turned on the auto-dictation machine to handle his mission report. Colonel Nichols was a stickler for getting as much information out of an operative as possible and Burke had learned to get his recollections down right away, knowing that the minor details would slip away from him with time. Practically everything they were doing was virgin territory and no one knew what detail, no matter how insignificant, might hold the key to giving them the upper hand in this seemingly never-ending war.

The luggage-size device hissed and clicked and whirred for ten minutes before it beeped to tell him it was ready. When it was, he began speaking clearly and slowly, listening as the automaton at the heart of the device pecked out the letters in short bursts that reminded him of the pecking of a woodpecker on the trees back home. Just under an hour later he had eight printed pages ready to send out. He summoned a runner and directed him to take the pages to Corporal Davis, Colonel Nichols's adjutant, who would give them to the colonel at the appropriate time. As MID resident expert on the undead, Graves would receive a copy as well.

Only when the runner was on his way, report in hand, did Burke turn to getting himself cleaned up from his mission. He stripped off his uniform, stiff with dried blood and seawater, and laid it aside. He'd set out a basin of water and a scrub cloth before heading out at 0-dark hundred that morning and he used them now to clean some of the grit and grime off his body before pulling on a clean uniform.

The very fact that he had spare water with which to clean himself showed how much things had changed since his transfer into the MID. Less than a month before he'd been on the front line with the men of the Fourth Platoon, facing daily attacks by shamblers and German infantry alike. They spent the day manning the trench and the nights sleeping in cavelike dugouts they'd excavated in the trench walls, wearing the same uniforms for weeks at a time. Wasting what little water they had on personal hygiene made no sense in those conditions; better to have something to drink than to use the water to clean something that was just going to be covered in filth again moments later.

Ready access to clean water was not the only thing that had changed. Sure, the missions might be a bit hairier, but there was a cot to sleep on at night and three square meals a day in the officers' mess that made up for the harrowing nature of the missions twice over.

And let's not forget the coffee, Burke thought. *Fresh grounds every morning!* Sometimes he thought he'd died and gone to heaven.

Thoughts of the Fourth Platoon brought with them memories of his former staff sergeant, Charlie Moore, and Burke's satisfaction with his new circumstances was quickly replaced with sadness at the thought of his missing friend. During their last mission together, Charlie had volunteered to lead the pursuing German troops away from the rest of the squad, giving them the time they needed to escort the man they'd rescued, Major Jack Freeman, back across the front lines to safety. Moore's fate was still unknown, as was the fate of Clayton Manning, the big-game-hunter-turned-soldier who had seen the gambit as a final chance to fulfill his mission of killing Richthofen. Burke had last seen Moore behind the wheel of the lorry they had stolen, Manning in the passenger seat beside him, as they'd sped off down the road.

I'll meet you farther down the line, Charlie said as they'd made their good-byes. That had been more than a week ago. Burke hadn't yet given up hope that his friend had escaped the Germans and managed to hook up with the partisan group outside of Reims that was the intended rendezvous point, but the odds were growing slimmer with each day that passed without word.

It had been Charlie who had saved his life by cutting off his hand just moments after it had been ravaged by a shambler's bite; Charlie who had gotten him back to the combat aid station where he would eventually be fitted for a predecessor of the mechanical arm that he wore today; Charlie who had saved his life more times than he could count in the bleakness and horror that was life in the trenches.

Burke knew he wouldn't be here if it hadn't been for Charlie's efforts along the way.

The hole in his soul that his friend used to occupy burned with an aching sense of loss that was terribly reminiscent of how he'd felt when his fiancée Mae had been accidentally killed while in the company of his half brother, Jack.

Burke missed his friend. Missed him terribly.

He walked over to his footlocker and dug out the half-empty bottle of whiskey lying inside. He twisted off the cup and held the bottle up in salute.

"Here's to you, Charlie," he said. "Wherever the hell you are."

He took a long pull; the cheap liquor burned harshly on the way down, but that was okay with Burke. It fit his mood perfectly. After a glass or two, he wouldn't notice anyway.

BURKE AWOKE SEVERAL hours later. He'd left the flaps closed on the tent, and the air inside felt hot and stuffy. So, too, did his head; he'd had several glasses of that less-than-premium-quality sour mash before falling asleep, it seemed. He pulled on his boots, splashed some leftover water on his face from the pitcher he'd filled the basin with earlier, and stepped outside.

The sun was going down in the west, the sunset filtered through the ever-present haze from the constantly burning corpse fires behind the casualty clearing station. The late hour, and his rumbling stomach, reminded him that he'd had very little to eat since earlier that morning, so he headed for the officers' mess to grab some dinner.

Afterward, given that he didn't have any particular duties to perform until the morning, Burke decided to drop in on Graves to see if he'd learned anything of interest from the captive shredder yet.

The bunker complex Graves had commandeered for his so-called laboratory was a fifteen-minute walk from the officers' mess. Ordinarily he would have caught a ride with a passing troop transport or staff adjutant, but today he decided not to bother.

It turned out to be a good choice; the walk cleared his head and allowed him to get his thoughts in order. If they were going to be facing more of these creatures in the future, then he wanted to know what he was up against and Graves was one of the few people who might actually be able to tell him something worthwhile.

The area Graves used as his laboratory and general workspace had started as a dugout designed to provide protection for senior staff during artillery and mortar attacks. Graves worked tirelessly to expand it to suit his needs, and now it was a warren of passageways of underground chambers where he conducted his research and experimentation.

As Burke rounded a bend and approached the U-shaped barrier of sandbags that surrounded the entrance to the bunker, he could see that the cast-iron door was propped open with the empty shell casing from a German howitzer round, allowing some air to flow inside. A guard stood outside smoking a cigarette. He snapped to attention the moment he saw Burke, doing what he could to hide the smoke in his left hand while saluting with his right. Burke had to suppress a smile as he returned the salute; he had done the same thing with his own smokes more times than he could count.

Beyond the doors was a set of steps, nineteen in all, leading down to the complex proper. Burke descended at a quickened pace; lights hadn't been hung in the stairwell and he hated being caught in the darkness between the daylight above and the artificial lights below.

The room at the bottom of the staircase was as long as it was wide and lit by several bare lightbulbs that hung down low from the ceiling above. The harshness of the lighting set Burke's nerves on edge, a situation made worse when he saw what was waiting for him on the long wooden table in the center of the room.

The shredder that his team had captured earlier that morning was lying naked on the table, its gray-black flesh glistening in the lights. Thick leather bands crossed its body at the forehead, shoulders, chest, waist, and knees, secured at the edge of the table with metal buckles at least an inch thick. Iron manacles locked its ankles and wrists to the table.

A thick rubber tube ran from the inside of the shredder's left elbow to a large bucket hanging from a nearby metal rack. Another ran from its right elbow to a bucket on the floor beside the table. Other sets of tubing ran from the buckets to a spot behind the table somewhere. From that same direction came the hissing inhalations and exhalations of an iron lung. Each time the machine breathed in, some of the shredder's black blood was pulled out of the shredder's left arm; when it breathed out, red blood—*was that human blood?*—was pumped back in through the other side.

Professor Graves sat at a nearby desk, his back to Burke, staring down into the eyepieces of one of his mysterious pieces of equipment and jotting notes onto a pad of paper beside him.

"Turn the left-hand dial to the third setting, would you please, Major?" Graves asked, without looking up from what he was doing.

"Uh . . . okay," Burke replied, startled by Graves's unexpected request and not really understanding what was being asked of him. *The left-hand dial? He didn't see any dials, never mind one on the left. Maybe he meant. . .*

"On the control panel hanging from the left side of the table."

"Right." Burke grimaced; he would have been perfectly happy staying on the opposite side of the room, away from the table and the shredder it contained.

Stepping closer, Burke saw the control panel that Graves was talking about. It wasn't anything fancy, just a couple of switches and a single dial cobbled together onto a flat sheet of metal about a foot square, hanging by two hooks from the edge of the table. Multicolored wires ran from the back of the panel and around behind the table, presumably to the iron lung that was still breathing in and out every few seconds.

As Burke reached out toward the dial, the shredder on the table opened its eyes and hissed at him.

"Aaagh!" Burke jumped in surprise. *The damned thing was awake!*

"Come, come, Major," Graves scolded him impatiently, looking up at last. "It's strapped down quite securely; it isn't going anywhere."

Burke scowled in Graves's direction. "You've tested the straps? You're positive it can't break free?"

"Positive? Well, no, not exactly. But I'm pretty sure."

Burke just stared at him.

After a moment filled only with the snarls of the shredder and the hiss of the electronic lung, Graves said, "Perhaps you should let me do that then, yes?"

"Be my guest, Professor."

Burke stepped out of the way, letting Graves handle whatever needed adjusting. The shredder couldn't move its head thanks to the wide strap of leather running across its forehead, but that didn't stop it from following the professor with eyes that showed a much greater sense of awareness than its shambler cousins and that made Burke distinctly uncomfortable. One of the few advantages they had in fighting the shamblers was the fact that the shamblers operated on an instinctive level and as a result were entirely predictable. You knew exactly what a shambler would do because it did the same thing every time. These new shredders, though . . .

Graves interrupted his thoughts. "Fascinating creatures, Burke. Truly fascinating."

Burke answered with a noncommittal grunt. *Fascinating* was not a word he'd ever use in conjunction with either shredders or shamblers, but then it wasn't his job to figure out what made them tick; all he had to do was kill them as quickly and as efficiently as possible.

"Just look at the way it reacts to our presence! It is aware of us on a level way above that of the average shambler. I wouldn't be surprised if it could even think independently to some extent."

Burke found the whole idea very frightening. *Self-aware zombies? No thanks.* The evidence for Graves being right was piling up, however. Knowing it was better to let him have all the facts at hand, Burke told him about the way the two shredders had split up while charging him on the pier, using the lamppost as cover for their two-pronged attack.

Graves was nodding before Burke was done. "Yes, yes, I read that in your report. Given the information I've collected to date, I'm beginning to believe that they can think *and* reason to a limited degree."

It wasn't a conclusion Burke was happy to hear. "What else can you tell me?" he asked.

"The physical exam uncovered a number of important facts. For one, they have excellent hearing. Equal to that of a dog, at the very least. Certainly much better than our own. On the other hand, their eyesight is rather poor, no doubt a result of these cataract-like changes in their irises. Dim light is probably very difficult for them. I suspect they react to movement and sound more than anything else."

Burke thought about that for a moment or two, not sure if the information would actually be useful in the field. A shredder's poor eyesight wouldn't be all that helpful to his squad if it could hear them coming from over a hundred yards away, though it was worth filing away for later reference if necessary.

"As you noted yourself, they are extremely quick and exceptionally strong," Graves continued. "Examinations of this specimen, along with the autopsies I performed on the bodies of two other recovered shredders, showed extensive growth of certain types of muscle tissue, particularly around the joints. That and a greatly increased metabolism appear to be acting together to allow them to operate at physical capabilities that you and I simply cannot match."

Great, Burke thought. *As if fighting shamblers wasn't hard enough. If these things spread to the Continent, we are going to be in serious trouble!*

In his mind's eye Burke could see them swarming a trench line en masse, like a colony of ants all working together toward the same goal, and knew instinctively that there was no way they would be able to withstand a charge like that. The very idea of it sent shivers up his spine.

To get his mind off the image, he focused on another question that had been bugging him since the encounter on the pier.

"What's driving these things? Why the hunger for human flesh?"

Graves frowned. "Initial tests seem to indicate that there is something in living tissue, particularly human tissue, that the shredder needs to maintain its current state of animation, but I've only begun my research so I can't say for certain. I do know this, though—deprive a shredder of living flesh for too long and it will begin to decay, just like any other corpse."

The comment caught Burke by surprise. "So are these things dead or alive?" He'd always thought of them as nothing more than reanimated corpses, but if they could think and reason . . .

"I guess it depends upon your definition of alive."

Burke laughed uneasily. "You lost me, Graves."

The other man moved to stand at the head of the table, directly behind the shredder's head. He reached over to a small tool stand next to him and picked up two metal rods. Each one was about half an inch in diameter and roughly six inches long.

"Think of it this way, Major. Life is nothing more than a combination of physical states. Our hearts beat to pump blood through our bodies. Our lungs inflate to push oxygen into our blood. We eat, we think, we breathe, and as a result we call ourselves alive."

Burke could see Graves fiddling with something behind the shredder's head, but from where he stood he couldn't see what the other man was doing. Something about the activity bothered him, though he couldn't have consciously answered what. He stepped forward, intent on getting a better look.

Graves, meanwhile, continued his explanation.

"Stop our hearts from beating and we die. Stop our lungs from breathing and we die. Interrupt the electrochemical processes of our brains and we die. Or so I've always thought."

He gestured at the shredder on the table before him. "Since we haven't had any reports of the London dead clawing their way out of their graves, we know this young man was alive when the bombs fell and the gas was released. He is clearly aware of us and is driven by an all-consuming hunger, and yet his heart does not beat, his blood does not flow, and his lungs do not breathe. By our definitions, he is dead. And yet . . ."

Burke's motion around the table finally allowed him to see what Graves was doing. As Burke looked on, Graves carefully inserted the rods into two holes that had previously been drilled into the shredder's head. Burke winced at the sight but the shredder didn't react at all. It was as if he couldn't even feel it.

Once the rods were in place, Graves clipped a tin wire to the end of each one. Burke could see that the other ends of the wires were connected to the bottom of a light socket that was clamped to a nearby table. A small incandescent bulb rested in the socket.

For a moment nothing happened, then . . . the lightbulb sparked and slowly grew brighter.

" . . . And yet there is more electrical activity going on in this shredder's brain right now than in yours and mine combined." Graves turned to face Burke squarely. "So you tell me, Major—is this shredder dead or alive?"

CHAPTER SEVEN

✪

BURKE WAS HALFWAY through his breakfast the next morning when a runner arrived with word that his presence was requested for a staff meeting at MID's headquarters at 0900 hours. A glance at his watch told him that he had less than ten minutes to spare, so he shoveled another forkful of syntheggs into his mouth and then headed outside. A staff car was waiting to take some fellow officers in the same general direction, so Burke caught a lift and arrived at MID headquarters with a minute to spare.

He'd spent a fitful night, tossing and turning as his mind wouldn't let go of the disturbing information Graves had presented in the laboratory earlier that evening, and he had awakened in a grumpy mood. The question of whether the shredders were living or dead was a profound one, with considerable implications for the war effort in the months ahead. Since the attack it had been the generally accepted theory that the gas had first killed, then resurrected its victims into the ghoulish zombielike creatures commonly known as shredders.

But what if they were wrong? Burke wondered. *What if the vic-*

tims of the gas never died at all? What if they were still in there some-where, their personalities subsumed by the transformation?

Burke shook his head, trying to clear it of all the extraneous thoughts. He wasn't smart enough to figure out the answers to such questions; he knew his own limitations. It would be up to guys like Graves to figure out the deeper questions, and hopefully they would come up with some answers.

For now, he had a briefing to attend.

Burke nodded at the guards out front and then entered the old farmhouse that the MID had claimed as its own. The first floor had been converted into the signals center, the communications officers stationed there working diligently to decode half a dozen enemy intercepts at any given time. Familiar with it all, Burke ignored them, slipping past the group to reach the stairwell leading to the upper floor.

Once at the top he moved briskly down the hall to the last room on the right. There he found U.S. and British officers and their aides milling about in a frenzied hive of activity. Burke spotted the new U.S. division commander, Lieutenant Colonel Ellington, talking with his opposite number on the British side, Brigadier Montgomery Calhoun, as well as several of the senior brigade commanders in charge of various sections of the front line. He nodded hello to several men he knew but avoided getting pulled into a conversation with anyone. After a moment or two, he saw his commanding officer, Colonel Nichols, waving to him from across the room. Burke cut through the crowd and headed in that direction.

As he approached, he saw that the sergeant he'd rescued the night before was there as well, dressed in a clean uniform but looking as uncomfortable as Burke felt among all the upper brass. Burke was surprised to see him up and on his feet, but apparently Bankowski's assessment had been correct. Exhaustion and dehydration—nothing a good night's rest and some fluids couldn't fix. The dark tartan of the man's kilt identified him as a member of a Scottish unit, though his unit recognition badge, a lion rampant over the field of white and blue worn proudly on one shoulder, was unfamiliar to Burke. The sergeant gave him a short nod when he stepped up, one professional to another.

The colonel turned at his approach. "Thank you for coming, Major," Nichols said with a smile. It didn't matter that Burke's presence was the result of an order, and therefore mandatory. Nichols treated him with courtesy; it was one of the many things Burke liked about the man.

Nichols turned to the British sergeant standing next to him and introduced the two men to each other.

"Mike, this is Sergeant Drummond of the Black Watch, Royal Highland Regiment. Sergeant Drummond, Major Michael Burke, formerly of the 316th Infantry Regiment and now part of my staff here in the Military Intelligence Division."

Drummond extended a hand. "I don't think I've ever been more pleased to see a Yank than when I saw your face yesterday," he said. "You have my thanks, sir."

Burke grasped the man's hand in his own, noting the other's considerable strength in the process, and then shrugged off the praise. "No thanks necessary," he said to Drummond. "I'm sure you would have done the same. Just before you passed out you mentioned you had a message from the King. What was that about, if I might ask?"

If Drummond intended to answer, he didn't get the chance, for at that moment Lieutenant Colonel Ellington stepped up to the head of the table and said, "If you would all find a seat, we'll get this meeting under way."

There were a few minutes of delay as the senior officers in the room settled around the table, their aides in chairs lining the walls of the room behind them. Burke was about to join the latter when Nichols caught his eye and pointed to a seat at the table on his left. Knowing there was no sense in arguing, Burke did as he was told, noting with amusement that Sergeant Drummond was grudgingly settling into the chair on Nichols's right, looking even less happy about it than Burke was. A glance around the room showed him another familiar face; Professor Graves was seated near the rear of the group.

Ellington waited until they were all settled and then got to business.

"As you all know, twelve days ago the Germans launched a devastating attack on the cities of London and New York. Using two armored airships designed to fly higher and faster than we believed possible, they evaded our air patrols and rained devastation down upon our countrymen in the form of a gas designed to turn the living into the walking dead."

The horror of the event, now nearly two weeks in the past, still had the power to bring the room to silence. You could have heard a pin drop as Ellington went on.

"What most of you don't realize is that Paris would have suffered the same fate if it hadn't been for the effort of a small team from our Military Intelligence Division who successfully penetrated enemy lines and, at a secret base outside of Verdun, were able to destroy both the airship and the gas supply it was due to carry."

A cheer went up at the announcement, causing Burke to shake his head in disgust and look away. Yes, he and his men had managed to destroy the *Megaera*, the Paris-bound airship, during their mission to rescue his half brother Jack, and yes, he was proud of that fact. But that pride was not enough to overcome the dismay he'd felt when he learned that just as her namesake had two sisters, so, too, did the airship he'd destroyed. The *Alecto* and the *Tisiphone* had launched from other facilities, miles away from where Burke had been at the time, and had carried out their missions with resounding success. Millions died, or worse, were turned into flesh-hungry zombies, because he couldn't see far enough ahead to realize that a ship named after the Three Furies of Greek mythology simply *had* to have two sister vessels.

No, he didn't deserve cheers for that at all.

Ellington went on.

"The strike on London decimated the city and severed contact with the palace. Our scientists tell us that the gas dropped on the city is similar to the corpse gas the enemy is using on the battlefield, but rather than raising the dead it is infecting the living, turning them into zombies. An evacuation effort was started almost immediately and has saved thousands of lives to date, but that's small potatoes compared to the population of London and the surrounding area."

He turned to an oversized map of London hanging on the wall behind him. "Units of the U.S. Engineer Corps and the Royal Corps of Engineers have managed to erect a makeshift barrier that completely surrounds the city of London—from West Thurrock in the east, north to Waltham Cross, west to Staines and south to Redhill and Seven Oaks—in an effort to keep the shredders, as the troops are now calling them, from turning the rest of the British populace into more of these undead creatures. As of this morning, the perimeter was secure and the threat contained."

Burke frowned. He wasn't an expert on the geography of greater London, Lord knew, but he was pretty damn certain that Southend-on-Sea, the resort community from which he'd plucked Sergeant Drummond less than twenty-four hours ago, was outside the line Calhoun had just described. *The perimeter was secured? Says who?*

He glanced at Nichols, looking for permission to interrupt, but the other man shook his head slightly. *Not now*, he seemed to be saying.

Fine.

Burke gritted his teeth and kept his mouth shut.

Ellington was still talking. " . . . For now. New information that reached us just last night has fundamentally changed our position on the issue. For that I'll turn you all over to Brigadier Calhoun."

Ellington sat down, yielding the floor to his counterpart on the British side, Montgomery Calhoun. The brigadier was a tall, thin man who was practically vibrating with excitement and urgency. His pencil mustache bobbed up and down as he spoke in short, clipped sentences.

"As of three days ago, the King and Queen were alive and well inside Buckingham Palace."

A roar of excitement erupted spontaneously from the British

officers in the room and even Burke couldn't help but smile at the news. The Windsors were well loved and the news that they had survived the bombardment would raise the morale of the troops all along the front.

Calhoun held up his hands for silence, but it still took a couple of minutes for order to be returned so he could continue.

"We intend to mount an immediate operation into the heart of the city to rescue the King and Queen. We're pulling three companies, two infantry and one mechanized, off the front and transporting them across the Channel to Dover."

He turned and pointed out the city's location on the southeastern coast of England. "From Dover we will travel overland to London, secure the royal family, and return with them first to Dover and then across the Channel once more to Le Havre."

A low buzz of excitement began to fill the room as the assembled officers and aides began to talk among themselves, discussing the pros and cons of the brigadier's plan. Pulling that many men off the front lines was going to leave some holes and it would be up to the commanders of the adjacent areas to plug them as best they could. Figuring out how to do that now, before the shortage was upon them, had clearly caught their attention.

Burke, on the other hand, was far from excited. In fact, he was surprised and angry at the news. Calhoun was talking as if they were just going to waltz into London and spring the royal family. After what Burke had gone through the day before, he knew things wouldn't be anywhere near that easy. If Calhoun thought the shredders had been contained, he was sorely mistaken.

The conversation went on around him, the brigadier doling out orders to various unit commanders around the table and they, in turn, discussed them with their staffs, as Burke sat there fuming.

Finally, he couldn't restrain himself any longer. As the chatter continued he rose to his feet.

"Excuse me," he said, trying, without success, to be heard above the crowd.

Colonel Nichols reached out and tugged on Burke's mechanical arm, but the newly minted major shook him off.

"Have you all gone nuts?" Burke asked, in a voice loud and sharp enough to cut through all the chatter.

The room fell abruptly silent in the wake of his remark, as all eyes turned toward Burke.

Brigadier Calhoun's head snapped around to face him.

"What did you say?" he asked.

Burke knew he was treading on thin ice but simply didn't care. The things he'd seen and done in the last few weeks had taken him way out on the edge, and he was finding it hard to come back again, to care about social niceties in light of the horror they were facing. They might throw him in the stockade for speaking up— hell, probably would—but there was no way he was just going to sit here while these idiots spouted such lunacy. Somebody had to derail this thing before it got completely out of control.

Burke went on as if he hadn't heard the brigadier's question. "Tanks?" he asked. "You want to take tanks into London with you? Against shredders?"

Calhoun's face was growing redder by the moment. He looked over to where Ellington was sitting. "Who is this man," he asked, pointing a finger at Burke, "and what the *fuck* is he doing in my meeting?"

Both Ellington and Burke answered at the same time, their voices drowning each other out until the sharp, clear voice of Colonel Nichols cut through the clamor.

"He's one of my people, Brigadier General," he said calmly. "Major Michael Burke. You might recognize him as the commander of the unit that destroyed that airship Lieutenant Colonel Ellington mentioned earlier, the one targeted at Paris?"

The others in the room were looking at Burke a bit differently now, but he barely noticed. His attention was squarely on the idiot at the front of the room.

Nichols went on. "While his decorum leaves much to be desired, something that he and I will discuss in detail immediately after this meeting, I assure you, he does have more firsthand experience in dealing with the shamblers and other classes of undead than anyone else in this room, save perhaps Professor Graves. I, for one, would be interested in what he has to say."

Burke knew a cue when he heard one. He jumped in before any of the other senior officers in the room could shut him down.

"Look, I'm all for rescuing the King and Queen, but what you are suggesting is way off the mark. A small covert team of operatives could probably succeed where a larger, heavily armed force might not, but you sure as hell can't go in there with infantry supported by armor. It will be suicide for all concerned."

Calhoun scoffed. "Suicide? I hardly think so. Fifteen tanks and over four hundred men should be more than enough against an unarmed mob. We'll drive a spearhead into the city with the armor and use the infantry to defend the palace while we get the royal family out."

Burke stared at him in disbelief. *Unarmed mob? Where was this idiot getting his information?*

"With all due respect, Brigadier, don't be an idiot. It's clear that you don't know what you are talking about. Suicide is exactly what that will be! The shredders will zero in on those tanks the moment you fire up the engines to roll them off whatever ship you're bringing them in on. As soon as they do, they'll all come running like you'd just rung the world's biggest dinner bell!"

Burke glanced around the room, looking for support and finding none. A little voice inside his head was telling him to shut up while he still had the chance, that antagonizing a room full of senior officers might not be the wisest thing he could be doing for his career, but Burke couldn't seem to make himself stop. Once the floodgates were opened, it was all going to come out, whether he liked it or not.

"How the hell are you going to use tanks against shredders?" he asked. "Do you think they are going to turn around and flee the first time you lob a shell into their midst?"

The room had gone deathly silent, but Burke barreled onward.

"I'll tell you exactly what is going to happen. You'll kill some with that first tank shell, but that will be the only shot you'll manage to get off. These things are relentless killing machines; they don't feel fear, they don't feel pain, hell, they don't feel anything! Those that survive the first shot from your tank crews will swarm the tank *and* the infantry it is supposed to be protecting faster than you can imagine. Before you know it, all you'll have is a bunch of corpses on your hands. Is that what you want?"

Calhoun frowned. "I hardly think . . ."

Burke cut him off. "That's part of the problem! You aren't thinking! If you were, you wouldn't be sending more than four hundred men to their deaths! For God's sake, General, wake up!"

For just a moment, Burke thought he'd done it, thought he'd talked some sense into the man, made him see that what he was suggesting was nothing more than a great big cock-up just waiting to happen.

Then the man's gaze drifted from Burke's face to those of the men sitting around them, all of whom were staring at the brigadier general, wondering how he was going to deal with this upstart major in their midst, and Burke watched his chance slip away. The man's ego was more important than the lives of the men under his command, a failure in more than one senior officer down through the years, and Burke knew the argument was lost then and there.

He slumped down in his chair, disgusted, as the room erupted in chaos around him. He barely heard the general's orders to have the idiot who'd disrupted his meeting forcibly removed from the room and didn't resist as a squad of MPs came in to walk him out. Thankfully, he wasn't in Calhoun's chain of command and so escaped a more serious punishment when, after a quiet word from Nichols, Lieutenant Colonel Ellington declined to press charges.

Colonel Nichols, however, was anything but quiet when he caught up with Burke outside the headquarters building moments later.

"Give me one good reason why I shouldn't shitcan your ass right now, Burke!" he hollered, oblivious to the other men passing around them as the meeting broke up. "Just what the hell did you think you were doing in there?"

Burke's common sense had finally caught up with him. He stood rigidly at attention in front of the colonel and prudently kept his mouth shut. Not that Colonel Nichols was looking for an answer; Burke knew a rhetorical question when he heard one.

"Get the hell out of my sight, Burke, before I bust you back down to private and return you to the trenches. Dismissed!"

As Burke turned and marched away, he missed the self-satisfied smile that crossed the colonel's face.

CHAPTER EIGHT

THINGS WERE QUIET for the next few days. Burke did his best to stay away from MID headquarters, knowing Colonel Nichols was still pissed at him for his outburst in front of Brigadier Calhoun.

No sense stirring up any more trouble, he thought with only the slightest bit of chagrin as he watched another group of refugees lining up to board a convoy of trucks bound for Marseille in the south, where they would be transferred to one of the steamers headed to India or Australia. London might be gone, but the British Empire lingered, and hopefully these people could build new lives for themselves. God knew an active war zone wasn't the place for them, no matter how many wanted to remain with the troops who had rescued them.

Burke had some time to think about his outburst at the meeting, and the truth was that he didn't regret what he'd said so much as the way he'd said it and then only because it had caused some issues for Colonel Nichols. The bottom line was that he'd said what needed to be said and to hell with the political issues it might cause anyone else. It was time the upper brass got their heads out of their asses and started fighting the war the way it needed to be fought, not as a conflict between nations but as a battle for the very existence of the human race.

He watched as a sergeant wearily explained to an elderly woman waiting to be helped up into the back of a two-ton lorry that she was going to have to leave her beat-up old sailor's trunk behind. Space was at a premium and they could fit at least one, possibly two more passengers into the back of the truck in place of the trunk. The sergeant was doing his best to reassure the woman that he would send it on to Marseille as soon as he could, but he wasn't fooling anyone; the resignation in his voice was plain for everyone to hear. As he droned on, the woman visibly gathered the shreds of her dignity around her like a tattered old cloak and turned away without saying anything more, turning her back on what had to be the last few things she owned in this world in order to give a total stranger a chance at a new life somewhere far from this place.

It was a brave and unselfish thing to do.

As she turned away, her gaze met Burke's and he could see the pain and misery floating there just behind her eyes, held at bay through nothing more than her own raw determination. In response to that burden, Burke did the only thing he could think of.

Holding her gaze with his own, Burke pulled himself up into a textbook-perfect salute, his back ramrod straight, his hand like a knife's edge against the side of his forehead, honoring not only the sacrifice she was making now but also those that they both knew were sure to come on the road ahead.

They stared at each other and for a long moment Burke thought his gesture would go unacknowledged, but then he saw the edge of the woman's mouth curl up into the slightest little smile and she nodded at him, noting his unspoken praise and solidarity. When she turned away, she stood a bit straighter and there was a spring to her step that hadn't been there moments before.

Feeling as if he'd done his good deed for the day, Burke turned to continue his walk, only to see Colonel Nichols's aide, Corporal Davis, racing toward him in an open-topped staff car and waving frantically to get his attention.

Looks like it's time to pay the piper, Burke thought.

Davis deposited him back at MID headquarters, with orders to see the colonel immediately. Burke slipped inside and found Nichols waiting for him in his office. With him was the Black Watch noncom from a few days before, Sergeant Drummond. The expressions on both their faces spoke volumes.

Burke's good mood evaporated.

"How bad?" he asked.

Nichols's mouth tightened into a hard, thin line. "See for yourself," he said, pointing to a table off to one side on which a stack of eight-by-ten photographs rested.

Burke stepped over, picked up the images, and began leafing through them one by one.

The photos were taken from several hundred feet up, most likely from the backseat of an Avro 504 reconnaissance aircraft or something similar. The photographer had been looking down upon the elements of Calhoun's rescue operation as they moved through the center of a small town somewhere outside of London. It was clear from the first photograph that the unit had already come under attack at some point; they were short several tanks from their initial complement, and more than a few men were being helped along by their fellow soldiers. The fact that the attack was continuing was made clear in the second image for it showed a handful of shredders charging out of a nearby alley on the column's left flank. The third image showed that those first few shredders were just the vanguard of an enormous mob of such creatures pouring out of every nearby street and swarming over tanks and soldiers alike.

By the time Burke got to the last of the ten photographs, there wasn't a single living soldier left standing in the final image.

Calhoun's rescue operation had been overrun before it had even reached the streets of London.

Just as Burke had predicted.

Putting the photographs down, he turned back to face the other two. "Did any of them make it out?"

Nichols shook his head.

"Sweet mother of God," Burke said under his breath.

The Scotsman laughed, a harsh, bitter sound. "You ain't heard the half of it yet."

"There's more?" Burke asked Nichols warily.

The other man cast a sour glance at the sergeant and then turned to face Burke.

"An hour ago the acting prime minister petitioned the president for help in rescuing the royal family. No doubt seeing an opportunity to stage another press conference to help him get re-elected, President Harper agreed to send his crack team of special operatives to do the job."

Burke frowned. "You don't mean . . ."

"I do indeed. This communiqué came right from the president himself."

Nichols handed over a slim sheet of telegraph paper.

As of 1100 hours this morning, Burke's Marauders are ordered to London with all necessary dispatch to locate and rescue the surviving members of the royal family.

Burke stared down at the orders in his hand without really seeing them.

"Fuck me," he said, after a moment.

Drummond laughed again. "From over here it looks like somebody already has."

Burke shot a withering glance in Drummond's direction and then followed his commanding officer as he headed back to his desk.

"With all due respect, sir," he said to Nichols's retreating back, "if Calhoun's three divisions couldn't pull this off, what makes you think we can?"

Nichols sat down at his desk and began hunting through a stack of papers in his in-box, clearly looking for something. "It doesn't matter what I think, Burke," he said. "It's what the president thinks. And after your success in Verdun, he apparently thinks you can walk on water. Besides, you said it yourself, 'A small covert team of operatives could probably succeed where a larger, heavily armed force might not.'"

Burke frowned. "I said that?"

"Right before you called Brigadier Calhoun an idiot."

That Burke remembered. One of his more accurate remarks from that particular morning, as the evidence now showed. Still, this wasn't the first time his tendency to tell it like he saw it had landed him in hot water.

"The next time I open my mouth in a meeting, do me a favor and tell me to shut up."

"I tried. Remember?" Nichols answered dryly.

Burke did have some vague recollection of brushing Nichols's hand off his arm, but there was no way he was going to admit that now.

Nichols went on. "I had the men in your unit recalled as soon as I knew what the president intended. Graves never bothered to take his leave, so he's been here since your last mission. Williams was on leave in Paris, but I managed to track him down and he will be arriving later this afternoon. I understand that you've already met your three new squad members, Cohen, Montagna, and Bankowski."

Burke nodded. That left one member of his team unaccounted for. "What about Jones?"

"He's in the stockade."

"Again?" Burke asked, exasperated. "What did he do this time?"

"Some foolishness involving General Harrington's staff car," Nichols said absently, as he searched his desk. After a moment, he found the set of orders he was looking for and passed them over to Burke.

"You'll need these to get him out."

Burke took them with barely a glance. "How long until we ship out?"

"There's a convoy leaving for Le Havre at 1500 hours. You and your men need to be on it. When you arrive, you are to seek out

Captain Wattley of the Royal Navy. He'll see you safely across the Channel."

Burke didn't question the hurried pace; time was of the absolute essence if they wanted to save the royal family. He just hoped they weren't too late.

The colonel inclined his head in the direction of the Black Watch noncom standing nearby. "I've spoken to British High Command and they've agreed to temporarily reassign Sergeant Drummond to your squad. He'll act as your advance scout, guiding you across the city to Buckingham Palace along the same route he used to escape from there several days ago. If that path is no longer secure, you'll be able to fall back on his knowledge of the local area to select an alternate route."

"Fine with me," Burke replied. Drummond had found his way out of a city crawling with shredders and done it in record time, it seemed. That fact alone was enough to tell Burke that he was more than competent. With Moore currently MIA, Burke needed a new sergeant.

Even if it was only temporary.

Burke turned and extended his hand to the other man. "Welcome to the Marauders," he said, as they shook.

"Thank you, Major. I'll try not to let you down," Drummond answered with a grin.

Nichols issued them a set of maps for the city of London and the surrounding area, as well as a series of requisition vouchers that would allow them to gather the weapons, ammunition, and rations they would need to make the trip. Burke handed them off to Drummond, with orders to gather up Cohen and Montagna for a trip to the quartermaster while Burke went to collect their final team member.

THE STOCKADE HAD once been a dairy barn and still smelled like one. The individual stalls had been raised to ceiling height and fitted with doors that came with small viewing slots from which to observe the prisoners, of which there were usually a dozen or so at any given time. Most of them were here for minor infractions like being drunk and disorderly or fighting with a fellow soldier. Those who committed more serious crimes might spend a night or two here while awaiting transport to the main correctional facility out of Paris, but that didn't happen very often.

The two guards standing outside the facility saluted when Burke approached and then opened the door to admit him. Inside Burke found a third man, the jailer, sitting astride a small stool. From somewhere deeper in the building came the sound of a man singing.

Singing *very* badly.

Burke handed his orders to the jailer, who glanced at them and then leaped to his feet.

"Thank you, Lord!" he cried, a wide smile spreading across his face. "And thank you, Major!"

For a moment, Burke didn't understand. Then, "Is that . . . ?" he asked, pointing deeper into the building were the awful cater-wauling was coming from.

"Yes, sir, it is, and can I just say how happy I am that you are taking him away from us?" The jailer was positively beaming at the thought of the prisoner being transferred.

Jones could have that effect on people.

The jailer led Burke down the center aisle and stopped before a cell about three-quarters of the way down. The cells all around it were empty; even the army can take pity on people sometimes, it seemed. From inside the cell came the strong smell of cow manure and the singing he'd heard earlier, if it could even be called that. It sounded like a moose was trying to mate with a mountain lion and neither animal was too happy about it.

The jailer stepped closer to the narrow slot cut into the door and said, "Quiet down, number 43. The major here would like a word."

Inside the cell, Corporal Harrison Jones went right on singing.

"I said quiet, 43!"

The singing continued.

The jailer bent over and glanced through the observation slot.

"You have got to be fuckin' kiddin' me!" he exclaimed.

Burke bent over to take a look for himself.

Jones was sitting on the floor of the cell with his back against the rear wall and his long legs stretched out in front of him. He was shirtless, the garment now tied securely around his head and over his ears.

No wonder his singing sounded worse than usual, Burke thought. *He can't hear himself!*

Burke had first met Corporal Harrison Jones just a few short weeks before. At the time, Jones had been undergoing what the British liked to call Field Punishment #1, where the victim was tied upright to the wheel of a convenient wagon or troop transport and left to stand there for hours in the hot sun to think about the actions, whatever they might be, that had landed him in hot water in the first place. Burke had given Jones a drag of his cigarette and had even taken a liking to the man's upbeat, yet defiant attitude. When he'd found out that Jones was being punished for taking a shot at a German officer when his lieutenant had ordered him not to, a shot that proved to be successful despite the thousand-yard difference that separated the gunman from his target, Burke knew he had to have him on his squad. Jones had been his first official recruit, if you didn't count Sergeant Moore who'd been reassigned when Burke had.

Since then Burke had learned that Jones sometimes had a bit of difficulty dealing with authority figures. He'd disobeyed a direct order in the field with Burke, who'd had no choice but to bust him down a rank as a result. The fact that his actions had probably saved the entire squad's lives was the only thing that had kept Burke from leveling a more severe punishment.

Despite all that, there was no doubt that Jones was perhaps the best natural-born sharpshooter Burke had ever encountered. When they got into the thick of it, Burke would rather have a man like Jones at his side than not.

Fighting to suppress a smile at Jones's ingenuity in finding a way to make his incarceration as unpleasant for his captors as it was for himself, Burke asked the jailer to open the cell door, then had to do it again when he couldn't hear him over all the noise Jones was making.

The jailer pulled a ring of keys off his belt and did as he was asked. When the door was open, he started forward, no doubt intent on using some physical persuasion to get Jones to quiet down, but Burke reached out with his mechanical hand and grabbed him before he could cross the threshold.

"No need for that, Corporal," Burke said. "I can handle it from here."

Grumbling darkly beneath his breath, the jailer stuck his fingers in his ears and headed back toward the front doors and his waiting stool.

Burke watched him go for a moment, just a little insurance to be certain the man's temper didn't get the better of him, and then stepped inside the cell. He let the blond-haired prisoner in front of him continue singing in that horrible off-key voice for another thirty seconds before gently clearing his throat.

The music, if you could call it that, immediately stopped. Jones was clearly far more aware of what was going on around him than he was pretending. He cracked an eye and looked at Burke.

"Let me guess," he said with a grin, "you've come to join me for the chorus?"

"Hardly," Burke replied. "Singing is not in my repertoire of skills."

"Nor mine!" Jones exclaimed with a laugh and broke into another round of the chorus.

Burke didn't hesitate, just drew back his leg and kicked the other man square on the sole of his foot.

"Ow!" Jones grabbed his foot and began massaging it. "Since when did you become a music critic?" he asked.

Burke was already turning away, heading back into the corridor outside the cell. "Come on. We've got work to do."

At the suggestion that they might have another mission before them, Jones leaped to his feet and followed. "What do they want from us this time?" he asked.

Burke glanced back over his shoulder. "What do you think they want? Nothing less than the impossible for Burke's Marauders."

Jones sighed. "Again?" he shot back, as he hurried to catch up, a grin spreading across his face.

CHAPTER NINE

AN HOUR LATER the team assembled together for the first time in a small room Colonel Nichols had arranged at MID headquarters for them. Looking around at the group, Burke was reasonably content that their wide range of skills could see them through the job ahead.

Closest to Burke sat the muscular, blond-haired Jones. Burke was going to be counting on Jones's ability as a sharpshooter to eliminate individual shredders from a distance as they made their way across the city.

Next to Jones was Professor Graves. His extensive knowledge of the shamblers and the occult processes that had been used to create them had been invaluable during their first mission together. The same could be said about the gadgets he produced when not examining undead specimens. They wouldn't have gotten off the burning hulk of the HMS *Victorious* without his personal gliding devices, and his pulse mortars had certainly saved their asses during the escape from Verdun. Burke was hoping Graves's presence would give them a leg up against the hordes of shredders they were sure to face once in the city of London; sometimes a little information made all the difference.

Next around the table were his three new squad members, Privates Cohen, Montagna, and Bankowski. The first two had performed well enough during their jaunt across the Channel to capture a shredder the day before, and Bankowski had dealt with Sergeant Drummond's injuries with quick efficiency. Cohen was a linguistics expert, Montagna a whiz with mechanics, and Bankowski a skilled physician. If they could keep their cool while moving through a city full of shredders and who knew what else, they should eventually become skilled veterans and welcome members of the squad.

The last man at the table was Corporal Benjamin Williams. A dark, curly-headed kid from rural Virginia, he'd been selected for their first mission as a result of his knowledge of things that go boom. He'd been a coal miner before the war, having started working in the mines at his father's side at the age of eleven. He could do things with dynamite that Burke hadn't even known were possible. Before joining the Marauders, Williams had been part of the team that had tunneled beneath the enemy lines at the Battle of Passchendaele and blown up the German company headquarters and half the Messines Ridge in an overwhelming display of military pyrotechnics.

The eighth and final member of the team was Sergeant Drummond, the Black Watch noncom who would be leading them across London to the last known location for the King and Queen. A veteran like Burke, Drummond would be invaluable once they were in the thick of things.

"All right, listen up!" Burke said, calling the meeting to order. "We've got a convoy to catch in under an hour and I want everyone to be clear about what's ahead of us before we head out."

He glanced around the table. "I shouldn't have to remind any of you that what is said in this room is Top Secret and can't be shared with anyone without specific permission from me or Colonel Nichols, but I'm going to do so anyway. Are we clear?"

A chorus of "Yes, sir"s came back to him.

Burke went on. "Our orders come direct from the president

himself and you all know what that means—no one wanted the job before they gave it to us."

A few quiet chuckles bounced around the room.

"By now most of you have probably heard about Brigadier General Calhoun's ill-fated attempt to enter London. What you aren't aware of is the reason for the attempt."

Every man had his attention squarely on Burke at this point.

"Calhoun was acting on credible intelligence received by the Military Intelligence Division that members of the royal family were alive and well inside Buckingham Palace."

"You can't be serious," Jones said.

Burke nodded. "But I am. Quite serious. In fact, it was Sergeant Drummond who brought that information to MID's attention in the first place," he said, pointing at the burly British sergeant in the process.

As one, the group turned to look at Drummond, but he had his attention on Burke and pretended not to notice.

"We'll get to Sergeant Drummond's role in all this in a moment. For now, it's important to know that Calhoun's mistake was thinking that he could get in, rescue the royals, and get out again if he had a large enough force—and it cost him three entire divisions. Clearly he didn't take the nature of the shredders into consideration during planning for the mission. Professor Graves?"

Graves cleared his throat. "Shredders not only have extraordinary hearing—several degrees better than a German shepherd's, if I had to hazard a guess—but some kind of innate sense that informs them when living beings are near, as well. They can remain unmoving for hours, even days at a time, until the proximity of a live human being wakes them up, so to speak, and acts like a homing beacon for them."

"In other words," Burke cut in, "Calhoun screwed up in more ways than one. The sound of all those men and machines, combined with the presence of such a large group of people, brought out every shredder for what must have seemed like miles to the beleaguered troops. They didn't stand a chance."

"Those poor bastards," Montagna muttered beneath his breath and Burke didn't disagree. Those poor bastards was right.

"So how do they expect *us* to pull it off?" Williams asked, unknowingly mimicking Burke's very question from several hours earlier.

"Number one, we're not going to go in there ringing the dinner bell like Calhoun did. A small, specially equipped team has a much better chance of penetrating the city limits and reaching the palace without being detected than a group the size of the one Calhoun utilized.

"Number two, we're not going to try and cross half of Great Britain on the way to the palace. A plan is in place to get us into the city before we move out on our own.

"And number three, we have a secret weapon in Sergeant Drummond."

Jones narrowed his eyes and stared at the recalcitrant sergeant. "And how's that now? Doesn't look like much to me."

Given his years in service, Burke knew that Drummond must have met more than one soldier with an authority problem and no doubt was more than capable of handling them. His hunch was proven correct when Drummond glanced in Jones's direction, winked, and said, "You should see the view from here."

Burke thought it was exactly the right kind of response for a guy like Jones: calm, confident, and without the need to pull rank or take umbrage at the remark. Jones must have thought so too, for the scowl vanished from his face to be replaced by a good-natured grin that told Burke Drummond had passed Jones's test.

Pretending not to have heard the exchange, and therefore avoiding any need to discipline either party, Burke continued his briefing.

"Sergeant Drummond is a member of the famed Black Watch regiment, Fourth Dundee Battalion, and served with distinction at Neuve Chapelle, the Somme, Arras, and Ypres. More important, his company was part of the King's Guard when the Germans attacked London. Unable to get word to Allied Command through the usual channels, the King ordered Sergeant Drummond to lead a squad through the city to the coast, where they hoped to meet up with other British units who could provide assistance to the beleaguered group holed up inside the palace."

He had their undivided attention now. "Sergeant Drummond fulfilled his mission by making his way out of the city and across forty kilometers of what can only be described as enemy territory before running into my patrol several days ago in Southend-on-Sea. He has agreed to lead us back across the city to the palace so that we can carry out our mission of rescuing any survivors that remain."

Burke picked up a large map of the city of London and unfurled it on the table in front of the team. Glancing up at Drummond, he said, "Sergeant? If you would be so kind?"

The other man nodded. "Righto. Here's the plan, boys."

Drummond stepped over to the table, pointed to the blue swatch on the map that represented the Thames River and then traced its route from the sea into the heart of the city. "Rather than trying to go overland like General Calhoun, we'll be taking a boat upstream as far as we can go. The river will help mask the sound of our passage and even if the shredders hear our motors, they won't be able to do anything about it unless they've suddenly developed the ability to walk on water.

"Our objective is the Westminster Bridge, which is here," he said, pointing to a spot just south of a major bend in the river and just north of the part of the city known as Lambeth. "From there we will move directly down Great George Street, past Parliament Square, until we reach the Birdcage Walk."

Drummond's finger traced a route across the bridge and along a road that ran along the southern boundary of St. James's Park.

"Birdcage Walk will take us directly to the Mall and Buckingham Palace. From there we can enter the palace the same way I got out, through the Ambassadors' Entrance on the southeast side of the complex."

Drummond leaned back and looked at them all. "From the bridge to the palace is roughly three kilometers. Shouldn't take us more than a few hours to get in and get out again, hopefully with His and Her Majesty in tow."

Seeing that Drummond was finished, Burke spoke up again. "It is unlikely that we'll be encountering any shamblers during the mission, but there will be plenty of shredders. Professor Graves has been studying one of the creatures firsthand for the last several days and I'm going to ask him to share what he's discovered so that we can be ready to deal with them when the time comes. Professor?"

As Graves began talking about the considerable differences between the two classes of undead, Burke leaned back in his chair and considered the mission ahead of them.

It all sounded so simple, he thought. *Just a quick little jaunt down to the corner and back again.* But he knew from personal experience that it was going to be anything but. Those three kilometers were going to be damned difficult, depending on just how many shredders were still hanging about and whether his squad's arrival was noted by them or not.

And getting back out again with nonmilitary personnel in tow?

Burke didn't even want to think about that.

Instead, he turned his attention to the question of arms and equipment. He was inclined to carry as little as possible, not wanting the equipment they carried to slow them down at any crucial moment, but at the same time he was worried that if they got stuck overnight, they were going to need everything they habitually carried in their haversacks for survival.

He began mentally going through their standard gear, trying to see what they could cut and what they'd have to carry with them on the mission ahead.

In addition to his bedroll and a change of clothing, each man carried a field kit that contained a mess kit with utensils and a condiment can, a personal kit with toiletries, and a first aid pouch with a couple of ready-to-use dressings and bandages, all jammed into a haversack.

Additional equipment—tents and pegs, coils of rope, candles, maps, compasses, matches, additional clips of ammunition—rounded out the rest of the gear the team usually carried, divvied up between them.

Armament-wise, each of the enlisted men carried a Lee Enfield rifle, the bolt-action magazine-fed repeating rifle that was the standard weapon of the American doughboy. The Enfield fired a .303-caliber cartridge, and a well-trained marksman could get off anywhere between twenty and thirty rounds in sixty seconds, making it extremely efficient.

A cartridge belt at the waist carried twelve clips of five rounds each for the rifles, while hanging from the outside of each man's pack was a canteen of water, a box respirator and gas mask, a trenching tool, and a sixteen-inch bayonet.

Given the gas the Germans had dumped on London during the attack, the masks were going to be incredibly important and Burke made a mental note to grab additional filters for each man.

The enlisted men might be carrying Lee Enfields, but Burke, on the other hand, was armed with a Thompson submachine gun, just as he had been for their last mission. The Tommy gun had, for the first time, provided the Allies with a portable machine gun that was as deadly as it was useful. The stocky weapon was fitted with a drum magazine that delivered its fifty-round capacity at a rate of six hundred rounds per minute and could be switched out in seconds by a trained operator. Burke had grown to appreciate the weapon's ability to knock down broad swathes of opponents with little effort; he just wished he had enough of them to hand out to all the men.

In addition to the Tommy gun, he also carried a Colt .45-caliber 1911 firearm in a holster on his hip. A double-pocket magazine pouch containing two full magazines for the pistol was attached to his cartridge belt. Both he and Sergeant Drummond also carried two British Mills bombs, or hand grenades, that could be set to a timed delay of four to seven seconds before throwing.

Burke wanted some of the special magnetism grenades he'd

used in the last mission, but Professor Graves hadn't had time to put them into standardized production yet. The ones he'd been given previously were all they had, and he'd used them during their escape from Verdun.

" . . . and that's all I can tell you at this point," Graves was saying, as Burke focused back on the conversation before him. The professor fielded a few questions from the team and then turned the discussion back over to Burke.

"All right, that's it for now," Burke told them. "We'll be traveling by convoy to Le Havre at 1500, so use the time you have left to check your gear and write any letters you need to write. This time tomorrow you'll be in London."

As Burke watched them file out of the room, he wondered how many were going to make it back again.

CHAPTER TEN

JUST A FEW hundred miles from where Major Burke was gathered with his team, Manfred von Richthofen swept down the hall of the Imperial Palace, intent on reaching the Throne Room without delay. At his heels was a squad of *Geheime Volks*, the undead supersoldiers that his pet scientist, Dr. Eisenberg, had created with his unique blend of alchemy, occult arts, and science. The squad was commanded by Richthofen's adjutant, Leutnant Adler. All of them, including Richthofen, were armed, the soldiers with standard Mauser rifles, Adler and Richthofen with Luger pistols.

Richthofen knew his supersoldiers were quite a sight to those who had never encountered them before. Their crisp black uniforms and black jackboots were designed to be intimidating and had the added benefit of making the black veins pulsing beneath their sallow skin stand out in sharp relief. The gleam of madness in their eyes and the guns in their hands were enough to send the palace staff scurrying out of the way at the first sight of them.

Of course, he was no picture of perfection himself, he knew.

The time he'd spent rotting on the battlefield before his first resurrection had left him with a gaping hole in the left side of his face, his teeth and jawbone clearly visible through his now ravaged flesh. He had always considered himself an intimidating individual, but now he knew he was downright frightening to behold. That didn't bother him at all; fear was a useful tool when utilized properly.

He had come prepared to deal with some resistance from the palace staff, but so far his squad hadn't encountered any, much to his satisfaction. The guards at the front gate, and then again those stationed at the doors of the palace itself, had let them in without hesitation. Perhaps even with a bit of eagerness. Nothing had been said about the weapons he and his men carried either, despite the fact that it was considered treason to bring firearms into the palace, never mind into the kaiser's presence. From Richthofen's viewpoint, the message had been very clear; it was time for someone new to sit upon Germany's throne and the guards' inactivity was tacit approval of his claim to that position.

They turned a corner and there, at the end of the hall, was the entrance to the Throne Room where the kaiser was having lunch with his senior advisers. Another pair of guards stood watch outside these doors as well. The younger of the two, a corporal, stepped forward, positioning himself between the Throne Room and the oncoming visitors.

Richthofen's eyes narrowed at the sight and he was about to raise his hand in a signal for Leutnant Adler to deal with the problem, when the other guard, an older sergeant, reached out and dragged the younger man to the side, out of Richthofen's way. When the corporal opened his mouth to protest, the sergeant clamped a hand firmly over it, cutting off whatever it was that he'd been about to say.

The squad closed the distance and formed up in front of the double doors to the Throne Room, preparing to make their entrance. Richthofen paused a moment before the guardsmen, head cocked to one side in amused interest. He eyed them one at a time, his gaze finally settling on the older of the two men.

"Is he going to be a problem?" the Baron asked. His voice was calm, unhurried, as if he'd been discussing the weather instead of a man's life.

From the way his voice shook, the sergeant did not miss the threat. "No, sir," he replied. "He's newly promoted and eager to do a solid job, sir, that's all. He won't be a problem."

There was a hint of similarity in the facial features of the two men and Richthofen correctly surmised that they were related. *Probably his sister's son*, he thought to himself idly.

The corporal mumbled something, but with the older man's hand over his mouth, Richthofen was unable to understand him. He waved the sergeant off.

Reluctantly, the older man let go and stepped back.

As soon as he was free, the corporal snapped to attention. "Corporal Manheim, at your service, Herr Richthofen!"

Richthofen eyed him for a long moment.

"At my service, you say?"

Over the corporal's shoulder, Richthofen saw the older man wince at the tone of Richthofen's voice, but the corporal had made his bed and would have to sleep in it now.

The younger man was oblivious to the silent exchange. "Yes, sir! For the glory of the empire, Herr Richthofen!"

Richthofen chuckled. *For the glory of the empire, indeed.* The young corporal had made his allegiance known at a most fortuitous time.

"Attend me, Corporal," Richthofen ordered. "I have just the task for you."

The corporal was practically beaming with pride at having been singled out in such a fashion and fell into step behind the German ace as he gave the signal to Leutnant Adler.

Adler turned, raised one booted foot, and then slammed it into the Throne Room doors. The flimsy locks holding them closed were no match for the enhanced strength of the undead soldier, and the doors sprang open with a crash. Adler's men had been lined up on either side of him and rushed into the room as soon as the entryway was breached, their weapons out and pointed at the men in the room just beyond.

Richthofen followed, with Corporal Manheim and Leutnant Adler at his heels.

The room was large and lavishly decorated with the kind of ostentatious display of wealth that normally disgusted Richthofen, but he barely noticed, for his attention was elsewhere.

The kaiser sat before a well-laid table on the far side of the room, eating lunch with General Ludendorff, his quartermaster-general, and Field Marshal Von Hindenburg, his chief of staff. All three men looked up in surprise as Richthofen's men crossed the room toward them.

"What's the meaning of this?" the kaiser demanded with as much bravado as he was able to summon at the sight of a dozen men pointing guns in his direction, but the quavering in his voice gave him away. The other two men didn't even do that much; they simply froze in place like deer trapped in a hunter's light. Richthofen wasn't sure which of the three he despised most.

The kaiser was weak; there was no questioning that fact. He'd had the opportunity to seize decisive control of the battlefield in the first few months of the war, but he'd surrounded himself with sycophants like Ludendorff and Von Hindenburg instead; men who would say whatever the kaiser wanted to hear, and as a result their greatest chance to squash the resistance of the Allies had been lost. Seven years of trench warfare with the two armies locked in a stalemate had been the result, and if things were left to continue as they were, Richthofen had no doubt that they would still be in the exact same place seven years from now as well.

Richthofen had hoped his bold attack on London and New York would provide the impetus needed to change the status quo. A strike at the heart of the Allied defense while they were still reeling with the destruction of those two great cities would have broken the back of the Allied line. Paris would have fallen and, with it, the rest of the Allied resistance on the Continent. Europe would have been theirs!

Rather than seizing the moment and exploiting the opportunity Richthofen had provided, the kaiser had instead done nothing.

It was time for a change.

As Richthofen stepped into view, the kaiser's eyes narrowed. "Richthofen! I should have known this was your doing."

There was no love lost between the two men.

Richthofen ignored the kaiser's outburst, speaking more for the others in the room than for the three condemned men at the table in front of him.

"Friedrich Wilhelm Viktor Albert," Richthofen began, addressing himself directly to the kaiser and refusing to give his ludicrous reign any further legitimacy by using titles, "I hereby charge you with treason, specifically with crimes against the people of Germany and against the empire itself. How do you plead?"

The look of confusion and abject fear that crossed Wilhelm's face at the word *treason* was like sweet ambrosia to the German ace. Even the lowliest private knew the penalty for treason in the German armed forces.

"Crimes against the empire? Treason?" Wilhelm blustered. "Have you lost your mind, Richthofen?"

Richthofen ignored the kaiser's response. "After due consideration of the facts before this tribunal, I find you guilty of treason and sentenced to execution by firing squad. Corporal Manheim?"

As the younger man stepped forward, Wilhelm began shouting at them both.

"Tribunal? What tribunal? You can't do this, Richthofen!" He turned to the soldiers standing around them and thrust a finger in Richthofen's direction. "I am the kaiser and I demand that you shoot this villainous bastard where he stands! Shoot him, I say!"

Richthofen's undead troops stared back at the kaiser, unmoved. It was clear where their allegiance lay.

Nervous sweat dotted Corporal Manheim's face as he stepped up next to Richthofen. "Sir?"

Without taking his gaze off the kaiser, Richthofen drew his sidearm and handed it to the young man.

"Carry out the sentence, please, Corporal."

Manheim took the gun and, with trembling hands, pointed it in the kaiser's direction. Richthofen watched him closely, enjoying the mental and emotional strain he'd just placed on the other man. Humans were weak, just like the kaiser, and if Manheim wanted to be a part of Richthofen's new world order, he was going to have to prove his support for the new kaiser.

Starting with killing the old one.

The only question was whether he'd have the backbone to do it.

"What are you doing?" the kaiser shrieked at him, holding up his good hand as if to protect himself from the bullet to come. "I am the kaiser! Shoot him, not me! Shoot Richthofen!"

Manheim's entire body was shaking with the strain, the muzzle of the gun wavering but still pointed toward the kaiser. The corporal brought his other hand up and wrapped it around the first in an effort to hold the gun steady, but that just seemed to make it worse.

Beside him, Richthofen leaned in close and said, "I gave you an order, Corporal, didn't I?"

"Yes, sir," Manheim gasped.

"Then what are you waiting for? Carry out the sentence."

Richthofen leaned back, glancing past the corporal as he did so to catch Adler's gaze with his own. He gave a slight nod. In response, the leutnant changed his stance slightly so that he was now facing the corporal rather than the senior officers at the table.

Manheim huffed several times, trying to get up the nerve. For a moment, Richthofen thought he might find the courage, but then the man's head dropped to his chest in shame and he lowered his arms.

"I can't, sir," he gasped.

Richthofen reached out and removed the gun from the young man's hands. "Leutnant Adler?"

Adler barked an order and the troops lined up in a semicircle around the table where the kaiser and his companions were having lunch and opened fire as one. The roar of their Mausers filled the room as bullets slammed into the three men at the table, making their bodies dance and jitter under the impact. Blood flew and the stench of cordite filled the air.

Richthofen watched it all with delight.

He let the shooting continue for another moment, then raised a hand, signaling the others to stop.

Wilhelm, Ludendorff, and Von Hindenburg were all slumped across the table, unmoving, their bodies covered in blood.

In the sudden silence Richthofen turned to Corporal Manheim, raised the pistol, and shot him in the head, splattering the soldier standing behind him with a mixture of blood, brains, and bone fragments.

As the corporal's body slumped at his feet, Richthofen handed the pistol to Adler.

The kaiser is dead, thought Richthofen. *Long live the kaiser!*

CHAPTER ELEVEN

THE CONVOY BURKE and the Marauders had been ordered
to catch consisted of four two-ton lorries packed full of salvaged
scrap metal and a Model T Ford ambulance with several medical
evacuees bound for the USS *Nightingale,* a hospital ship docked in
Le Havre that would eventually take them back across the Atlantic and home to the States.

After arriving at the staging area, Burke checked in with the
captain in charge of the convoy, offering to have his men take their
turns at watch along the way. He knew the planned route would
take them through Paris to Rouen and then on to Le Havre. At no
time would they cross into German-held territory, but they would
be traveling very close to the front for much of the way and would
most likely come under attack of one kind or another at some
point. The captain was all too happy to add several more rifles to
the convoy defense should they need them and stationed Burke
and his men in the last two trucks in the group while consolidating
his own men in the front vehicles. The vehicles were refueled, the

wounded loaded aboard the Model T, and the convoy got under way reasonably close to the planned departure time.

As Burke and the convoy captain had feared, they were attacked twice while en route by German aircraft patrolling behind the lines. The first time it was by a lone Fokker D.VII biplane that must have been low on fuel, for it strafed the convoy just once before continuing on its way. The second time they were caught on the open road by a trio of aircraft, Albatroses, Burke thought, given their rounded tails, and took some heavy fire for several minutes before a pair of Sopwith Camels turned up and chased the German fighters off. Having come under fire from a determined fighter pilot in the past, Burke knew they got away pretty easily.

Night had fallen by the time they reached the city. They said their good-byes to the convoy crew and headed for the docks. Once there, Burke sent the men over to the enlisted mess while he slipped into the officers' club to try to track down their contact, Captain Wattley.

It took a few tries, but eventually Burke was directed to berth number eighteen. He headed in that direction, expecting to find another fishing trawler like the one that had taken him to Southend-on-Sea just a few days before, and was shocked upon arrival to find a submarine bobbing gently in the waters at the end of the dock, a British flag flying over it. Two sailors stood guard duty at the end of the gangplank leading to the deck of the submarine and they watched him cautiously as he approached.

"I'm looking for Captain Wattley," Burke told them.

One of the guards looked him over for a moment, then said, "Wait here," and disappeared up the gangplank and through the hatch.

The other guard wasn't the talkative type, replying to Burke's inquiries with one-word responses, so after a few attempts at conversation Burke moved to one side and shook out a cigarette to smoke while he waited. He'd just about finished when the guard returned, this time with a lieutenant in tow.

"Major Burke? Lieutenant Sanders, HMS *Reliant*."

The two men shook hands.

"I'm Captain Wattley's executive officer. The captain is asleep at the moment; it's his off-shift. Can I help you with something?"

"Sorry to spring this on you unannounced, Lieutenant, but I'm afraid you're going to have to go wake the old man up. I've got sealed orders for him and him alone and we're on a bit of a timetable on this one."

The lieutenant didn't look happy, but he didn't have much choice in the matter. Sanders led Burke up the gangplank, across the deck, and over to the conning tower hatch from which Sanders had emerged moments before. With a warning to watch his head, Sanders led him below.

Burke had never been aboard a submarine before, and the tight quarters were the first thing he noticed. It was hard not to when the ceiling seemed to press down from above and the walls felt closer than he knew they actually were. He couldn't imagine being trapped inside this contraption with thousands of pounds of pressure pushing in on it from the outside; the thought made him claustrophobic.

Sanders slipped past the crew members working around them and led Burke to a bulkhead door at the back of the room. He knocked and then slipped inside the door, leaving Burke standing there alone under the curious eyes of the crew for several minutes. Eventually Sanders stepped back out and gestured for Burke to go on in.

The room was tiny and clearly served two purposes, if the radio he glimpsed behind the captain's hammock was any indication. Captain Wattley turned out to be a slim, narrow-faced man with a shaved head and the bushiest set of eyebrows Burke had ever seen. He stood next to his hammock, a cup of coffee in hand, and glowered at Burke.

"What's this about, Major?"

Burke didn't say anything, just took the envelope containing their sealed orders from inside his uniform shirt and handed it over.

Wattley tore it open and read the orders it contained, his scowl deepening as he did so.

"Is this a joke?" he asked finally, when he was finished.

Burke did his best to hold on to his temper. So far the reception he'd received had been less than stellar. He wondered if the man had a thing against the Yanks. *Would explain his behavior, at least . . .*

"I'm not privy to what your orders say, Captain, but I have my own and I assure you that this is not a joke. Far from it, in fact."

Wattley stared at him for a moment and then stepped to where a talking box was bolted to the wall beside his bed. Picking up the receiver, he spun the crank several times to build up a charge and then pressed the red button on the front of the base. He waited a moment until someone picked up on the other end and then said, "Get me Davis at the Admiralty, Lieutenant."

Burke stood by politely while the other man waited for the connection to be made and then spent several minutes arguing with whoever was on the other end of the line about the orders he'd just received. That someone must have pushed the issue higher up the chain of command, though, for Wattley's attitude underwent an abrupt change a few minutes later, his speech suddenly interspersed with short silences followed by several "Yes, sir"s and "Of course, sir"s. When at last he hung up the phone, his attitude was noticeably improved.

"It seems that my boat and I are at your disposal, Major. I don't suppose you'd care to tell me what this is all about?"

"What did the Admiralty say?"

"Just that this is a highly classified mission and that I am to take you to London as quickly as possible."

Burke had no doubt that the mission would go much more smoothly if the captain's assistance was given willingly, so he decided to trust the man and give him a little more information.

"My men and I have been tasked with rescuing several individuals from the heart of London. We need you and your boat to take us as far up the Thames as possible. Getting us all the way to the Westminster Bridge would be ideal, but if you can't make that, then the Waterloo or Blackfriars Bridge will have to do. Any farther east of that point and we probably won't live long enough crossing the city to reach our objective."

From the look of surprise on the captain's face it was obvious that he hadn't expected Burke to answer him and the extension of trust seemed to go a long way, just as Burke had hoped. The captain's annoyance was greatly mitigated as he turned his full attention to dealing with the issue at hand.

"Normally we'd have no problem making Westminster Bridge," he told Burke. "The river's deep enough to carry us through the city and out the other side for that matter when the tide is high. But that was before the Germans tried to bomb us back into the Stone Age. Who knows what's in the water at this point?"

The captain pulled a chart from a nearby shelf and spread it out on his desk. He stared at it for a moment, his fingers tracing the course of the river as it made its way through the heart of the city, and then looked up at Burke.

"If the bridges are intact, we should be fine." He paused, glanced at the map, and then up again at Burke. "Are the bridges intact?" he asked.

"Reconnaissance photos show the London, Southwark, Millennium, and Blackfriars Bridges to be undamaged. The Westminster Bridge has taken some hits, but appears to be mainly intact as well. We're less certain of the Waterloo and Hungerford Bridges, however, as smoke from a large fire burning out of control in South Bank has obscured every attempt we've made to get a decent look at them."

"Nothing to do but wait and see then," Wattley said. "I'll get you as close as I can, you can rest assured of that."

Burke nodded; he'd expected as much.

"How many men are we talking about?" the sub captain asked.

"Eight. Myself, plus seven others."

"And for the return?"

Burke shrugged. "Unknown. Might be one. Might be a dozen or more. We really won't know until we get there."

He could see by Wattley's face that he didn't care for that answer, but there wasn't much Burke could do about it. Drummond had reported that the party had consisted of the King, the Queen, and fifteen soldiers when he'd been sent for help. But that had been days ago; there was just no way of knowing how many had survived at this point.

The submarine captain must have worked that out for himself, for he shrugged and said, "Good enough, I guess. Let's just hope they don't expect first-class accommodations."

Burke was certain they'd be too thrilled at being rescued to care and said as much.

"I suppose you've got that right, Major," Wattley said with a laugh. "You know, you should feel right at home here."

"Really? Why's that?"

"The *Reliant*'s an H class submarine, built by you Yanks in the Quincy Navy Yard outside of Boston."

"Good old American engineering, is that what you're telling me?"

Wattley shrugged. "She hasn't let me down yet," he said, with a grin.

Burke very carefully avoided mentioning that there was a first time for everything.

The captain didn't notice Burke's hesitation. "Ever been aboard a submarine, Major?"

"Can't say that I've had the pleasure."

"Well, then, how about a quick tour while we make the necessary arrangements to get your men aboard and squared away?"

"Sounds good to me," Burke replied, thinking the more he knew, the better chance of survival they all would have should something go wrong.

They left the radio room and stepped back into the control room. Lieutenant Sanders glanced in their direction, but Wattley waved him off with a quick shake of his head and led Burke to the right, toward the aft section of the boat.

"The *Reliant*'s one hundred seventy-one feet long, with a beam of just over fifteen feet. We're slightly smaller than the older E class subs, which makes us a bit more maneuverable when we need to be, especially in tight quarters."

Burke stiffened; he hadn't even thought about maneuverability, particularly within the confines of the Thames. A mental image popped into his head of the bulkhead in front of him tearing open as the boat ran hard aground deep beneath the surface of the river and he could almost hear the shouts and cries of the wounded as the water began to pour into the compartment . . .

Focus, Burke, focus.

"This here's the main battery compartment and crew accommodations. Since my men will be at their posts during the run across the Channel, your men can use this compartment for the passage," Wattley told him.

Burke nodded; the space looked like it would be more than adequate for their purposes. After all, there wasn't much for them to do but sit around and wait for Wattley and his men to take them to their destination. Hopefully the *Reliant*'s fate would turn out better than that of the *Victorious,* the British airship that had ferried the Marauders across the lines into German-held territory in eastern France just a few weeks before.

That had not ended well, Burke remembered, with a rueful shake of his head.

Just beyond the battery compartment was the engine room. Looking in through the hatch, Burke saw a burly chief directing several sailors as they stripped the covers from two large engines, one on either side of the compartment.

Wattley pointed in their direction. "The boys there are giving our electric motors a final once-over and should be done within the hour. The motors deliver 160 horsepower each and provide us with nine knots of speed when we're submerged."

Burke did the math in his head and realized that nine knots

was only about ten miles per hour. Not all that fast, but he supposed speed was less of an issue when you were down deep beneath the waves where no one could see you.

"What about while on the surface?" he asked.

"That's the job of our primary diesel engine," Wattley told him, pointing to another hulk of machinery deeper in the compartment. "Without the water resistance, we can make eleven, sometimes twelve knots on a good day."

Burke frowned. That didn't sound like much compared to the twenty or so knots he knew a German König class battleship could reach. While he didn't expect to meet a vessel like that on the Thames—*Good God, he hoped not!*—he was still surprised that the disparity was so high and mentioned it to Captain Wattley.

"You're thinking like a surface captain and not a submariner, Major. Follow me."

Wattley waved to the engine room chief and then turned and headed back the way they had come. He passed through the control room and into the wardroom where the crew took all their meals. Beyond that was another crew accommodation space, this one with hammocks still hung throughout the compartment, and then finally a large space with racks of torpedoes on either side.

"You're standing in the forward torpedo storage compartment. From here the weapons chief arms the eighteen-inch torpedoes we carry and loads them into the bow tubes for use against the enemy."

Wattley smiled. "We don't need to be faster than the König or Kaiser class dreadnoughts. We just need to be able to sneak up on them long enough to fire a few of these pretties in their wake and sit back to watch the fireworks."

Burke would feel much more comfortable knowing he could escape an engagement if it went wrong, but he'd give Wattley the benefit of the doubt given that he was the submarine captain and Burke was not.

Wattley asked about the state of things at the front, and Burke was happy enough to share what he knew as they made their way back to the control room and the exit from the boat. Wattley didn't follow him topside but bid him good-bye at the base of the ladder, returning to his preparations while Burke went to round up his squad.

BACK AT THE mess hall, Burke waited for his men to finish eating and then led them outside. Commandeering a truck and driver, he had the driver take them back over to the docks to where the *Reliant* was berthed. From there it was a simple five-minute walk to the *Reliant*'s individual slip.

Burke was walking next to Jones, his haversack slung over one shoulder, when the conning tower of the boat came into view and Jones stopped short at the sight of it. "That's a submarine," he said.

"That's right," Burke replied. "The HMS *Reliant*. Quite the modern vessel, I'm told."

"But . . . it's a submarine."

Burke frowned. "Yes, a submarine. What's the problem?"

Ahead of them, the rest of the squad slowed, then stopped as they realized that Jones and Burke had fallen behind.

Sergeant Drummond turned and headed back in Burke's direction. "Everything all right, Major?" he called.

Burke waved him off. "Go on and get the others settled, Sergeant. I'll be along directly."

Drummond nodded and did as he was told, heading for the gangplank with the rest of the squad in tow. There were a few curious backward glances, but that was all. Once they'd passed out of earshot, Burke turned and faced Jones directly.

"What's the problem, Jones?" he asked.

A look of embarrassment crossed the man's face as he said, "I can't swim, sir."

His answer caught Burke off-guard. *Can't swim? What the hell does that have to do with anything?*

"I'm not following you."

"I can't *swim*, sir," Harrison said, stressing the latter word as if that was enough, but to Burke it still didn't make any sense.

"What in the blue blazes does swimming have to do with the submarine?" Burke asked. "It's not like you have to get out and push!"

You hope, his conscience said.

Burke ignored it.

"I told you, sir, I can't swim. What if there is a . . . a *problem*, sir?"

A look of horror crossed the man's face at the word *problem*, and at last Burke began to understand. It wasn't his ability or lack thereof that was bothering Jones; it was the idea of getting trapped in what was little more than an oversized tin can hundreds of feet beneath the surface in the event of an emergency.

Jones was afraid.

Burke almost didn't believe it. Of all the men under his command, Jones was the last person he'd expect to balk at the sight of the boat. He'd personally seen Jones jump out of a burning airship with nothing more than an experimental gliding device strapped to his back, go toe-to-toe against the twin Spandau machine guns on a diving Fokker D.VII with just a Lee Enfield rifle, and face down ravaging hordes of the undead with a smile on his face. A quick submarine ride across the Channel should be easy after all that.

Jones, however, didn't think so.

"I . . . I can't go in there, sir."

Burke laughed, trying to make light of the situation. "Sure you can, Jones," he said, clapping the younger man on the shoulder. "Nothing to it."

But Jones was shaking his head. "I can't, sir. I really can't."

The corporal took two steps back as he said it, as if to punctuate his statement.

Burke frowned, uncertain of what to do next. Manhandling Jones aboard the boat didn't seem to be the answer; the man's fear would make him go hog-wild the moment he thought they were going to force him aboard. Doing so would just give the British sailors aboard the boat a reason to ridicule the U.S. Army, never mind one of his men.

No, that wasn't any kind of solution at all.

If he couldn't force him aboard or convince him to make the choice on his own, there seemed to be only one other solution.

"It's all right, Jones," he said, not unkindly. "You've done enough. I'll find something for you to do here at the port until we get back and keep the reasons to myself; no one else needs to know."

The original squad had been made up of volunteers, including Jones. As much as he wanted Jones by his side for the mission ahead, he couldn't, in good conscience, force him to come along. The man was terrified, that was easy to see, and Burke had no doubt that the fear would get worse if Jones couldn't conquer it before boarding. Being trapped inside the *Reliant* was going to be hard enough on all of them; they didn't need a raving lunatic along to keep them company.

Burke clapped a hand on Jones's shoulder, gave it a reassuring squeeze. "See what you can do about arranging transportation for us back to MID headquarters for when we return, yeah? And make sure it's something reasonably comfortable. I don't want to be the one to tell the Queen of England that she's going to have to ride in the back like some common piece of luggage, understand?"

Jones was staring at his feet, refusing to meet Burke's gaze, but he nodded slightly to show he understood. Burke decided that was going to have to be good enough.

He clapped Jones on the shoulder one more time and then turned away, his steps heavy as he covered the last few dozen yards to the submarine slip. Jones was a helluva soldier, for all his authority issues. Burke was going to miss having his skill with a rifle . . .

The sound of running feet behind him drew Burke's attention. He turned and was just in time to see Jones jog up the gangplank behind him. There was still fear in the man's eyes, but Burke could see he had it under control. His next comment proved that was the case.

"If I drown in this blasted tin can, I swear I'll haunt you forever, Major!"

Burke laughed. "Welcome aboard, Corporal, welcome aboard."

CHAPTER TWELVE

LONDON WAS ALL but unrecognizable.

From his position in the conning tower next to Captain Wattley, Burke stared out at the devastation around him and wondered just how Sergeant Drummond had ever managed to cross more than forty kilometers of such destruction and live to tell about it.

After boarding the HMS *Reliant* earlier, Burke and his men settled into the compartment that had been assigned to them. Some, like Sergeant Drummond and Private Bankowski, slipped into the canvas hammocks hanging from the ceiling and tried to catch some sleep while the rest simply found a convenient stretch of decking out of the main traffic pattern running through the compartment and did the same.

It was raining when they slipped their berth but Captain Wattley made the decision to remain on the surface; the winds weren't strong enough to kick up the kind of swells that would necessitate a dive beneath the surface, and the low cloud cover would make it unlikely that any German aircraft would be patrolling in this weather. It was a decision that pleased Burke almost as much as it did Jones. As far as

Burke was concerned, boats were made to stay on the surface of the water, not dive beneath it.

At twelve miles per hour he knew that it was going to take them practically all night to cover the 150 miles between Le Havre, their starting point, and their destination midway along the Thames estuary. Perhaps longer, if they ran into any trouble.

Burke kept his eye on Jones, who had borrowed a deck of cards from one of the British sailors and was passing the time by teaching Private Cohen to play poker. Jones seemed to be doing just fine, his initial fear of the boat not showing at all, and eventually Burke stopped worrying about him.

Somewhere along the way, Burke had fallen asleep, only to be woken up several hours later by Sanders, the executive officer, who told him Captain Wattley was looking for the major to join him in the conning tower.

Now Burke and Wattley stood side by side, gas masks securely on, staring out at the devastated city as they headed into the heart of London.

The Tower of London rose on their right as they slipped beneath the Tower Bridge, and Burke could see that while some of the lesser buildings had taken some damage, the White Tower, the oldest of the group, still stood tall in the early morning light. The sight of the age-old edifice still standing despite the Germans' bombing of the city gave him a small bit of hope amid the destruction he was witnessing around him.

They motored onward and glided beneath each of the other bridges connecting the north side of the city with its counterpart on the south. The London Bridge, the newly built Southwark Bridge, the Blackfriars Bridge—all were intact and provided no barrier to their passage. There were a few anxious moments when they came up on the old Waterloo Bridge, site of so many of London's suicides in its early days, and found the crossing tilting dangerously to one side, but they managed to maneuver around the impediment and continue on their way without striking anything.

All the buildings they could see as they made their way deeper into the city were in various states of destruction. Some had been hit by falling bombs, some by falling buildings as the bombs took out the structures around them. Runaway fires claimed a lot of the rest, and Burke could still see patches of flame burning here and there against the dark night sky. Billowing clouds of smoke and ash drifted here and there amid the ruins, a visual reminder of all that had gone before.

Looking around, Burke knew it would be a long time before London was once again considered the jewel of the British Empire. There was *that* much destruction.

And he and his team were headed into the heart of it.

Burke reached up and adjusted the gas mask slightly, trying, and failing, to make it more comfortable. The rubber mouthpiece tasted like old tires and the clips on his nose pinched uncomfortably, but he guessed he'd have to make do until Professor Graves had a chance to check the air once they arrived at their destination. For now, he'd just have to deal with it.

Captain Wattley nudged him with an elbow to get his attention and then pointed across the water. A large freighter had run aground on the other side of the river, tipping up at an angle, and even from here Burke could see the bodies of the dead lying on the deck and hanging partially off the edge of the ship. Although he couldn't see their bodily injuries in any detail, the dark red stains covering most of their torsos didn't require much explanation.

Wattley said something to him, but Burke didn't hear it clearly; the sound was muffled thanks to the hoods of the gas masks each of them wore. He leaned in closer.

"What was that?"

Wattley gestured at the boat as they slipped past in the gray light of the early morning. "Why are they still dead? Why aren't they up and walking around again?"

It took Burke a moment to understand what it was that Wattley meant.

Shambler bites were infectious and those who survived being bitten by one often suffered a hideous death shortly thereafter as the virus or whatever it was spread through their system. Inevitably, those who died ended up rising again to join those resurrected by the gas, like one big happy family of flesh-eating undead. The same might be expected here. The victims on the freighter had clearly been killed by shredders and, given that this new breed of undead were cousins to the shamblers, it made sense that their attacks might have the same effect.

Or, at least, Burke would have thought so.

Now he wasn't so sure.

Perhaps those who had survived the attack unscathed had returned to deliver the coup de grâce, a bullet through the skull, to their less fortunate comrades?

He suggested as much to Wattley.

"Come on, you can't be serious!" the captain replied. "Look at them over there; there must be nearly four dozen or more! It would have taken forever and the noise would have brought dozens more shredders down on them in the process."

Wattley shook his head. "Nah, I'm betting there's more to it than that."

But without stopping and boarding the freighter, which neither man wanted to do, there was no way of knowing for sure. As the wreck slipped into the distance behind them, Burke wondered if anyone would ever know what had happened aboard the vessel in its final hours.

Less than ten minutes later the bulk of the Westminster Bridge loomed out of the gray light of dawn ahead of them, Big Ben and the ruins of the Houses of Parliament rising behind it, and the captain began quietly passing instructions through a series of sailors stationed as relays to Lieutenant Sanders in the control room. The boat slowed as it approached the bridge and then slipped into its shadow. Burke stepped out of the way as men dashed up from below to handle the anchors and soon the vessel was at a full stop, bobbing gently in the waters beneath the bridge.

They had arrived at their destination.

Captain Wattley disappeared below to arrange for their transport ashore. Professor Graves took his place out on deck, lugging his haversack behind him. The gas mask he wore made him look particularly insectoid given his height and narrow frame, like a weirdly mechanical praying mantis, and Burke found that he had to resist the urge to laugh lest he insult the man.

Graves dug around in his haversack for a moment, removing an assortment of items.

"Here, hold this," he said, his voice muffled from the mask. He handed Burke a small automaton that looked like a mechanical dragonfly, but with eight wings instead of four. A small glass jar hung from its belly.

"What is it?"

Graves ignored him. "Use this to wind it up, please," he said, handing Burke a wooden hand crank.

Burke sighed, but did as he was told. He had come to know Graves a bit better over the last several weeks of working together and knew that once Graves tuned into a particular project, getting three words out of him was tantamount to getting blood from a stone.

He inserted the crank into a hold designed for it in the side of the dragonfly's body. He held the wings flat against the dragonfly's back with one hand while turning the crank with the other.

"Fifty times, please. No more and no less."

Right.

While Burke was doing that, Graves pulled out several bottles filled with different colored powders or liquids and arranged them on the decking next to him. When he was satisfied with the arrangement, he took a roll of string from his pocket and tied the loose end of the string to a ring in the nose of the dragonfly.

"Now I want you to take the EDFFAMD and raise it . . ."

Burke interrupted. "The what?"

"The EDFFAMD."

At Burke's continued blank look, Graves said, "The electronically driven free-flying atmospheric measuring device," and pointed at the device in Burke's hands.

"Right. Got it."

"Raise it over your head and loft it into the air like you would a pigeon."

The wings lay flat and unmoving as it headed skyward and for a moment Burke thought it was going to reach the top of its arc and drop like a rock right into the waters of the Thames, but then the eight little tin plates that served as wings popped out and flapped wildly, sending the little device soaring into the air.

Graves kept control of it via the string he held in his hands, and after it had buzzed around above them for a few minutes, he quickly reeled it in. Burke could see that the collection bottle hanging beneath the automaton was filled with some of the dense smog that was drifting across the city. Graves quickly popped a cork in the bottle and slipped it free of its clamp.

Burke watched as Graves set the bottle aside and mixed some of the powders and liquids from the other jars together in a mortar and pestle. He ground them into a dark-gray-colored powder, then he turned and handed the mortar to Burke.

"When I open the collection bottle, I want you to pour that mixture inside as quickly as you can."

Graves was hard to understand through the hood, but Burke thought he'd gotten the gist of it correct and he did as he was asked, tapping the edge of the mortar against the side of the bottle gently to get as much of the gritty-looking mixture out as he could.

When he was done Burke stepped back, expecting some strange chemical reaction to occur as Graves corked the bottle back up and gave it a good shake.

Nothing.

The mixture inside the bottle stayed exactly the same.

"Excellent!" Graves exclaimed, then reached up and removed his gas mask.

"No, Graves! What are you doing?" Burke shouted, reaching out to forcibly return the mask to the man's face, but Graves shook him off.

"Now, now, Major. I assure you I'm just fine. The gas has dissipated and we are in no danger of it from here."

Burke reached up to remove his own mask, and then stopped.

"You're certain?" he asked.

Graves cast a withering look in his direction but didn't say anything.

"Okay, okay," Burke replied, holding up his hands in surrender. He loosened the strap on his mask and slipped it off his head. Realizing he was holding his breath, Burke relaxed and tried to breathe normally.

The air held the acrid scent of burned concrete and steel, along with the stink of bodies decaying in the wind, but that was all.

Perhaps their mission just got a little easier.

CHAPTER THIRTEEN

★

BENEATH WESTMINSTER BRIDGE
LONDON

ONCE PROFESSOR GRAVES determined that gas masks were
unnecessary, communication was no longer hampered by the thick
material of the mask hoods, and the squad's efforts to get under
way sped up appreciably.

A wooden-bottomed rubber raft was brought up from below
and Burke's men inflated it with the help of a pressure hose run up
from the engine room below. As the squad climbed aboard, Burke
ran through things one more time with Captain Wattley.

"Forty-eight hours," he told him. "If we're not back in that time
frame, we're probably not coming back at all. Get your men out of
here and see to it that Colonel Nichols in Military Intelligence has
all the details you can give him. That's all I can ask."

Wattley nodded grimly. "I'll keep an eye out, Major, and I'll
be sure your man knows what happened if things go sour for you."

The two men shook hands, and then Burke joined his men
aboard the raft. Moments later they were rowing for shore, doing
their best to keep the noise levels down to the barest minimum.

After anchoring the boat on some convenient rocks, the team disembarked and formed up as a unit, with Sergeant Drummond on point and with Corporal Williams watching their six. Major Burke was near the front of the column, just behind Drummond, with the others spaced out in a single-file line with about a yard between them.

Burke's rules of engagement were simple. They were to avoid any and all contact with the shredders for as long as possible. If it looked like they were about to be attacked, they were to try and eliminate the threat without resorting to gunfire. Gunfire would be used as a last resort and then only so long as the threat remained active. By limiting the noise they were making, Burke was hoping to avoid attracting large groups of shredders to the team before they reached their destination.

The streets weren't much better up close than they had been from the deck of the *Reliant*. Many of the buildings had been reduced to rubble; soot, smoke, and ash lay everywhere thanks to the fires burning out of control in other parts of the city; and they were forced to move at a slow, measured pace to limit the noise they were making so as to avoid attracting wandering shredders.

With Drummond leading the way, they managed to leave the river behind and make their way into the city without incident. They spotted more than a handful of the creatures moving through the streets, but each time they did so Drummond led the squad away from any potential confrontation, moving down an alternate route that allowed them to skirt the creatures before they were noticed.

What they couldn't avoid, however, were the remains of the shredders' victims. Bodies lay everywhere, the violent evidence of death that many of them sported on their bodies proof enough that it hadn't been the German bombing run or subsequent gas attack that had done them in.

Wanting a closer look, Burke stepped over to the nearest corpse and squatted next to it.

The victim had been male, most likely in his late sixties. He was wearing the remains of a dressing gown, so had likely been chased out of bed by either the bombs or the shredders themselves after the attack. The shredders had made a mess of the man's chest cavity, burrowing into it with all the ferocity of rabid dogs. Burke could see the shattered remains of the corpse's ribs jutting up through the ruin of his chest and the empty space between them where his internal organs had once been.

Remembering his conversation with Captain Wattley on the deck of the *Reliant*, Burke checked for a coup de grâce shot but didn't see any sign of one. He didn't know how it was possible, but this man seemed to have died at the hands of the shredders but hadn't gotten up to walk again in their wake, just like those on the ship they'd passed on the Thames. A quick check of some of the other bodies nearby showed him the same.

Drummond appeared at his side. "Find something, Major?" he asked in a low voice, leery, like the rest of them, of attracting the shredders unnecessarily.

Burke shook his head. "Not particularly. Just verifying a pet theory, that's all."

Drummond nodded, as if doing so made perfect sense while they were trying to clandestinely make their way through the city to Buckingham Palace without getting eaten by shredders. "Righto. Perhaps we can get a move on, then?"

"Of course, Sergeant."

A scream split the morning air.

Burke leaped to his feet, turning in place as he tried to pinpoint the source of the sound. The others were doing the same, their weapons at the ready, but without a target to shoot at there was little they could do.

"Where is it?" Jones said urgently, but all Burke could do was shrug. He didn't know.

The scream came again, and this time it was long enough for them to get a fix on it.

"This way!" Jones yelled and dashed off down a side street before Burke could say anything.

"Damn it, Jones!" Burke muttered as he set off after him.

The rest of the squad had no choice but to follow.

They left the main street and cut down an alley, following in Jones's wake. Another cry split the air, helping them better triangulate the source of the anguish. Fear, pain, and horror were at the root of those cries, and the hair on the back of Burke's neck stood on end to hear them. Whoever she was, she was in dire need of help.

Burke and the others skidded around a corner to find Jones staring at a maze of rubble strewn along and across the road in front of them, uncertain which way to go. Having caught up with his wayward corporal, Burke took command and led the way, making certain that Jones stayed to the middle of the pack.

They found her moments later.

The woman lay on her back in the middle of the street, her arms and legs flailing as she tried to beat off the pair of shredders who crouched over her using their nails and teeth to tear at her flesh. Blood was splashed everywhere, on her clothes, on the ground, on the faces and chests of the shredders preying upon her.

The squad was crouched along the ruined wall of a nearby building, perpendicular to where the woman lay. They had good, clean shots at both shredders. Jones took one glance and brought his rifle up, ready to take down the undead creatures in front of him with or without orders. He was lining up the shot when Sergeant Drummond snatched the weapon from his hands.

"What the hell are you doing?" Jones whispered. "Give me that gun!"

Drummond shook his head. "If you fire that thing, you'll bring every damned shredder within half a mile down on our heads!"

Burke moved to intercept the two before things got out of hand.

Jones wasn't one for subtleties. "Give me that fucking gun, Sergeant, or so help me God I'll . . ."

"You'll do nothing, Corporal," Burke said, placing himself bodily between the two men. "And that's an order." He faced Jones directly, crowding into his personal space. "We're not going to jeopardize this mission for the sake of a single shredder victim."

Jones was shaking his head, refusing to accept that they were just going to leave the woman to her fate. "Major, that woman . . ."

" . . . is dead," Williams cut in from behind them.

Burke turned, saw Williams's face, and rushed back over to the ruined wall beside him. One glance was all it took; the shredders were still feeding, but the woman lay unmoving beneath them now, her empty eyes staring skyward unseeingly.

The group slipped quietly back the way they had come, not wanting to disturb the shredders now that there was no urgent reason for doing so. Burke could tell Jones wasn't happy, and the murderous glances he was casting Drummond when he thought no one was looking weren't exactly reassuring either.

I'd best keep my eye on him, Burke thought, and he reminded himself to warn the sergeant when they had a private moment. For now though, they had to keep moving.

It wasn't long after that when they reached the edge of St. James's Park and the street that would lead them to the palace itself, Birdcage Walk.

St. James's was the oldest of the royal parks, originally constructed by Henry VII in 1532 and greatly expanded during the reign of Charles II. Its fifty-eight acres were thick with forest and included a large lake running the length of the park.

More important from Burke's perspective, the park ran parallel to Birdcage Walk, the road leading to the palace, and provided them with considerably more in the way of cover than the streets they left behind.

Drummond led them through the park and around the northern shore of St. James's Park Lake. He approached the palace from the southeast and it wasn't long before they could see a massive marble building looming ahead of them out of the trees.

Burke and company had reached Buckingham Palace.

CHAPTER FOURTEEN

SERGEANT DRUMMOND POINTED to the northern section of the palace, just visible from where they crouched among the trees in the Mall. From what they could see, there wasn't much left of that wing.

"The King and Queen's private apartments were in that section of the palace. The bombardiers must have been aiming for them because at least half a dozen bombs came down smack in the middle of it."

Burke shook his head, imagining what it must have been like to be inside the building at that moment. The entire wing had been pulverized; there probably wasn't an intact wall in the whole section.

"Thankfully, the royals were in the East Gallery courtyard at the time, on the opposite side of the building, and escaped without injury. My comrades and I hustled them inside the building and to one of the hardened rooms near the Blue Drawing Room, built to act as a temporary retreat when danger threatens."

Drummond pointed to a large, raised roofing area in the south-west corner of the building, which, from Burke's perspective, was in the back corner to his right.

"See that raised section?" he asked Burke. "That's the State Ballroom. The safe room was just north of that, in the corner area there."

Burke nodded as if he knew exactly what Drummond was talking about, but the truth was he did not. The palace was huge, easily one of the larger structures he'd ever seen, not counting the skyscrapers in New York City back home. Drummond had told him earlier that Buckingham Palace had 775 rooms, including 19 state rooms, 52 bedrooms, and 78 bathrooms, never mind all the staff apartments and business offices used for the day-to-day running of the kingdom.

Without Drummond's help as a guide, Burke had to admit that he could probably wander through the building for days before finding the room where the King and Queen were currently holed up for protection.

"So that's where they are?" Burke asked. "By the State Ballroom?"

But Drummond shook his head. "That's where they were immediately after the Germans' attack, but we didn't keep them there for long, especially not after the damned shredders began making an appearance. There's a series of private apartments above the staff quarters that are occasionally used for diplomatic visitors and we moved them up there. It's a more defensible position; only one way in and out."

Drummond's remark about the shredders set off a twinge in the back of Burke's mind. Given what they knew about their behavior, he'd expected to see dozens of them milling about outside the palace and yet he didn't see one anywhere he looked. There were several in the park, wandering aimlessly among the trees, and they'd passed more than a handful on their way here, but not a single one within a hundred yards of the palace.

"Where are the shredders?" he asked, more to himself than anyone else.

Drummond must have heard him, but not well, for he leaned in closer. "What's that?"

"Where are the shredders?" Burke asked again, louder this time. He waved a hand toward the palace. "If the rest of your squad has been holed up inside that building for the last week protecting the King and Queen, shouldn't there be a mob of shredders surrounding the place right about now?"

He knew he was right and by the way Drummond began swiveling his head back and forth, searching the front of the palace for any sign of a shredder, so, too, did his companion.

Something was terribly wrong.

Burke was as sure of that as he was of his own name.

He could feel Drummond's anxiety ratcheting upward and was suddenly worried that the other man would break cover and rush into the open, so he reached out and put a hand on Drummond's shoulder, turning his attention away from the scene before him and pulling him back down to earth before he did something rash.

"Easy," Burke said. "We've come this far, let's not do anything stupid and screw it up now."

Drummond nodded and took a couple of deep breaths, but his eyes were still full of anxiety as he looked out at the palace.

"How do we get in?" Burke asked, when it looked like the other man was thinking clearly again.

Drummond pointed to a one-story extension jutting off to the left of the main building. "Behind that wing is the Ambassadors' Entrance. It's half hidden in that thick copse of trees. We barricaded the entrance and posted several men there to guard it. When I left, I slipped out through that door and made my way through the trees to the street beyond."

"What about the fence?" Burke asked, pointing to the tall iron fence that separated the palace grounds from those of the Mall.

Drummond shrugged. "You can climb, right, Major?"

Provided I don't have a horde of shredders grabbing at my heels, Burke thought.

Then again, that might make me climb even faster.

Aloud, he said, "Sounds good. Let's do it."

He carefully didn't mention that the presence of the guards, or the lack thereof, would also tell them if the situation inside the building had changed and possibly just how badly things had gotten out of control.

For a hundred yards before the fence and maybe half that again after it, they would be out in the open, exposed. They could creep a little closer under the cover of the trees they were now hiding in, but they were going to run out sooner rather than later, and when they did, they wouldn't have any options left. There simply was no way of approaching the palace from this side without crossing that space. When they did, they would be exposing themselves to view from both inside and outside the building at the same time.

Can't be helped, he thought. Going around the complex seemed fraught with more danger than the few seconds of exposure in front of it; who knew what was lurking around the other side.

Yeah, well no one said this would be easy. Get off your ass, Burke, and get moving!

Word was passed back to the others in the group and when they were ready, they made their move. Burke figured they'd have a better chance of survival if they were all together should shredders decide to break up their little party, so they left the cover of the trees as a group and raced over the open ground to the fence as quickly as they could. Jones, Williams, and Burke stood watch while the others scrambled over the fence and then Drummond, Cohen, and Montagna did the same from the other side while the others joined them.

Nothing raced out of the building to confront them, nor did anything emerge from the trees in their wake.

So far, so good.

They crossed the open space on the other side of the fence and then slipped into the trees governing the approach to the Ambassadors' Entrance, leery of anything hiding within their shade, but their fears were unnecessary.

There were no shredders in the trees.

Nor was there anyone manning the barricade at the entrance.

As they approached they could see that a pitched battle had been fought just in front of the doors and recently, too. Dozens of shredder corpses lay scattered about, along with the bodies of several of the King's Guard.

Drummond let out a cry and rushed over to the nearest one, but the man was long past help. His head had been nearly severed from his neck by a sweep of a shredder's claws, and his eyes stared up at Drummond without seeing.

The same held true for all the rest.

They'd fought hard, but eventually they'd fallen, and the shredders had made their way into the palace, if the destruction in the hallways just beyond was any kind of evidence.

Drummond led them through the building, down hallways and up staircases, and everywhere they went they saw the same thing—scores of shredder bodies lying beside the bodies of a few of the King's Guard. The soldiers may have paid with their lives, but they'd made damned sure the enemy had paid a high price for each and every one.

By the time they reached the entrance to the third-floor apartments where the King and Queen had taken refuge, the hopes of finding them alive had dimmed considerably. Here, too, another pitched battle had been fought, and the dead were piled high in the corridor and around the doors. Shredder and human alike had fought with a ferocity that Burke found disquieting, and he wondered how many other places across the city held scenes just like this one. Was this what all of England was destined for in the days to come?

It was a horrifying thought.

They found the King and Queen in the back bedroom, lying side by side on the bed with identical bullet holes in the middle of their foreheads. Slumped against the wall nearby was the body of a British officer, a colonel by the look of the insignias on his uniform, the gun he'd used to blow off the top of his skull still in his mouth.

It wasn't hard to figure out what had happened.

The King's Guard had fought to protect them as long as they could, judging from the number of shredders lying dead in the hallway. When it became obvious that there was no way out, the King and Queen had retreated into the bedroom with the colonel in tow. Not wanting to die at the hands of the shredders, the King must have given orders to the colonel and then lain down beside his wife. Steeling himself, no doubt with very little time left, the colonel must have shot the Queen first, then the King, and, after taking a seat beside his now-dead monarchs, shot himself.

It couldn't have happened all that long ago, either, for the bodies had yet to start any kind of significant swelling.

A day, maybe a day and a half at the most, Burke thought.

At the sight of the King and Queen, Sergeant Drummond nearly collapsed, and it was only Burke's quick reflexes that kept the man from hitting the floor. Burke helped him over to a nearby chair and lowered him into it. Tears streamed down Drummond's face and he couldn't seem to pull his gaze away from the deceased couple. Burke could guess how he was feeling, simultaneously full of grief and the nagging suspicion that the royal family might still be alive if he had returned with help sooner.

It wasn't true; Drummond had done all he humanly could have done to rescue the King and Queen, but time and circumstances had been against him from the start.

Of course, if General Calhoun had not wasted time with staging a massive assault just to make himself look better . . . Burke shook the thought away before it could take hold.

Nothing he could do about it all now.

They had done their best, but the mission was a failure through no fault of their own.

Knowing he couldn't just leave the bodies of the British heads of state to rot in their bombed-out and shredder-infested palace, Burke made the decision to wrap them up in a set of sheets, bind them with ropes, and carry them back to the *Reliant* for transport back to France where they could be given a proper burial as befitted their station.

He explained what he wanted to do to the others and they all, solemnly, agreed that it had to be done. Sergeant Drummond seemed particularly grateful.

"All right then. Doc, why don't you grab some sheets from the other room? Jones and Williams, you're in charge of lifting and moving the bodies while Cohen and Montagna will find us some rope to use to secure them."

Burke clapped his hands. "Let's move, people. The faster we get their Royal Majesties ready for transport, the faster we can get back to the *Reliant* and head out of here for good. I've had my share of shredders, if you know what I mean."

The men snapped into action, and soon they had several sets of sheets laid out on the floor next to the bed. They moved the Queen first, being as gentle with her corpse as they could, sliding it off the bed and lowering it into the center of the sheets for Cohen and Montagna to bundle, wrap, and tie under Doc Bankowski's supervision.

But as they stepped up to move the King, Burke noticed something peculiar. The King's right hand was clenched tightly around something. He could see it, just a hint of white, maybe a piece of cloth or paper, sticking out at the bottom of his palm.

Doc Bankowski was about to tell Jones and Williams to lift up the body when Burke stepped in their way.

"Hold on a minute, guys."

Burke knelt by the edge of the bed, being certain to avoid the blood that had dripped down from the mattress and pooled on the floor, and then lifted the King's arm so he could get a better look.

Yep, definitely something in his hand.

Holding the King's wrist in one hand, he tried to pry his fingers apart with the other.

Nothing. Whatever it was, the King had it clenched in a death grip. If he wanted to get it out, he was going to have to break the man's fingers.

Leave it alone, a dim voice at the back of his head said. *It's got nothing to do with you. Probably just the man's handkerchief anyway.*

But something about the way the King was holding on to it so tightly kept nagging at Burke. *It was almost like he wanted it to be found . . .*

"Sergeant Drummond, could you come here, please?"

Drummond, who had been watching the proceedings from the far side of the room, came over as he'd been bid.

"Major?"

"I believe King George has something in his hand, Sergeant. Something important, though I can't really explain why. As the only representative of the British Crown here at the moment, I'd like to ask your permission to retrieve it. Before you answer, understand that I'm going to have to break one or more of the King's fingers in order to get it out."

To Burke's surprise, the sergeant didn't even hesitate. "If you don't mind . . ." he said, then held out his hands as if to take the King's forearm himself.

Of course.

"Certainly, Sergeant. And thank you."

Drummond nodded but didn't say anything as he sat on the edge of the bed and laid the King's arm across his lap. Holding the dead man's wrist securely with one hand, he took hold of the King's thumb with the other hand, took a deep, calming breath that everyone in the room could hear, and then snapped it with a dull crack.

When that didn't prove sufficient, he repeated the same action with the King's index finger.

In the end, the King didn't want to give up his secrets lightly, and it took three broken digits before Drummond was able to slide the piece of paper King George was holding free and pass it to Major Burke.

Burke opened the slip of paper and read the two words that were written there in a hurried scrawl.

"What the hell is Bedlam and who is Veronica?" he asked aloud.

CHAPTER FIFTEEN

The object of Major Burke's attention was at that moment staring out the window of the third-floor ward for female patients, wondering how she was going to get her men down three floors and out of the building proper without losing them to the horde of ravaging undead that still wandered the hospital grounds.

Frankly, she didn't have the bloodiest idea.

No pun intended.

Veronica Windsor, princess of Great Britain and Ireland, continued loading rounds into the cylinder of the Webley Mk VI revolver she'd picked up from a dead soldier as she pondered the question. She knew they were running out of ammunition as well as food and wondered which staple would ultimately be their undoing.

Would they die of starvation or fall victim to the rampaging creatures that had once been their friends and fellow workers?

Neither opportunity sounded all that enticing, actually, but without a plan she was effectively stuck for the time being.

Which was all the more frustrating, as she shouldn't have been here in the first place.

On the morning of the attack, her mother, Queen Mary, had been due to make a planned visit to Bethlem Hospital. More commonly known as Bedlam, the hospital was both a medical facility and a sanatorium for patients with various medical afflictions, and the Queen's visit was to show her support of the changes the hospital board had made in recent months to improve the facility's reputation. Having awoken with a severe headache, the Queen asked Veronica to come in her place. She was halfway through the tour when the bombing started.

At first the leader of her protective detail, a Black Watch captain from the King's own Guard named Samuel Morrison, hadn't wanted to expose her to the danger presented by the bombs hammering the city streets. "We'll stay here, hunker down, and return to the palace when the attack has passed," he said. By the time they realized that the green gas that was starting to flow through the city streets was a far greater threat than the bombs themselves, many of the patients and staff inside the hospital had been exposed to the chemical agent through the windows that had been broken in the bombing run and had become infected. Within minutes dozens of them had been transformed into flesh-hungry ghouls who then fell on their comrades, ripping and tearing their flesh with their teeth and bare hands.

Veronica had never been more terrified in her life.

None of the protection detail had been carrying gas masks and there were a few frantic moments spent assembling makeshift ones from portable respirators and oxygen tanks in a supply room off the main ward while two of her guards stuffed wet towels into the cracks around the door in an effort to keep the gas out.

Their efforts had given the others time to get their masks in order, but the two soldiers had paid the price, transforming right in front of Veronica into horrible, undead creatures like those she'd heard roamed the battlefields of the Continent.

The next several days had been a blur, with Captain Morrison and his men doing their level best to protect her from the ever-increasing number of creatures wandering about the hospital grounds. Each time they thought they'd found a safe haven to hide and let their wounds heal, the damned zombies found them again. *It was almost like they were sniffing them out, like hounds on a fox!*

Her protection detail started with six men, plus Captain Morrison. Now they were down to her, Morrison, and three others. All of them had suffered minor wounds of one kind or another, mostly cuts and bruises from fending off the undead, but Veronica knew it would only get worse as they grew weaker from lack of food and water.

After noticing the zombies seemed to be a bit less active in the bright sunlight, Veronica and her team had waited until the middle of the day and then had slipped away to the third floor. They had piled several corpses in front of the first set of double doors and then retreated behind them, locking several sets of double doors between them and the entrance in the hope that they might manage to escape notice until they could figure out what to do next.

Thankfully, their plan worked.

Now, days later, they had exhausted their supplies and needed to make a decision about what to do next.

"I think we should stay put," Morrison said, his voice intense despite the whispering. "Someone is eventually going to come looking for us, and if we start wandering around, we might miss the rescue team when it comes."

Staring out at the ravaged city from her window perch, Veronica knew there was no rescue coming, however.

They were on their own.

"Look out the window, Sam," she said softly, using his first name for emphasis. "Where do you think this hypothetical rescue is coming from?"

Sam refused to do as she asked, however. He kept his eyes on the floor and waved his hand in the general direction of the rest of the European continent.

"I don't know," he said sharply. "Out there somewhere."

Veronica stared at him, until, feeling the weight of her gaze, he looked up to meet it.

"We both know that's not going to happen," she said. "Have you seen even one emergency response crew in the last few days? A fire brigade? An ambulance team? Hell, even a bloody bobby would do! Anybody?"

Morrison shook his head.

"Nor have I. I'm starting to suspect that there won't be any, either. They would have been here by now if any were still in operation. This is a hospital, for heaven's sake!"

Veronica shook her head. "No, we're on our own. And that means we need to stop sitting around on our asses and see about rescuing ourselves instead."

Morrison sighed, though whether that was the belief behind her statement or the words she'd used to express herself, Veronica didn't know. Given he was twenty years her senior, and full of what she considered some rather antiquated beliefs as to how a lady, never mind a princess, should behave, she suspected the latter.

"What would you suggest?" he asked.

"We need to get to a wireless set, let someone know where we are and that we're all right. They couldn't have bombed the entire country! Someone must be out there, someone who can help us."

The guard captain looked at her like she'd lost her mind. "Where did you expect to find a wireless set, Your Highness?"

"The British Museum."

Morrison shook his head. "The museum doesn't have a wireless."

"Yes, it does. Trust me when I tell you that there is more to the museum than you know, and a wireless is definitely on the premises. Get me there and I'll handle the rest."

"I don't know . . ."

The museum was north of Charing Cross Station, close to Covent Garden. If those flesh-eating fiends had spread through the city as easily as they'd spread through the hospital, it was going to be quite the trip. But there were things she needed to get at the museum, things that couldn't be left behind for the enemy to find, if they were audacious enough to invade.

Veronica didn't know what had happened to her parents, and she prayed that they were all right. But she had specific orders she was required to carry out in the event of an emergency and recovering certain items from the British Museum was one of them. Now that she decided they shouldn't wait to be rescued, those orders took priority. If her parents lived, a big "if" in her view, given how extensively the Germans had bombed the city, then she could always turn her charge over to them when they were all reunited. For now, though, she had a job to do; and the longer she waited, the more she worried that someone would beat her to it.

The *wrong* someone.

"I'm not asking, Captain."

Morrison had been in the service of the Crown long enough to know an order when he heard one.

"Yes, Your Highness. The British Museum it is."

HALF AN HOUR later they made their move.

The ward they were in looked down upon a large, outdoor garden. An iron fence ran completely around the entire property, including that garden, but one thing made the garden section of that fence different from most of the other sections of the fence.

The garden had a gate.

It was currently chained and locked; they could see that from the room they were in. But Veronica didn't know a lock yet that could stand up to a couple shots from a .455-caliber Webley revolver and she fully intended to blow that particular lock right to hell.

Once outside the gate, they would do their best to hook up with another group of survivors or locate a vehicle they could use to take them most of the way to the museum.

After that . . . well, after that they'd figure something out.

"Ready?" Morrison asked.

Veronica nodded.

Two of the soldiers—Veronica was embarrassed that she couldn't remember their names—stood guard on either side of the window while Morrison carefully opened it and then tied one end of their makeshift rope around his waist.

Directly below them was the roof to the first-floor extension that jutted out from the side of the building. The plan was for Veronica and the other soldier, Stevens, to lower Morrison down to that roof. He would hold up there and stand guard while the rest of them came down one at a time. From there they would take out the ghouls in the garden, three of them, sprint for the fence, and be gone before any of the creatures inside knew what had happened.

They hoped.

Along with her partner, Private Stevens, Veronica braced herself to bear the captain's weight and then said, "Go!"

Out the window Morrison went. It took only a few minutes to lower him to the rooftop below and then it was Veronica's turn.

One of the guards took her place and then helped Stevens lower her down the side of the building. She watched the undead creatures stumble around in the ankle-high grass of the garden as she slowly descended. They were not yet aware that fresh prey was only a dozen yards away, but she knew that it wouldn't take them long to head in their direction as soon as they noticed.

Drawing close to where Morrison was waiting for her below, she was suddenly glad that she'd taken up wearing men's-style trousers and button-down shirts several months ago. As with her language, it was another thing that some of those of the older generation, like her mother and father, frowned upon, but she had to admit that it was going to make running for the gate much easier than if she'd been wearing a corset and skirts.

Never mind avoiding the whole embarrassing situation of having Captain Morrison looking up at her as she came down the rope.

Morrison reached up and grabbed her around the waist with both hands and helped her the last few feet to the rooftop. Untying the rope from around her waist, he left it to hang there in case they needed to go back up in a hurry.

"Okay?" Morrison asked.

Veronica nodded.

Out in the garden, roughly thirty feet from their position, one of the monsters cocked its head to the side as if it had heard them.

No, that can't be, she thought. *Morrison had barely raised his voice.*

But as the next soldier began making his way down the rope, the ghoul turned its head in their direction and looked right at them.

For a moment Veronica's gaze met that of the creature and she saw that there was nothing human left in those eyes, just a bottomless sense of hunger . . .

It lurched into motion, headed in their direction.

"Company, Captain," she said.

Morrison turned, saw the oncoming ghoul, and raised his right arm.

The creature's head snapped back a split second before the sound of the shot reached her ears. Veronica watched as the thing toppled over backward to lie still in the grass.

As if they shared one mind, the two remaining ghouls turned in their direction at the exact same time.

"I think we should be quieter . . ." she began to say and then two more shots rang out and both those creatures dropped dead as well.

By then events were too out of control for her to do anything about and all she could do was get carried along in their wake or get left behind.

The last two soldiers slid down the ropes, their boots thunking onto the steel roof. From somewhere below them Veronica thought she heard several of the creatures snarl in reply.

"Run!" Morrison yelled and that's exactly what they did.

The three soldiers with them grabbed hold of the edge of the rooftop, swung their legs over the side, and hung there for a second before dropping down the last few remaining feet into the grass below. Instantly two of them turned and raised their arms, ready to help Veronica do the same, but she'd been a tomboy all her life and certainly didn't need any help swinging down from so low a height. Ignoring their hands, she dropped down right next to them.

Captain Morrison quickly followed suit and no sooner was he on the ground than the group headed out, running hell-bent for the gate on the far side of the garden, with Veronica in the center surrounded by the four soldiers, all that remained of her guard detail.

She could hear her heart pounding in her chest, her breath hissing in her ears, and over both of those the howl of those things as they caught sight of their little party.

Faster! she thought and flung herself headlong toward the fence.

Before she knew it they were skidding to a stop in front of the wrought-iron structure and Veronica was pushing Private what's-his-name out of the way as she wrenched her Webley out of the leather belts she had crisscrossed over her chest. She pointed it at the padlock holding the gates shut.

Boom!

Clack.

The lock fell to the ground.

"Move! Move! Move!" Morrison yelled as he hauled open the gate. The little group poured through it and turned to the left . . .

Veronica could see that for ten, maybe twenty yards ahead of them the space was clear, but just beyond that a literal wall of ghouls was moving in their direction, arms outstretched, with fingers grasping, and a horrible grunting-snarling sound of need, of hunger, coming from their mouths.

Veronica glanced the other way, only to find more of them coming from that direction.

It's the noise, she thought dazedly. *The noise attracts them!*

"Get back! Back to the room!"

Veronica didn't need to be told twice.

She turned and ran for the gate, Captain Morrison at her side. Behind her she could hear the others firing their guns, doing what they could to give them time to make it to the ropes.

My fault. This is my fault.

It didn't matter whose fault it was if they didn't live through it.

A blackened, hideous form lurched toward her and Veronica turned, Webley in hand, and fired off a shot before she'd even consciously thought about it.

The ghoul's head exploded in a colorful explosion of blood, flesh, and bone.

Don't you dare be sick, she told herself sternly and thankfully she was not.

Morrison was firing beside her now and she realized, albeit belatedly, that more of the monsters were swarming out of the ground floor wards on either side of the garden. It was going to be a race to see who was going to get to them first.

Behind her, Veronica heard one of the other soldiers scream in pain but she didn't dare turn to look. She kept her eye on the ground-floor extension in front of her and the ropes dangling from the window high above. She drove her boots into the grass beneath her feet as she charged forward, willing herself to go faster, faster . . .

Two of the creatures outdistanced the others and closed in. As she raised her pistol two shots rang out from beside her and both of the horrible things were tossed to the side by the impact of Morrison's bullets.

Then she had no more time to look, no more time to think, as the wall from which they'd descended loomed before her.

"Here," Morrison gasped, "let me help you!" He laced the fingers of both hands together to form a stirrup and extended it toward her.

Veronica barely had her boot in it before Morrison was heaving her upward.

She grabbed the edge of the roof and pulled herself up with strength born of pure terror. Without even bothering to stand up she spun around, her body stretched out on the rooftop for balance and her feet wedged into the crack between two tin sheets for support as she dropped her arm over the side, reaching for Morrison.

Behind him, she could see several of the ghouls closing in, but no sign of the three men who had remained to guard the gate.

Morrison jumped, caught her wrist in his, and nearly pulled her from her perch as he swung his legs upward . . .

Veronica pulled with all her might, and the captain slipped up and over the edge of the roof just as the ghouls reached for him with empty hands.

Morrison sent her up the makeshift rope first and then followed close behind. Once back in their room, they pulled the sheets back up behind them, and slumped in exhaustion to the floor, their backs to the wall beneath the window.

Their escape attempt had failed and they'd lost three men in the process!

Veronica put her face in her hands and wept.

Outside in the garden, dozens of the creatures stared up at them, milling about while groaning and gnashing their teeth.

CHAPTER SIXTEEN

IMPERIAL PALACE
BERLIN, GERMANY

NO LONGER ENCUMBERED by the need to sleep in any real sense of the word, His Imperial and Royal Majesty, German emperor and king of Prussia Manfred von Richthofen stared at the battle plans laid out on the table in the Throne Room, despite the fact that it was still an hour before dawn and the sun had yet to even peek its head above the horizon, and considered how he was going to break the back of the combined Allied armies where they were dug in along the Western Front.

Even the sun trembles at my power, Richthofen thought and then laughed at his own hubris. He might rule the mightiest nation in the history of the world at this point, but the stars, oh, the stars were still their own masters.

For now.

He was paging through reports of unit strengths along the Belgian border when there was a knock at the door and a second later Leutnant Adler's voice reached him from across the room.

"Dr. Eisenberg to see you, Your Majesty."

Richthofen didn't bother to look up from his work, just waved for Adler to send him in.

"Busy day, *Doktor*," Richthofen said without looking up from his work. "What do you have for me?"

"Your predecessor's dear cousin, George the Fifth, lives."

Richthofen froze, then slowly looked up at his chief scientist, the man who was also the inventor of the gas that Richthofen had used to turn England into a nation of flesh-hungry ghouls.

"How . . . interesting. Do tell, *Doktor*."

"My man inside the American's Military Intelligence Division smuggled a message out to me this morning, reporting that General Calhoun had not been trying to retake London, as we had assumed, but rather rescue the King and Queen from where they were hiding inside the remains of Buckingham Palace."

Richthofen frowned. "Calhoun's command was wiped out, was it not?"

"Indeed, Your Majesty. They had barely reached the city limits when they were torn apart by a seething mob of their own countrymen who had been infected by the gas."

"So what's the problem? The heir apparent, Prince Andrew, died on the battlefield at Amiens. He has no other brothers, only a younger sister, leaving the succession unresolved. King George and his annoying little wife will eventually fall victim to the same fate as their subjects." Richthofen glanced at the pile of maps and battle reports on his desk, impatient to return to them. Breaking through the Allied line at Nogent might be the easiest way to go . . .

"My man reports that a second force has been dispatched in an attempt to rescue King George—Major Burke and his so-called Marauders."

Richthofen's hand involuntarily clenched around the report he was holding, crumpling it up into a ball as anger surged. His body went stiff as he fought back against the red tide that threatened to overwhelm him, succeeding only after several long moments of effort.

When he was at last back in control, he turned his now murderous gaze on Eisenberg.

"Burke, you say?"

Captain—no, *Major*—Michael Burke. The man who had invaded his secret installation in the Verdun forests, destroyed his gas production facilities, and burned the *Alecto* at her mooring post, thereby ruining Richthofen's attack on Paris. The man who had stubbornly refused to die no matter how many times Richthofen had tried to kill him and who had ultimately helped Richthofen's greatest prize, the Allied ace Julius "Jack" Freeman, escape his control. The man Richthofen wanted to get his hands on more than any other in the entire war effort was in charge of the rescue operation?

Eisenberg nodded. "Yes, Burke."

Richthofen's eyes narrowed at Eisenberg's tone. "If I didn't know better, I would think you were almost happy about this development."

"Your perception is as strong as ever, Your Majesty. I want to get my hands on Burke as much as you do, and his reappearance now gives us an opportunity I have been waiting for."

"Go on."

"With your permission, I would like to send a team of our own to London, for a variety of reasons. As you know, the *Geheimnisvollen Bruderschaft* have been making great strides in increasing their power and effectiveness over the last several years."

Richthofen nodded. It was true; the Arcane Brotherhood had increased their numbers and had managed to bring several operations to fruition that had led to serious breakthroughs on the empire's behalf, including the final formulation of the gas that had been used on London and New York.

"For some time now, the Brotherhood's leader, Heinrich Himmler, has been pushing for permission to send a group of agents into London in an attempt to recover the philosopher's stone, an arcane artifact of some antiquity, which some say has been the cornerstone of British success for hundreds of years.

"I have denied Himmler's request in the past for obvious reasons, but with the city now in ruins thanks to your brilliant attack, now might be the time to make the attempt."

Richthofen had heard of the philosopher's stone but had always considered it a myth, much like the Holy Grail or the sword of Excalibur, other symbols of British power and might.

"You believe this stone exists and can be useful to us?"

Eisenberg nodded. "The research I've done suggests that the stone is genuine and that it does, indeed, provide the individual who possesses it with considerable power. The Brotherhood wants to use it for several select rites, which we can discuss later, but even if you keep it in your possession, I think it is worth going after, if for no other reason than to deny it to the Allies. Eventually someone in the British High Command is going to mention it to the American commander and the last thing we want is for the stone to fall into their hands."

That, Richthofen could agree with. Giving the Americans an opportunity to bolster their already considerable ability to put men and equipment on the battlefield made very little sense.

"You propose sending a team of Himmler's men to carry this mission out?"

"Good heavens, no, Your Majesty! Himmler's far too unstable to trust something of this importance to directly. No, I suggest sending a team of our own *Geheime Volks* to handle the job, and I have just the man to lead them. May I invite him in?"

A laugh burst out of the emperor's mouth. *Leave it to Eisenberg to come prepared for any eventuality.*

"By all means, *Doktor.* Is he waiting in the hall?"

"Yes. I didn't want to trouble you with him if you were not interested in the mission."

Eisenberg walked back to the door, opened it, and spoke a few words to the guards waiting on the other side. Moments later the door opened and Richthofen watched a large, hulking fellow cross the room, snap to attention, and salute.

Richthofen recognized him immediately as the U.S. Army sergeant he'd pulled from the wreckage of the stolen transport truck in the wake of the attack on the Verdun facilities, despite the changes the transformation process had wrought in his appearance. The man's skin had turned ash gray, his veins now black as pitch and standing out sharply beneath the skin. His eyes had the yellow cast to them so common to the new breed of *Geheime Volks,* and what little hair he had started out with had turned limp and sallow. He was dressed in the black uniform worn by all of Richthofen's new supersoldiers, and there was no denying the strength infused in the man's impressive frame nor the light of intelligence in his eyes.

Eisenberg walked over to join them.

"This, Your Majesty, is my latest success. May I present *Vizefeldwebel* Karl Jaeger, leader of the first *Totenkopf* Strike Force."

Moore bowed his head slightly in the emperor's direction and said, "'Tis a pleasure to meet you, Your Majesty."

Richthofen stared at the man for a moment. "Is that . . . ?" he began.

Eisenberg nodded. "Yes, Your Majesty, it is. Or, should I say, was."

Richthofen laughed in delight. "Well done, *Doktor,* well done indeed!"

CHAPTER SEVENTEEN

ACCORDING TO SERGEANT Drummond, Bedlam had been in continual operation since 1247 and had earned its nickname from a time when chaos had reigned inside its walls and those who went in rarely came out.

An asylum where the doctors were as crazy as the inmates. Wonderful.

"And this 'Veronica' person?" Burke asked.

"Veronica Windsor, Major, the princess royal."

"Ah." That should have been obvious and Burke mentally kicked himself for being slow-witted. He glanced behind him at the bodies, thinking, *Princess no longer. Now she's the Queen of England.*

Which meant his mission wasn't yet over after all.

Burke dug the map out of his pocket and spread it out on a nearby table. "Show me where this hospital is."

Drummond pointed to a spot on the other side of the Thames, just south of Lambeth Castle. "Here," he said. Anticipating Burke's next question, he went on. "If we backtrack along the same route we took to the palace," he said, tracing the route on the map with his finger, "we can cross the Thames at Westminster Bridge and follow Kennington Road south to the hospital."

The distance wasn't far; probably less than two miles total. But it wasn't the distance that Burke was worried about. They'd been lucky so far and had managed to avoid any confrontations with the shredders roaming the city, but eventually their luck would run out.

Especially if they kept trooping back and forth across the city.

But Burke also knew there was no way he could morally justify leaving London without verifying whether or not the princess— *the Queen, she's the Queen now*—was still alive. He had no choice but to make the trip to the hospital and see for himself.

It was barely midmorning; they had plenty of time to make the trip across the Thames, check out the hospital, and then return to the boat, hopefully with the new Queen in tow.

After that it was mission accomplished and back to France.

Or so he hoped.

"Good enough," Burke said, folding the map back up and slipping it into his pocket. "Let's get Their Majesties squared away and then we'll go see what's waiting for us at Bedlam."

Drummond looked like he was going to cheer, but in the end settled for a simple thank-you. Burke didn't blame him; these were his countrymen, after all.

The men made short work of wrapping up the bodies of the King and Queen and soon the squad left the palace behind and set out for the Thames. Burke put Drummond back on point, trusting in his ability to steer them around any trouble spots, which was more important than ever now that four of them—Bankowski, Cohen, Montagna, and Graves—were burdened down with the bodies of His and Her Majesty. Burke, Williams, and Jones formed the other three points of the diamond around them, ready to come to their defense should circumstances require it.

They hadn't even left the palace grounds when a lone shredder erupted from the undergrowth and raced right toward them.

"Major! On your right," Williams shouted.

The warning was unnecessary; Burke had already seen it coming.

As the creature rushed toward him, Burke let his Tommy gun fall to his side so that it hung by the strap around his shoulder and then drew his combat knife with his right hand. He turned slightly so that his mechanical hand was closest to the shredder and waited for it to reach him.

It didn't take long. The shredder, a stooped older fellow who moved much quicker than anyone his age ever should, rushed forward with the single-minded obsession of a starving man seeing his first meal in a week.

For his part, Burke was unconcerned. Shredders might be slightly smarter and a whole lot faster than their shambler brethren, but in the end they were still nothing more than zombies and, as such, reasonably easy for an armed and able-bodied man to handle on his own if he could keep his wits about him.

Given everything he'd been through recently, it was going to take a lot more than a single shredder to ruffle Burke's calm.

The creature slammed into him without slowing down, but Burke was ready for it, falling over backward and taking the shredder down with him. He flipped the two of them over in midfall, so that they landed with the shredder on the bottom and Burke on top. The creature's jaws snapped open and shut, open and shut as it sought to reach him with its teeth, but Burke pinned its head on the ground sideways with his mechanical arm to keep it from sinking its teeth into him.

The research Graves had done before they'd departed France on the mission taught them that shredder bodies were much less fragile than those of their shambler cousins. A solid blow would often stave in a shambler skull, if for no other reason than the fact that the bodies from which they were formed most often had already started to decay before they were exposed to the corpse gas that resurrected them. Once that decaying process started, there was no turning back the clock; eventually the shambler was going to fall apart where it stood.

But try that same blow on a shredder and you'd better be ready to run for your life because that strike was just going to bounce off the creature's head more often than not. Shredders were once living people transformed through the strange science and arcane magick of Richthofen's unique gas and weren't, as far as anyone knew at this point, subject to the same slow but relentless decaying process.

So while you were still trying to figure out what happened, that shredder was going to slip inside your guard and rip out your throat.

Burke had all that in mind as he pinned the side of the shredder's face flat against the ground with his mechanical hand and then jabbed his combat knife savagely into the creature's temple where the skull was soft and wouldn't be an impediment to his blade.

The thing gurgled once in protest and then died.

Just to be sure it didn't get back up again, Burke gave his knife a bit of a twist as he pulled it free of the shredder's skull and then climbed to his feet.

The entire attack had lasted less than a minute, but off in the distance Burke could already see several shredders turning in their direction. It was time to go.

"Get us out of here, Drummond!" Burke ordered, and the group set out once more.

They were attacked three more times during the remainder of the journey back to the submarine, once by a pack of five shredders that required the pallbearers to put down their load and get in on the action. Each time, however, the Marauders came up victorious and they returned to the *Reliant* without suffering anything more dangerous than a few cuts and bruises.

After speaking with Captain Wattley and arranging for the bodies of His and Her Majesty to be properly stowed for transport back to Allied Command, Major Burke asked to have the radio man put in a call to Colonel Nichols at the MID.

Five minutes later Burke was led into the tiny room that served as both the captain's cabin and radio room. The operator, a corporal named Symington, offered Burke the room's only stool but he waved it away, preferring to stand.

Symington extended a set of headphones in his direction. "Here you go, sir; put these on and we'll . . ."

The corporal caught sight of Burke's mechanical hand and stopped in midsentence, his eyes going wide.

Having lived with his mechanical wonder for long enough that he no longer thought of it as anything other than a natural part of himself, Burke often forgot how others initially reacted to it or how strange it must seem to them. Most mechanical hands were primitive devices, a far cry from the five-fingered multijointed version that was grafted directly to the stump of his forearm and used a combination of clockwork mechanisms and his body's own electrical impulses to power it. He could do almost as much with his artificial hand as the average person could do with one made of flesh and blood.

Burke pretended the man hadn't stopped in midsentence and took the headphones, slipping them on over his ears. He'd had some experience working with a trench telegraph and recognized them for what they were. The headphones were a snug fit but would work well enough for the time being.

By the time he looked up again, Symington had recovered from his embarrassment and was settling in behind the radio panel. He began flipping switches and setting the dials to their necessary positions.

"Ever used a radio, sir?"

"No, just a talking box aboard a dirigible."

The corporal laughed nervously. "They're pretty much the same thing, sir." He pointed to a tabletop microphone with a button on the front of the base. "When you want to say something, push this button and speak into the microphone. When you want to listen, let go of the button and wait for the voice to come over your headphones."

"Press the button to talk, let go to listen. Got it," Burke said.

Symington made a few more adjustments to the settings then asked over his shoulder, "What's the frequency?"

"Frequency?"

The corporal glanced over his shoulder at Burke. "The frequency that you're supposed to use to . . ."

This time he paused at the blank look on Burke's face.

"You don't have any idea what I'm talking about, do you, sir?"

Burke sighed. "Can't say that I do, Corporal."

The younger man nodded sagely, as if this kind of thing happened all the time. When it came to newfangled technology like radio, Burke could well imagine that it did.

"I'm sure I can get this sorted, sir," Symington said. "Give me a moment, would you?"

"By all means."

The corporal was nothing if not resourceful. A quick check revealed that Captain Wattley's orders contained the radio frequency they needed. With typical bureaucratic reasoning, someone, somewhere, had apparently decided that Burke didn't need that information himself because he didn't have a radio.

With that snafu solved, Burke turned his attention to the issue that started this all, namely, bringing Colonel Nichols up to speed on the mission thus far.

The corporal dialed in the proper frequency and then reminded him, "Your call sign is Eagle One. MID headquarters is Nest."

"Understood."

The corporal excused himself and slipped out of the room, giving Burke privacy.

Burke hit the on switch, waited for the light on the console to go green, and then pressed the transmit button.

"Eagle One to Nest. Eagle One to Nest. Acknowledge."

The response was almost immediate.

"Nest to Eagle One. Pass phrase 'I'm looking over . . .'"

Burke had expected the need to confirm his identity and was ready with the next half of the phrase from the song popularized by both Nick Lucas and Ben Bernie. "A four-leaf clover," he replied.

Upon hearing the correct phrase to complete the pass code, the radio operator on the other end gave him the go-ahead.

"Message to Condor," Burke began. "Mama and Papa Bear have fallen asleep. Reports state Goldilocks may still be awake. Will check before calling it a night."

His message was circumspect enough to confuse any enemy agents who might be listening in, Burke hoped, but should make sense to Colonel Nichols, a.k.a. Condor.

Burke waited, didn't hear any response, and was about to transmit again when he realized he still had his finger on the button. He pulled it back as quickly as if he'd been scorched by a hot stove and a voice immediately filled his earphones.

"Repeat Eagle One, do you copy?"

"Negative, Nest. Sorry. Please repeat."

"Coup in Germany. Richthofen has declared himself emperor. Be advised Condor expects he'll send troops after Goldilocks and the Bears. Copy?"

"Copy and understood. Eagle One, out."

Burke stripped off the headphones and sat there for a moment, thinking about Colonel Nichols's warning. London might have been attacked, but England was still in Allied hands and sending an enemy unit into British territory was such a bold and audacious move that Burke hadn't even considered that the Germans might try it. A bit shortsighted on his part, he mused. Especially since it was that same tendency toward nearsightedness that had allowed him to take a squad of his own behind *German* lines recently to rescue his brother, Allied ace Major Jack Freeman.

Far more disturbing, however, was the news that Richthofen had staged a coup. Burke had interacted with Richthofen briefly during that very same mission to Germany and had read the extensive reports Jack had written on his time in Richthofen's captivity. Burke had no doubt in his mind that the new German emperor was certifiably insane. Whether he was that way before he'd undergone his transformation or after was debatable, but the end result was the same; a bloodthirsty megalomaniac now sat on the

German throne and directed the course of the war. That was not good news for the Allies by any stretch of the imagination. They had held on this long in part because of the kaiser's bungling of the situation at the front; the generals he'd put in charge really didn't know how to conduct a war in this new day and age, and their mistakes had allowed the Allies to regroup and dig in before all could be lost.

Richthofen wouldn't make the same mistakes, Burke knew. Unlike most of those who rose as a result of exposure to corpse gas, the German ace had not only retained full use of his mental faculties but had effectively had those same faculties enhanced, bringing his natural brilliance to near genius levels. Freeman's reports had made it quite clear that the man—if you could even call him that now—thought like a world-class chess player, staying eight, nine, even ten moves ahead of his opponent at any time. Now that same devious intelligence would be directing the enemy forces arrayed against them.

It was exceedingly bad news for the Allies.

Should have let Manning kill him when he had the chance.

That decision was going to come back and haunt them all, he knew.

With nothing more he could do at the moment, Burke flipped off the radio set and went in search of his squad. They had an asylum to visit.

CHAPTER EIGHTEEN

✪

THE PARK WAS empty, devoid of the life that usually filled it, and as a result felt particularly desolate. Even in the midst of war people often gathered here, to find that sense of community that told them they weren't alone; but no one was here today. It was as if the universe understood what was to come and worked to keep the innocent from being here.

Had people been standing in the park, they would have heard a faint thrumming sound coming from their surroundings. The sound would have grown slowly louder, filling the air around them, until it would have seemed to be emanating from the very ground on which they were standing.

But no one was there and so the noise, and the earth tremors that accompanied it, went unnoticed.

The earth shook and then split apart, the thrumming sound filling the air as a metallic behemoth emerged from deep within the earth to breach itself like a whale on the grassy sward, the three circular drills on its snout spinning wildly now that there was no resistance for them to chew through.

Some ten yards away another similar craft burst into the open air, adding its own mechanical whirlings and clankings to the already considerable din, and then a third did the same a short distance from them.

When the drills stopped spinning, there was a hiss of escaping steam and then hatches on the sides of all three vehicles dropped open with a clang of steel. Troops poured out and set up firing positions around the vehicles, rifles at the ready.

The empty park stared back at them.

A man in the uniform of a senior NCO, or *vizefeldwebel* in the German army, appeared in the doorway of the first drilling machine. He glanced about, satisfying himself that they weren't in any danger, and then descended the ramp to stand for the first time on British soil.

He was a big man, both in height and in breadth. He stood several inches over six feet, allowing him to see over the heads of the others during routine exercises, and he had broad shoulders that strained the fit of his uniform. His skin was the color of wet ashes, his veins standing out against it like lines of black pitch, thick and dark, and his once blue eyes were now cast in yellow.

Friends had once called him Charlie, but he would answer to that name no more. He was Karl Jaeger now, Vizefeldwebel Jaeger. The transformation that had altered his physical form, that had morphed him into one of the new breed of *Geheime Volks*, had changed his mental state as well. Put him in the same room with his former comrades and while he would have recognized them, he would not have understood them. Their wants and needs were so far from his wants and needs at this point as to be almost alien.

All he cared about right now was pleasing his superior officer by carrying out the mission to the best of his ability. Nothing else mattered.

His team was made of three squads of eight men each, plus

one unit of several Death Hounds (*Tot Hunde*) and their handlers under the command of a hound master who reported directly to Jaeger. Two of his squads were *Tottensoldat* infantry units, while the third was a machine-gun unit armed with a Maschinengewehr 08, or MG 08.

As a whole, the unit was armed heavily enough to deal with anything from a company on down but still light enough that they could make good time in their pursuit of the Americans. Satisfied that his men were getting sorted out properly, Jaeger turned his attention to their current location.

He knew right away that they were not where they were supposed to be; if they had been, he would be looking out across a lawn of well-kept grass to the wall of Buckingham Palace. Instead, he was staring at footpaths and flower patches.

"Navigator!" he barked.

A moment later a man wearing a white lab coat over an engineer's jumpsuit and boots stuck his head out the door of the drilling machine. He had a pair of goggles pushed back on his forehead over thick, unruly hair, making him look like he'd just woken up.

"Sir?"

"I want to know where we are, Navigator. And I want that information yesterday, do you understand?"

"Ja, *Vizefeldwebel*. At once."

The man disappeared for a moment back down inside the depths of the drilling machine and then returned with a black case in one hand and a rolled-up map in the other. From inside the case he withdrew an auto-sextant, wound it up, and then set it on the ground in a wide patch of sunlight. The clockwork mechanisms that controlled the device went to work, moving the viewfinder and sighting scope and then calculating their present position from the measurements taken. When the machine stopped, the navigator checked the position noted against the map of London in his hands.

"We're more than a mile south of our intended destination, *Vizefeldwebel*. According to my readings, we are in a place called Ranelagh Gardens."

The name meant nothing to Jaeger, just another location on the map. But that location allowed him to triangulate on his destination and determine how much longer it was going to take to get there.

The kaiser wanted the stone recovered as quickly as possible; he intended to deliver on that desire.

He turned to the soldiers standing nearby. "Release the hounds," he ordered.

A few minutes later he watched as half a dozen of the strange, twisted creatures were led up from the storage units down in the hold. He checked their control harnesses himself, not wanting any of them to fail over a trivial issue, and then signaled to the controller that they were ready.

Commands were given, doses of the gas topped off inside their masks, and then the hounds were released to hunt those they had come here to find.

As he watched them slink sinuously away into the trees at the edge of the park, Vizefeldwebel Jaeger smiled to himself.

Wouldn't be long before they had the stone, and the princess, in hand.

CHAPTER NINETEEN

THE SQUAD REPLENISHED their ammunition, packed some extra food to take with them, and filled their canteens with water from the boat. It was midafternoon and Burke fully expected to be back to the sub before dark, but they didn't know what condition any survivors they discovered at Bedlam might be in and it seemed prudent to have something to offer if the need arose.

After a quick lunch consisting of bread, cheese, and hard salami eaten on the deck of the *Reliant,* Burke and his team clambered back into their inflatable dinghy and pushed off from the submarine for a second time that day. This time, however, they were headed for the opposite side of the Thames.

They hid the boat in the shadows beneath Westminster Bridge and got under way as swiftly as possible, not wanting to linger in any one location very long. Due to the nearness of Waterloo Station, one of London's largest railway terminuses, this side of the river had suffered as much heavy bombing as the other. Many of the buildings along the river were in ruins, and more than once they could see corpses lying among the rubble.

It was less than a mile to Bedlam and they saw only a single shredder, easily dispatched, during that entire distance. The reason for this was only made clear when they arrived at their destination.

Bedlam Hospital was a long, three-story building with a tower-like structure at either end and a colonnaded entrance with a soaring domed roof in the very center. The entire property was walled off from the surrounding neighborhood by an eight-foot brick wall along the front and sides and a cast-iron fence with a small gate in the back. Sergeant Drummond explained that brick walls had also been used to separate the grounds inside the fence into individual courtyards for use as "airing yards" for the patients and a garden for the staff. A larger, more prominent garden stretched out from the colonnade surrounding the main entrance to the front gate.

They had hoped to slip in through the back gate and gain entry to the hospital from the rear, but a quick bit of reconnaissance showed that entrance to be blocked by a milling crowd of more than three dozen shredders. The front entrance wasn't much better; shredders pressed against the doors with single-minded determination and the never-ending hunger of the undead.

Drummond cursed at the sight.

Burke, however, was a bit more upbeat about their presence. "Look at it this way, Sergeant. This many shredders is a good indication there's still someone alive in there."

All they had to do now was figure out a way to get them out.

The squad hunkered down amid the ruins of a doctor's office across the street from the western wing of the hospital and tried to come up with a plan. Drummond had been to Bedlam several times in the past with the Queen, so Burke had him draw a rough map to allow him to better visualize the place. It wasn't perfect, and nowhere close to scale, but it would have to do.

After studying it for a moment, Burke decided that a full frontal assault was out of the question. Although they had enough arms and ammunition to make short work of the shredders crowding the entrance, the noise they would generate would simply bring more of them running. The same held true for any attempt to get in through the back gate. What they needed was a spot where they could go over the wall and reach the main structure quickly enough that the shredders wouldn't have time to do anything about it.

"What about here?" Burke said, pointing to a spot about midway along the western wall where the building seemed to come quite close to the edge of the property. "Is there a way into the tower if we climb over the wall at this point?"

Drummond thought about it for a moment before eventually nodding. "I haven't been inside for a while, but I think that's the wing for female patients. If so, there's a small courtyard on the other side of the wall that's only accessible from the offices at the end of the ward."

That should do the trick, Burke thought.

While there was usually safety in numbers, in this case he thought a smaller group might give them the best chance of success. They wouldn't have as much firepower at their disposal, but they'd be able to move a bit quicker and a whole lot quieter, two things that would come in handy if they had to evade a pack of shredders.

"All right, here's what we're going to do . . ."

BURKE RAN ALONG the outside of the brick wall surrounding the hospital grounds with Sergeant Drummond and Doc Bankowski on his heels. The ground here was free of undergrowth and the soft earth beneath their boots did a good job of absorbing the sound of their footfalls. Once or twice he thought he heard a shredder moving about on the other side of the barrier, but without being able to see over it, there was no way to know for sure.

When he drew opposite the tower marking the end of the building, Burke came to a stop and leaned his left side against the wall. Lacing his fingers together to form a cradle, he bent slightly, braced his feet, and then turned to nod at Drummond.

The British sergeant took a couple of steps forward, put his foot into the makeshift stirrup Burke had created, and then used that plus the momentum Burke imparted to him to spring upward and grasp the top of the wall several feet above their heads. Burke steadied the man's feet until Drummond could get a solid grip and pull himself up to straddle the wall.

"Clear," Drummond called down.

They repeated the process with Doc, though he had it a bit easier than Drummond since the other man was in a position to help pull him up. The two men then straddled the wall and extended a hand down for Burke.

He needed a running start to vault himself high enough to catch them both about the wrists, but once he had, it was a simple matter for them to pull him the rest of the way to sit between them.

Drummond had been right; the section of the wall on which they now sat looked down on a small, isolated courtyard that backed up to the end of the west wing of the main building. The yard was empty and the building didn't offer much in the way of clues as to what the conditions inside would be like for there were no windows on this level, only a single door hanging sagging in its frame.

Burke had left Corporal Williams in charge in his absence, with orders to wait two hours for their return. If they weren't back by then, he was to get the rest of the squad back to the boat and report to Colonel Nichols. Jones had protested against leaving him behind, but Burke had been adamant. Bedlam was only so big; if they weren't back in two hours, they weren't coming back.

He'd have preferred to leave Drummond in charge, as he clearly outranked all the others except the major himself, but Burke needed his knowledge of the hospital's interior and couldn't spare him. Burke had a quiet word with Jones before leaving as well, telling the other man that he was counting on him to get the squad back in one piece under Williams's leadership if Burke and the others didn't make it. Jones had sworn on his mother's grave that he would.

Anticipating that those inside Bedlam might be in need of a doctor, Burke had asked Doc Bankowski to join their party and the three men had then set off, conscious that the day was growing later and wanting to be back on the river before sundown.

With that thought still playing out in his head, Burke swung his legs over and dropped to the ground on the other side of the wall.

Behind him, first Sergeant Drummond and then Doc Bankowski followed suit.

Burke advanced slowly, his Tommy gun in hand and ready at a moment's notice should he need it. Due to the way the light struck the side of the building, he couldn't see inside the partially opened door in front of him and that worried him a bit. A dozen of the things could be waiting just beyond the doorway. He might be able to handle one or two by hand, but any more than that and he was going to need some firepower, hence the Tommy gun. If he ended up facing that many of the creatures, noise would be the least of his worries.

Step by step, he continued forward, his gaze fixed firmly on the doorway in front of him.

He was halfway across the courtyard when the first of the shredders reared its head.

It stumbled past the partially broken door and into the sun-lit courtyard. It stood there a moment, blinking in the light, and Burke had a chance to get a decent look at it. Between its gray-green flesh, its bulky, oversized straitjacket, and head shorn free of hair, it was hard to tell if it had been a man or a woman. Burke supposed it didn't really matter; given its transformation, all it would ever be now was hungry.

The straitjacket was a dead giveaway that this had once been a patient rather than a member of the staff, which made Burke wonder just how many more of them were loose inside the building. He'd been hoping they wouldn't have to fight for every inch inside the place, but that might have been wishful thinking.

A few seconds passed and finally the creature's cerebral processes caught up with what its eyes were seeing as it focused on Burke. It opened its mouth, let loose some kind of strange half groan that sounded like it was gargling with fist-sized rocks, and then it rushed toward him on unnaturally agile feet.

The major sized up the threat the creature posed with a single look; with its arms buckled behind its back, it couldn't do anything but try to sink its teeth into him. If he could get it on the ground, he shouldn't have too much trouble pinning it down while waiting for one of the others to step up and finish it off with a quick smack of their gun butt.

It was a plan he was perfectly happy with until he looked over its shoulder and saw the swarm of other shredders pouring out of the doorway after it.

CHAPTER TWENTY

★

SURROUNDED BY WALLS at his back and sides, and with that many shredders rushing toward him from the front, Burke made the only reasonable choice available to him. He brought his Tommy gun up and opened fire.

Nicknamed the "trench broom" for its ability to deliver a fair amount of firepower quickly and reasonably accurately, the Thompson submachine gun Burke carried was fitted with a hundred-round drum magazine loaded with .45 ACP ammunition. It was also set on full automatic fire, rather than the single shot select fire setting, which meant that when he opened fire, the gun sent out a steady stream of bullets and made one hell of a racket.

He couldn't be worried about noise at this point, though. If he didn't live through the next couple of minutes, attracting more shredders would be the least of his problems.

Smoke and empty shell casings kicked to the right as he sent half a dozen rounds into the skull of the straitjacketed shredder directly in front of him, literally blowing it apart. The body was still on its way to the ground as Burke pulled the gun back down on target, never taking his finger off the trigger, sending a steady stream of bullets into the mob of shredders coming up from behind.

Blood and flesh flew through the air as several shredders in the front ranks were cut down, but still the rest came on.

Burke lowered his aim, sweeping the muzzle of the Thompson back and forth across the line of oncoming shredders at knee height, chopping their legs out from under them, hoping to trip up the ranks farther back on the bodies of those in front. Seconds later the staccato chatter of Drummond's Tommy and the heavy bark of Doc's Enfield joined the cacophony as they took their cue from Burke and added their firepower to his.

The last of the shredders fell less than three feet from where Burke stood. It continued to crawl toward him, pulling itself forward with its hands while dragging its shattered legs behind it until he stepped forward and put a bullet through its brain.

The smell of cordite filled the air as the three men lowered their weapons and looked around. Close to twenty of the creatures littered the ground between them and the entrance to Bedlam.

Burke glanced back at the others.

"Keep your wits about you," he told them. "There could be more inside."

As if on cue, the shredder hiding in the darkness just beyond the doorway chose that moment to explode into action. It charged out of the doorway and hit Burke like a freight train while his attention was still on the men behind him, bowling him over backward and knocking the Thompson free of his grasp as he slammed into the ground. His head rang from the impact and darkness threatened at the edge of his vision, but he fought back against it, knowing he wouldn't wake up again if he lost consciousness now.

Teeth snapped at his face as the shredder tried to reach him, but he'd managed to get an arm across his chest as he'd fallen and used that to push back, holding it at bay, but just barely. It kicked and squirmed, trying to get closer, while Burke fought to push it off him enough to find some leverage that he could use to his advantage.

"A little help here!" Burke shouted.

He was answered by the crack of a gunshot, so close that his ears rang from the sound, and a grisly splatter of blood, bone, and brain matter splashed across his face as Doc's bullet took the top of the creature's head clear off.

The body slumped down on top of Burke, soaking the front of his uniform with blood and other bodily fluids.

"Bastard!" he cursed quietly as he pushed it off him and, with the help of the others, climbed to his feet.

That had been too close for his liking.

As Burke wiped the worst of the detritus off his face and went to retrieve his weapon, he noticed Drummond kept glancing at the walls on either side of them, a nervous expression on his face.

"You hear that?" Drummond asked.

Burke paused, listened; he did hear something.

It sounded like someone shuffling his feet in the dirt.

A lot of someones, in fact.

He was suddenly very happy that there was an eight-foot wall between this courtyard and the next. He just hoped the shredders didn't figure out how to climb.

"Come on," he said, waving the others forward. "Let's get this done and get back to the boat."

They entered Bedlam through the door at the western end of the building and, just as Drummond had predicted, found themselves in a set of administrative offices that had certainly seen better days. Light came in through several windows, making it easy to see. Desks and chairs were smashed. Bookshelves and filing cabinets were knocked over and their contents scattered all over the floor. Blood was splattered across the walls and ceiling in more than one location. The bodies of two of the former staff lay in the doorway to the hall beyond, their chests and throats torn open, most likely by the very same shredders that Burke and his two companions had just dealt with out in the courtyard.

The trio left the offices behind and stepped into a long hallway that appeared to run the length of the west wing all the way to the main building. Doors lined either side of the hall, one every six feet or so, and the observation windows set in each and every one of them made it clear that the rooms had once housed the hospital's patients. More than a few of the doors were open, and from where they stood Burke and his men could see corpses lying in the hall.

Step by step they made their way slowly forward, leapfrogging each other over and over again as they checked each and every room, not wanting a shredder to come charging up behind them unexpectedly.

Each time they came to a corpse Drummond had the unpleasant task of trying to determine whether the ravaged and decomposing mess of flesh in front of them was that of the missing Queen, as he was the only one who had met her.

Three-quarters of the way down the hall they discovered an open doorway on the left that led to a stairwell going upward. As they had yet to check out the main structure ahead of them, they bypassed it for now and continued forward.

Burke was tempted to cry out, to see if anyone would answer his calls, but he knew that was just asking for trouble. For all they knew, the next door he opened might lead them into a room full of shredders and he would be much happier to surprise them with his sudden appearance than to find them waiting on the other side of the door for him to open it.

At the end of the hall a set of double doors led from the west wing into the main building, but when he tried them, Burke found them locked. Peering through the window in the door revealed a large open room with what looked like a receptionist's desk and several couches; perhaps the waiting room by the main entrance.

Something thumped.

Burke went still, holding up a fist in a signal for the others to do the same.

He glanced around and then up at the ceiling, trying to pinpoint the sound, and after a moment it came again. It seemed to be coming from the room above them.

Shredders?

He didn't think so. The sound had a furtive quality to it, as if who or whatever had made it hadn't meant for it to be heard. Shredders weren't exactly known for their subtlety.

The Queen? Some other survivors?

There was only one way to find out.

They backtracked a little until they came to the stairwell they'd passed a few minutes before and then headed up toward the second floor.

On the second flight they found several bodies littering the stairwell, but this time they were shredder corpses rather than those of murdered staff. They checked the features of each corpse, making sure none of them were the royal family. Doing so made Burke aware that they probably should have done the same thing with the shredders in the courtyard and he made a mental note to check them on the way back out if they didn't find anything on the floor above.

Satisfied that their target was not among the dead, they continued upward.

They slipped through the door at the top of the steps and found themselves in another corridor like the one they'd left below. Just beyond the stairwell they found their first barricade.

It was a thick pile of furniture, pillaged no doubt from patient rooms. Bed frames, mattresses, bureaus, desks, nightstands; you name it, it was in there. Whoever had built the barricade had piled it nearly to ceiling height and, as a result, completely blocked the way forward.

It looked intact.

Burke took that as a good sign.

A few minutes of cooperative effort allowed them to clear a small section on the edge of the barricade. From atop the pile they could see another barricade about twenty feet farther down the hall. The area in between looked clear, so Burke clambered through the opening and then stood watch as the other two followed suit.

The next barricade looked more extensive and, after a few moments of investigation, proved to be about twice as thick. Drummond and Burke were just beginning to pull material from the top when Doc's whispered voice broke the silence.

"Major! Over here!"

For a moment Burke was certain that it was going to be bad news, that Doc was going to reveal the body of the woman they'd come to find, but as Burke drew closer he saw that Bankowski was grinning.

"What have you got?"

Doc stepped out of the way, revealing an opening low to the ground. "A tunnel."

Indeed it was. By getting down on his hands and knees, Burke could look down its length and see clear to the other side of the barricade. There was just enough room for a man to pull himself through lying flat on his back or his stomach, though only if he didn't mind tight spaces.

Very tight spaces.

Burke sat back on his haunches, thinking. He guessed that the barricades had been set up as two separate lines of defense. Those they were designed to protect would make their stand at the first barricade and then, if events got away from them, they could retreat behind the second, using the tunnel to reach the safety of the hall beyond without the need to scramble over the unsteady pile. He had no doubt that there would be some way of closing off the tunnel on the other end once the retreating soldiers reached the safety of the hallway beyond. It was a clever setup and, in usual circumstances, would probably work pretty well.

These were not usual circumstances, however; far from them.

Shredders were exceptionally fast, and the narrow confines of the tunnel would create a bottleneck at precisely the wrong time for the retreating defenders. The fact that the area between the two barricades was empty of bodies told him more than anything else that the defenses had yet to be tested.

And that meant the defenders might still be hiding out somewhere beyond the barricade.

He made up his mind.

"I'm going to check it out," he told the other two. "Watch my back."

But Drummond grabbed his arm before he could lower himself to the floor. "You shouldn't do this," he said to Burke. "The squad needs you to get us back to the *Reliant*. Let one of us handle this."

Burke shook his head.

"You're the only one who can identify the Queen on sight, so sending you doesn't make any sense. Neither does sending Doc, as I'm sure we're going to need him to provide medical attention if we find any survivors. That leaves me."

Burke wasn't the type to order his men into any situation that he wasn't willing to risk himself, which made his decision even easier. Logically, he was the best choice for the job.

"Here, hold this for me till I get back," he said, handing his Tommy off to Drummond. "I don't want the strap getting caught on something halfway through."

The other man took it wordlessly, clearly not happy with Burke's decision but understanding that he didn't have any choice in the matter.

Burke drew his pistol, took a deep breath, and then slid into the makeshift tunnel on his stomach, headfirst. It was a tight fit, but he managed to move forward through a combination of pushing off with his feet and pulling with his free hand, squirming his body back and forth as he went. He did his best not to think about the massive mound of furniture just inches over his head, nor what it would do to him should it collapse.

Inch by inch, he slid forward.

As he neared the other end of the makeshift tunnel, he paused, surveying the area in front of him. The hallway beyond the tunnel looked empty but also intact; there was none of the destruction they'd seen elsewhere that indicated that shredders had come through at some point in the recent past. It was a good sign and gave him some hope that they might actually find who they'd come looking for.

With his free hand he reached out, grabbed the upper edge of the tunnel mouth, and pulled himself clear of the obstruction, only to find himself staring down the muzzle of a pistol very much like his own.

The man who held it stood with his back to the barricade a foot or so to the side of the tunnel mouth. He was a grizzled-looking veteran in a stained uniform with a tattered bandage wrapped around his head and at least three days' worth of unshaven beard on his hard-lined face.

His eyes showed no amusement or relief at Burke's appearance. "That's far enough," the soldier said.

CHAPTER TWENTY-ONE

ENSIGN LOWELL STARED at the group of shredders on the riverbank fifteen yards away and wondered if he should alert the captain to their presence. He counted six, maybe eight of them; it was hard to tell exactly, given the smog that hung about everywhere in the city and the fact that the shredders were constantly moving about, slipping in and out of view.

They hadn't been there at the start of his watch, he was certain of that. What he wasn't certain of was just when they had appeared. He'd been staring out into the afternoon haze, doing his best to stay awake during what was turning out to be a very long and boring watch, when the faintest of sounds caught his attention. It sounded like a large fish jumping out of the water and at first he looked for it eagerly, having loved to fish in the cold waters of the lake just outside the borders of his hometown in Wales while growing up. In the process, he'd seen movement on the bank, and a few moments later he realized there were several shredders stumbling about over there.

That they were aware of his presence was clear; he'd seen them stop and stare in his direction often enough that he was starting to doubt the briefing they'd received about the creatures' allegedly poor eyesight. *Seemed the buggers could see him just fine, thank you very much.* Still, he kept as still as he could and didn't make any loud noises that might serve to attract their attention more than he already had.

Lowell raised his rifle and pointed it at the shredders milling around on the bank. "Pow! Pow! Pow-pow!" he muttered softly. He wasn't a bad shot; a few minutes with his rifle and he could take care of those shredders right quick. And so what if the noise attracted more of them? They could sit out here all day and all night, picking off shredders until the sun came up. There wouldn't be anything the shredders could do about it either; they were out here in the middle of the river and last he heard shredders couldn't swim.

Unfortunately for Ensign Lowell, he was about to learn how wrong he was.

Twenty feet below and fifty feet farther back from the conning tower, a shredder's hand broke the surface of the water and slid upward along the steel hull of the submarine.

Its fingers grabbed hold of a slight metal protuberance jutting out from the side of the vessel and the shredder pulled, dragging its head above the waterline so it could take a look around. From that moment on, the minutes left in Ensign Lowell's life were numbered.

Lowell was correct—shredders couldn't swim, not really—but they could walk just fine and didn't have to worry about something as petty as breathing. This particular creature had been roaming back and forth along the shoreline with its brethren, attracted by the nearness of living prey but unable to understand just how to reach them when it had slipped on the wet rocks and fallen off the jetty into the river.

Righting itself, it began to move forward, following its innate attraction to the living, walking out across the muddy river bottom in the direction of the HMS *Reliant*.

It was simply Ensign Lowell's bad luck to let his guard down, believing he was safe out on the water.

Bad luck that the shredder didn't get stuck somewhere in the mud along the way.

Bad luck that it walked into the anchor chain securing the *Reliant* in position in the middle of the river, for another foot to either side and it would have missed entirely, would have continued walking until it reached the far bank.

Bad luck that some deeply buried instinct floated to the surface of its mind at that moment and it began pulling itself up the chain toward its prey at the other end of the chain.

Hand over hand.

Foot by foot.

Until it encountered the smooth hull of the submersible.

Sensing humans on the other side of the steel, it began climbing upward, looking for a way in.

LOWELL HAD NEVER been this close to a pack of shredders before, and the nearness of the creatures everyone was talking about back in Le Havre made him long for a better look. He wanted to have stories to tell his friends when he returned to base. Figuring he might be able to see more a little closer to the action, he slipped out of the conning tower and made his way across the hull until he stood next to the deck gun. He left the hatch open behind him; that way the executive officer, Sanders, wouldn't take him by surprise if he decided to check up on him.

He squinted in the afternoon light, trying to get a better look at the creatures on the shore, but the dust and haze in the air kept defeating him. To keep himself amused he began to mimic their motions, lurching back and forth in that oddly disjointed way they had, copying their head and hand motions so he'd be able to better describe them back at base.

The sound of a footfall on the deck behind him caused him to turn, still laughing at his own antics, expecting to find one of his crewmates standing there, but instead he found himself face-to-face with a shredder.

As the sight of the dripping wet creature was still registering in Lowell's mind, it lunged for him. It seized him in its iron grip and its mouth clamped down on the flesh of his face, its jaws snapping shut like a steel vise and removing most of the flesh from just below his eyeballs to the edge of his chin, including his nose and both lips.

Reeling in shock, Lowell opened his mouth to scream, the gun in his hands completely forgotten, only to have the shredder tear his throat out with a single swipe of its overgrown fingernails, silencing him forever.

His body dropped and the shredder fell on it, claws and teeth working feverishly as it burrowed into the man's soft flesh, seeking the organs deeper inside.

Lowell's decision to leave his post damned him forever. His decision to leave the hatch open damned the rest of the crew.

Long moments passed before the shredder raised its head. Sensing the presence of more humans inside the boat beneath it, the shredder headed for the open hatch. It didn't know how to use the ladder, but that didn't stop the creature. It simply stepped into the opening and let gravity do the work.

The first man to rush over to help what he thought was a fallen crew member ended up with half of his calf being bitten off for his trouble. Within moments the infection had spread through that man's system and suddenly the crew of the *Reliant* had two shredders to deal with inside the narrow confines of its hull.

The odds were not with them, and the screams of the dying continued for some time.

CHAPTER TWENTY-TWO

BEDLAM HOSPITAL
LONDON

BURKE STARED DOWN the barrel of that pistol and thought how ironic it would be to survive three years of fighting in the trenches and a secret mission behind enemy lines only to wind up dead in the British capital thanks to a trigger-happy Allied soldier.

Crazy laughter bubbled up inside but he stomped on it immediately. Laughing at the man pointing a gun at him was not a good idea.

Instead, he opened his hands so his own pistol hung by only a finger and said in a calm, clear voice, "Easy there, Tommy. We're on the same side."

The other man visibly started at Burke's accent, and then a grin wider than the Brooklyn Bridge spread across the soldier's face.

"Bloody hell!" he exclaimed. "You're an American!"

"Major Burke, American Expeditionary Forces. I'd appreciate it if you'd stop pointing that gun at my face."

"What? Oh, right. Sorry about that." The gun was withdrawn

and the other man helped Burke to his feet. "Thought you might have been the Boche, actually."

Burke shook his head at that one, thinking the Germans wouldn't have bothered climbing through the barricades; they'd have simply blown the things up.

The other man extended a hand. "Captain Morrison," he said, "Black Watch, Royal Highlanders. A pleasure to make your acquaintance."

They shook and Burke asked, "Are you alone?"

Morrison's tone grew wary as he said, "There are . . . others with me."

Burke nodded, pleased to hear that not everyone had perished in this mess. He jerked a thumb in the direction of the barricade. "I've got some men on the other side of this thing, one of whom is a doctor. If any of your people need medical attention, we can deal with that before we get you all out of here."

"Out of here?"

Burke bent down, put his fingers to his lips, and whistled down the length of the tunnel. An answering whistle from Drummond quickly came back. They were ready. Over his shoulder, Burke said, "Right. Allied Command sent us to be certain that Queen Veronica gets out of the city safely."

Morrison hesitated. "*Queen* Veronica?" he said at last, putting emphasis on the first word.

As Burke straightened, he realized his faux pas and mentally kicked himself for being such an idiot. The captain was a British subject and therefore no doubt loyal to the King and Queen. Burke had just told him, in no uncertain terms and with absolutely no tact whatsoever, that the King and Queen were dead.

Burke opened his mouth, intending to apologize, only to have a woman speak up behind him.

"My parents . . . they're both dead then?"

Burke winced and shot a glance of apology at Morrison, but the furious expression on the captain's face told him he'd be getting no sympathy there. Burke knew that Veronica was probably here somewhere, but he certainly hadn't expected her to be within hearing distance. She should have been under guard somewhere away from the barricades.

Unless of course it was just Morrison and her.

He turned to face her . . . and was momentarily at a loss for words.

Queen Veronica was not what Burke was expecting.

She stood just beyond the doorway from which she'd emerged, a dozen feet away, but he could feel the impact of her personality just the same. She was younger than he—mid to late twenties would be his guess—with long auburn hair that was pulled into a loose braid on one side of her smooth-skinned face. Her eyes were a deep green, almost luminescent in the light, and they caught and held his glance without flinching.

She was dressed in a button-down blouse, now smudged with dirt, blood, and other unrecognizable stains, and a pair of men's pants that tapered to calf-high riding boots. A pair of leather belts crisscrossed her chest and stuck through them on either side was a large-barreled revolver.

She was dirty, disheveled, and obviously distraught at the news he'd just inadvertently delivered, but she was also the most beautiful woman he'd ever seen.

He took a few involuntary steps forward and then nodded once, briefly, before bowing his head for a moment in recognition for her loss. When he thought he'd given it sufficient time, he introduced himself.

"Major Michael Burke, Military Intelligence Division, American Expeditionary Forces, Your Majesty," he said.

He expected her to fall apart at the news about her mother and father, to turn away weeping and need to be consoled, but she simply closed her eyes for a moment, gathering her composure as she digested the news.

When she opened them again, there was determination in her eyes and in the hard set of her jaw.

"All right, Major. We will be happy to accompany you and your team back to Allied Command. We will need to retrieve several items from the British Museum before doing so, but after that . . ."

She stopped when she saw Burke shaking his head. "Is there a problem, Major?"

"No offense, Your Majesty, but yeah, there is. We're not going to be making any side trips. We're going right back to the *Reliant* and getting the heck out of London as quickly as we can."

The Queen frowned. "Perhaps I wasn't making myself clear, Major."

She walked over, her back straight, her eyes full of determination as she stood in front of Burke and glared at him, trying to stare him down from her position of a foot shorter in height.

"The items I intend to secure from the museum are directly relevant to the national security of the British Empire and I will not leave them behind."

Burke bit back the quick retort that sprang to mind. *This was the Queen of England,* he reminded himself. *Behave accordingly.*

"That's all well and good, Your Majesty, but I have orders to take you back to the *Reliant* as swiftly as possible. Once there I am to turn you and your party over to the captain of the vessel, Captain Wattley. What he chooses to do at that point is entirely up to him. Unlike me or my squad, Captain Wattley is a British citizen."

Which makes him one of your subjects and therefore bound by his oath to you and the Crown, Burke finished silently.

His orders were to see to it that Her Majesty made it back to the *Reliant* alive and in one piece. What happened after that . . . well, that was in someone else's hands, not his. He was here to do a job, and that was what he was going to do.

Noise behind him caught his attention and he turned to see Doc Bankowski squirming his way out of the barricade. Once he was clear, Sergeant Drummond followed suit. Introductions were made and Doc politely offered to see to the injuries of anyone in the Queen's party.

"We're all that's left," the Queen said sadly as she came forward and let Doc examine her briefly. She was a bit bruised and battered, but otherwise unharmed, as it turned out. Captain Morrison, on the other hand, had a nasty cut across his scalp, which Bankowski cleaned with the help of some alcohol from his medicine bag, and then Doc bandaged it with clean gauze to try to keep infection from settling in.

While Bankowski worked, Morrison explained how they'd been in hospital when the German bombing run had begun and about how they'd subsequently made the decision to stay put and wait for rescue when the bombs finally stopped. They hadn't anticipated the effects of the gas and had almost been overrun when the transformations had first begun.

It had been the Queen's idea to seal off the stairwells and the upper floor, an idea that would cost the lives of several of her men but that would, ultimately, mean the difference between life and death for the Queen and Captain Morrison. Just the same, it had effectively trapped them here ever since.

In turn, Sergeant Drummond gently explained to the Queen what he knew regarding the fate of her parents, how he had stayed with them following the initial attack, how the palace had ended up surrounded by shredders in the wake of the gas, how the King had eventually ordered several of them to try and reach help. He told her about his journey to Southend-on-Sea and of how he'd stumbled upon Major Burke and company just in time to escape with them back across the Channel to France and then of their subsequent return to Buckingham Palace. A tear slid down the Queen's cheek when Drummond told her that they'd removed the bodies of her parents in order to give them a proper burial and Burke, watching from the side, was struck with the sudden uncharacteristic urge to reach forward and gently wipe it away.

When Drummond finished and Doc signaled he was done treating their injuries, Burke explained that the rest of his squad was waiting in the buildings just across the street from the hospital. It was his intention to leave the hospital the same way they'd gotten in—through the courtyard at the end of the west wing—

and then regroup with the rest of the squad for the short trip back to the *Reliant*.

Morrison wasn't thrilled with the plan, but he also recognized that they couldn't stay there; eventually, the shredders would find their way inside. After a short consultation with the Queen, he, too, agreed that it was the best option available to them and soon they were ready to go.

They made their way over the barricades one by one, with Sergeant Drummond and Captain Morrison leading the way to secure the area on the other side, followed by the Queen and Doc Bankowski, with Burke guarding the rear. Thankfully none of the shredders had yet found their way to the second floor, and they were able to retrace their steps down the stairwell and back to the first floor without difficulty.

Drummond ducked around the corner, saw the coast was clear, and led the others back down the long hallway toward the administrative offices at the end of the west wing. As they approached the door to the courtyard, however, Drummond slowed so dramatically that Captain Morrison nearly ran into his back.

"Sergeant! What do you . . ." Morrison began indignantly, but Drummond cut him off with a single whispered phrase.

"Shut up!"

Drummond's voice was full of such deep fear that it shocked even Burke into silence, and he was at the back of the group. He understood what had frightened the man a moment later when the people in front of him shifted position slightly and he was able to see past the others to the courtyard outside.

It was teeming with shredders.

They were wandering back and forth, their attention caught by the walls that held them in place more than the building behind them. As a result, they had yet to notice Burke and the others. The minute they did, however, they'd be on them like lions among the sheep.

Which was why Drummond began moving backward slowly and quietly, taking short little steps to keep from stumbling and drawing attention to their group, forcing the others to do the same lest he walk right over them.

The shredders had found some way to climb the fence; that was the only logical explanation. Although that didn't make Burke happy, it was a hell of a lot better than thinking the shredders were getting back up again after taking a bullet to the skull. Semi-intelligent shredders were bad enough; shredders that could resurrect themselves repeatedly, no matter the injury, was a nightmare of epic proportions.

He prayed like hell that it was the former.

After moving backward for several yards, the group swung about and started running back the way they had come, trying to put as much distance between them now that the shredders weren't right on top of them. If they could reach the stairwell and get back behind the safety of the barricades, they could still get out of this alive. They could contact Jones somehow, figure out a new plan . . . there were plenty of options available.

First, they had to get to safety.

They might have made it, too, if it hadn't been for the hound.

Burke was now in the lead and he was racing for the entrance to the stairwell, Queen Veronica on his heels, when something stepped into the hall from a room to their right.

Burke recognized it immediately.

The last time he'd seen one he'd been running for his life over no-man's-land, a wounded Private Williams in his arms, while a pack of such creatures chased after them and Richthofen tried to gun Burke and his companions down from above in his brilliant red aircraft.

Burke didn't know their official designation, or if they even had one for that matter, but his half brother Jack had called them hounds and in Burke's mind the name had stuck.

They were one of the new breed of zombies produced in the hell of Eisenberg's secret labs, their bodies and senses twisted and warped by the gas to meet the specific needs of the German war machine. In this case, trackers.

The hounds ran on all fours, faces close to the ground, and had their sense of smell constantly enhanced by a cloud of gas that filled the strange helmetlike contraptions that covered their heads. How they could smell anything through the glass faceplates they wore was more than Burke could fathom, but then again he couldn't have imagined morphing the bodies of the dead into these hideous creatures in the first place.

This one looked up, saw them, and let out the ear-shattering howl that called the rest of their pack.

The answering bark of Burke's Thompson submachine gun mingled with the boom of Veronica's Webley, and in the next instant the creature went over backward, its mask and skull shattered from both bullets.

But the damage had been done.

The shredders in the courtyard behind them turned at the sound, saw their prey racing away down the hall, and charged after them in hot pursuit.

CHAPTER TWENTY-THREE

WITHOUT THINKING, BURKE reached back, grabbed Veronica's free hand in his own, and took off running, no longer concerned with trying to be quiet. Behind him he could hear the others follow suit.

Already the shredders were starting to close the distance.

The stairs to the second floor were out of the question now. They would barely make the first barricade before the shredders would be upon them, and they wouldn't have the time needed to scramble over the top to safety. Caught with their backs to the enormous pile of junk the Queen and her troops had previously erected, Burke and his little group would be cut down where they stood.

Burke glanced around frantically as they ran. They needed an alternate route, and they needed it now!

His gaze fell on the double doors at the end of the hallway, the ones that led to the main building, and he headed for them as fast as they could go. They could shoot out the locks and then find something to brace the doors with from the other side against the oncoming horde . . .

Gunfire filled the hallway as Drummond and Morrison began

firing into the oncoming shredders, knocking down the front ranks and causing those just behind to stumble over the bodies as they charged forward. It would only gain Burke and the others a few seconds of respite, but even a few seconds might make a difference.

Burke skidded to a halt in front of the double doors, a good half-dozen yards ahead of the rest of the group. He dropped Veronica's hand and brought up his gun. He was about to fire into the locks holding the doors closed when Veronica stepped in front of them, fumbling with something in her hands. Burke opened his mouth, intending to holler at her and tell her to get the hell out of his way, when he realized that what she had in her hands was an iron ring full of keys.

She started shoving them into the keyhole one at a time, testing each one, hoping to find the correct one before it was too late.

Come on, come on, Burke thought, willing the next key to be the right one. If it took much longer, they were going to be fighting the shredders hand to hand, and in these tight quarters they didn't stand a chance. Doc Bankowski had already caught up to them and was standing off to the side, taking shots with his Enfield past the forms of Morrison and Drummond as they continued their orderly retreat in the face of the oncoming shredders. Less than fifteen feet now separated the two groups.

The Queen let out a whoop of success as the lock clicked open. Before Burke could stop her, she shouldered the door open and stepped inside.

For one heart-stopping moment Burke imagined her stepping into the waiting arms of a pack of shredders, but she stuck her head back out a second later, a grin spreading from ear to ear.

"It's clear!" she called to the others. "Hurry!"

Burke and Doc Bankowski scrambled through the open doors, with Captain Morrison and Sergeant Drummond right on their heels. The four men grabbed the doors and swung them shut just as the shredders slammed into them from the other side. Burke was convinced there was no way they were going to hold, that another blow like the last was going to knock them all aside, leaving the door open and them to their fate, but suddenly the Queen was there, a long, thick crossbeam in her hands, and the men were able to get it up and into the slot across the door where it belonged just before the shredders tested their defenses a second time. There was a thunderous crash from the other side as multiple bodies slammed into it, but the door held.

Just to be extra safe, the Queen used the keys to relock the door from their side. It might not add that much more protection, but Burke still felt safer seeing her do it.

They found themselves in the grand lobby of the main building. It featured a wide reception desk and several rows of comfortable chairs for those waiting to see doctors or loved ones. Another set of double doors opposite the entrance led to the east wing, identical to the west but for male patients rather than female.

Burke didn't care about any of that; he had eyes only for the afternoon light coming in through the front entrance. Now was the time to make a break for it, he realized. He could see shredders wandering around the grounds outside the front door, but they had not focused their attention on the entrance yet, had not gathered outside it in a mob so dense that it would be impossible for Burke and company to fight their way through. The time to go was now, while they still had the chance!

He gathered the others about him, speaking quickly but calmly, showing his confidence in voice and deed. They were only going to get one shot at this . . .

"We're going out the front door and through the gate at the end of the drive while the opportunity is still available to us. Don't shoot until you absolutely have to, for the minute we do we'll be calling the others down on our heads. Stay close, keep the Queen in the middle, and whatever you do, don't stop moving. Let's go!"

He didn't give them time to think, just stepped over to the front door, hauled it open, and headed out into the open air beyond.

Thankfully, they all chose to follow.

For the first few seconds it seemed that things might go their way. The steps outside the doors led to a circular driveway that surrounded a large flower garden several dozen yards wide. Grassy lawns and well-trimmed hedges spread out on the far side of the driveway, ultimately leading to the tall iron fence that surrounded the entire property. A few shredders could be seen milling about the garden and the lawn areas, but if they hurried, Burke thought they might just make it to the main gate.

He led them down the front steps to the crushed gravel of the driveway.

There were two large courtyards on either side of the main entrance, nearly impossible to see from the front steps due to the thick green hedges that covered all but the narrow gates leading into them. The dozen or so shredders milling about in the courtyard, worked up by all the noise coming from inside the building, caught sight of Burke right about the same time he saw them.

That's when all hell broke loose. The shredders didn't hesitate; they came charging forward with the relentlessness of the tide, spilling through the gate and across the lawn toward Burke and his small company.

Burke brought his Tommy gun up, his finger already pulling back the trigger, only to have the weapon cough out a few shots and then fall silent. Thinking it had jammed, he hauled back on the charging handle, only to find an empty chamber; he was out of ammunition!

He tried not to think of how quickly the shredders were closing on them as he hit the release, dropped the empty drum magazine to his feet, and jammed another in its place, noting that it was his last.

As the others continued to fire, holding the shredders at bay, Burke used the moment it gave him to look around. More shredders were closing in from the front now, as well as the side. Not seeing any way forward and worried that the shredders would get around behind them and cut them off, he was about to order them all back inside when the sound of a racing engine reached his ears.

He looked forward, over the heads of the oncoming shredders, and watched in surprise as the black iron grille of a truck came into view through the front gates of the hospital complex. The engine was whining, sounding as if it were being pushed too hard, but the driver didn't let up; if anything, he pushed it even harder.

Burke glanced away long enough to put a bullet through the skull of a shredder that was trying to flank Captain Morrison while he was otherwise engaged with another of its ilk, and then he looked back in time to see the truck smash through the gate without stopping.

Iron fencing crashed to the ground, pinning several shredders beneath it as the truck roared over them, leaving still corpses in its wake.

Due to the afternoon sun reflecting off the glass, Burke couldn't see who was inside and a sudden surge of fear washed over him as it occurred to him that this might not be help at all.

What if it was that German special ops team Colonel Nichols had mentioned?

Thankfully, he didn't have to find out, for even as the truck raced toward them, someone clambered out the passenger-side window, raised a rifle to his shoulder, and began shooting the shredders that were drawing too close to Burke and his group.

The unerring accuracy of the shots brought a smile to Burke's face; he knew only one man who could shoot like that, never mind doing so from the front of a speeding vehicle.

Corporal Jones.

The noise of the truck caught the attention of the shredders, and several of them paused in their headlong rush toward Burke and company to look back at the oncoming vehicle. Jones took them out like ducks in a shooting gallery.

The driver swerved to deliberately run down three shredders on the edge of the road and then bounced over the curb into the flower garden forming the centerpiece of the circular drive. Earth and flowers went every which way as the churning tires tossed them aside, and then the truck was bouncing over the curb and slewing to a stop in front of Burke and his bewildered crew.

Jones looked down from his perch on the passenger door with a grin.

"Need a lift, Major?"

For once, Burke didn't find the need to yell at him for disobeying an order. "Don't mind if we do, Corporal," he said with a grin of his own.

The canvas flap in the back was thrust aside as Cohen and Montagna made an appearance, adding their firepower to that of Sergeant Drummond and Captain Morrison and making short work of the closest shredders. Graves, meanwhile, was leaning out the back, extending a courteous hand to the Queen and helping her up into the rear of the vehicle. As soon as she was situated, Burke gave the order to retreat, and the rest of the squad turned away from the fight and scrambled into the back. They'd barely settled into place before Williams put the pedal to the metal and got them the hell out of there as fast as the truck would go.

CHAPTER TWENTY-FOUR

En Route to the *Reliant*
LONDON

HAVING SEEN THE photographs detailing what had happened to Brigadier Calhoun's column when he'd brought motorized vehicles into the city, Burke was understandably worried about their use of the vehicle salvaged by Corporal Williams. He knew the trip back to the Thames was a short one, however, and decided that getting the Queen to the *Reliant* as quickly as possible was worth the risk of attracting shredders with the engine noise.

Besides, after spending an entire day in the city, he was starting to think the vast majority of shredders had headed elsewhere the minute the easy food supply had grown scarce. With all the people living in the city limits at the time of the initial gas attack, he would have expected there to be massive hordes of the creatures roaming the streets. Instead, they'd only encountered a few individual creatures here or there or, when they did run into a larger group, it was as a result of a living survivor having attracted them to that locale.

Lieutenant Colonel Ellington's words came back to him. *We have the perimeter secured and the threat contained.* Now, more than ever, Burke believed that to be untrue and he wondered just where the hell the shredders had gone if they were no longer in the city.

At least, not the part of the city they'd seen so far.

As Williams drove, Major Burke had Cohen fill him in on how they came to be riding in a salvaged lorry in the first place.

"Corporal Jones had us scout the area around our position, which is how we came across the truck," Cohen told him. "It was parked just up the street and, miraculously, hadn't suffered any damage during the bombardment or in the days thereafter. Figuring you might have need of a quick escape, Jones, Montagna, and I pushed it back to our position, at which point Corporal Williams had a go at the engine. Didn't take him long to get the thing running at all!"

No, I don't suspect it did, Burke thought. Williams, as well as knowing his way around explosive devices, was a genius with anything mechanical. He probably could have gotten the truck started even if half the engine had been missing.

Jones and Williams were a formidable team, it seemed, and Burke made note to put them both in for a medal when they returned. Without a doubt, the truck had saved the Queen's life and that, at the very least, deserved some notice.

Satisfied that things were well in hand, Burke shot a glance in Veronica's direction. She sat between Captain Morrison and Dr. Graves, her head back against the canvas side of the truck and her eyes closed. A dark smudge ran across one smooth cheek—Gunpowder? Grease? he wondered.

She must have felt his scrutiny at that point, for her head came forward and she opened her eyes, catching his gaze with her own and smiling slightly.

Burke felt the jolt of her stare right down to the base of his bones, so strong and so unsettling that he had to turn away. It had been many years since a woman had affected him in such a way and to experience those feelings here, amid the ruins of a once-great city, with a member of the British royalty no less, felt completely surreal. He had no idea what to do with those feelings and so he did what man, from time immemorial, had been doing in such situations.

He ignored them.

To get his mind off Veronica, he got up and made his way forward, squatting down just behind the two front seats so that he could talk to the driver, Williams, and look through the windshield at the same time. He could see Westminster Bridge, with the skeleton of Big Ben looming over it, coming up ahead of them.

"How are we doing, Corporal?"

"Good, sir," Williams replied. "Another five minutes or so should bring us back to where we left the boat."

"Excellent. Any sign of gathering shredders?"

This time it was Jones who answered from his overwatch position in the passenger seat. "None. If I didn't know any better, I'd say they've all flown the coop, Major."

They arrived at the point where they'd beached their boat just a few hours earlier, parked the truck, and cautiously climbed down, looking about. The riverbank seemed deserted and the noise of their truck didn't appear to bring any shredders out of the woodwork, for which Burke was thankful.

Shielding his eyes against the afternoon glare, he looked out across the water, to where the *Reliant* was anchored.

He could see several figures moving about on the deck of the *Reliant*, and more than one appeared to be wearing the characteristic uniform of a British sailor, but something about them just didn't seem right.

It took him only another moment to focus in on the quick, jerky nature to their movements to realize what he was looking at.

Shredders.

Burke didn't know how it had happened, but somehow, the sub had been lost.

He stared across the water in shock, his thoughts a chaotic mess.

What the hell were they going to do now?

That boat had been their lifeline, their transportation home, and without it they were now in serious danger. Everything they needed was aboard that vessel, from fresh food and water to the communication equipment necessary to report back to headquarters. Hell, they couldn't even let anyone know they'd rescued the Queen, never mind set up an alternate plan for getting her out of London without that boat!

Beside him, Jones raised his Enfield, intending to take out the shredders on the deck of the boat. Burke reached out and pushed the barrel of the man's weapon down before he could fire.

"Save the ammo," he told Jones. "We're going to need it."

Ammo and a hell of a lot of other things, including food and water, before this was over. Thank God they'd taken the time to replenish their supplies before going to Bedlam.

He didn't notice the Queen standing at his elbow until she spoke up.

"I take it there's been a change of plans, Major?"

He nodded, gestured across the water to where the *Reliant* was bobbing gently with the tide. "Shredders have taken the *Reliant*."

She glanced that way and then back at Burke. "Can you and your men take it back?"

"Yes," he told her and it was the truth. He didn't relish the idea of fighting in those close quarters, but it could be done. There was no sense in doing so, however. "Yes, we could take it back, but doing so won't help. None of my men are sailors; we'd never get out of the Thames, never mind back across the English Channel with what little we know. We'd be lucky if we didn't drown in the first five minutes."

He wouldn't say it to the Queen, but they were pretty much fucked. He stared at the shredders lurching about on the deck of the *Reliant* and, not for the last time, found himself cursing their very existence.

He had no idea what they were going to do next.

Veronica, however, wasn't at such a loss.

"There's a wireless set at the museum."

Burke blinked, then slowly turned to face her, not certain that he had heard correctly.

"I'm sorry?"

"There's a wireless set at the British Museum. We can use it to let your people know what's happened and arrange for some other means of rescue."

The British Museum. Where she'd wanted to go in the first place.

She was persistent, he had to give her that, but her suggestion also made sense, Burke thought. The wireless would be invaluable, both in bringing Colonel Nichols up to speed on the latest developments as well as allowing them to consider options open to them to get the Queen out of London safe and sound.

He glanced at the chronometer on his wrist and noted that there were still several hours before nightfall. They had plenty of time to make the trip, even if they were to do so on foot. He knew the men must be feeling the same sense of hopeless despair at the loss of the sub, knowing just as he did that the boat had been their ticket home. He needed to keep them occupied, keep their minds off the ugliness of their situation. Sure, they were effectively marooned in the midst of the city, surrounded by legions of the undead, but they didn't need to worry about that, did they? No, that was his job. The museum would give them a target and a focus, both of which were in high demand right now.

Besides, he thought, *they were going to need a place to hole up for the night. Someplace they could reasonably defend with a group their size. There had to be an office or an exhibit hall inside the museum that fit the bill.*

Burke was nodding to himself as he turned to the Queen and smiled.

"All right, Your Majesty, the British Museum it is."

CHAPTER TWENTY-FIVE

BURKE MADE THE decision to stick with the truck, if for no other reason than it allowed them to make the two-kilometer trip to the museum in less than fifteen minutes. They crossed the Westminster Bridge and then turned north, passing through Leicester Square and the western edge of Covent Garden in order to reach the area around Bloomsbury Street where the museum was located.

Given how close the museum was to the British seat of government, Burke was surprised to find that it had survived the bombing campaign intact. As there weren't any shredders in sight—they had, in fact, seen very few during their short drive—they parked the truck out front, slipped between the massive stone pillars that formed the central colonnade leading to the building's entrance and walked inside right through the front doors.

Amazingly, the lights were still on inside, their soft glow illuminating the entryway and seeming to lead them forward, deeper into the building.

Seeing Burke's surprise at the lights, Veronica told him, "The museum has its own internal energy supply that provides constant power to the facility, day and night."

And on such was the British Empire built, Burke thought.

Just past the foyer they entered what was known as the Great Court, a massive square-shaped room that served as the gateway to the rest of the museum. The entrances to the gallery areas on either side of the room had been constructed to look like ornate Greek temples, giant columns and all, and rising in the center of the court was an enormous circular room two stories high that functioned as a combination library and reading area.

Burke sent Jones and Williams up the steps to check the room above while the rest of the squad fanned out through the court, verifying that there weren't any shredders inside. Once the room and immediate surroundings were declared clear, the major asked the Queen to lead on.

Veronica, however, had other ideas.

"We may be allies, Major, but I'm afraid I can't reveal national secrets to your entire squad, trusted as they may be. Perhaps your team can wait here until my men and I retrieve what we need?"

Burke shook his head. "With all due respect, Your Majesty, I can't do that. I've been ordered to be certain that you make it back to Allied Command alive and unharmed, and I can't do that if I'm not with you at all times. It would make my job easier if I had several of my men with me as well."

"That's just not acceptable."

Burke did his best to remain calm. He wasn't the diplomatic type, and the seriousness of leaving the Queen exposed for any longer than necessary was testing his social graces to the limit.

"My apologies, Your Majesty, but without my squad, you and your men have little chance of surviving an attack by any sizable group of shredders you might encounter. You need us."

The Queen's nostrils flared as her own irritation threatened to break loose. Her tone was icy as she answered his remark with an observation of her own. "And without the equipment I'm going to provide access to, *Major,* you and your men will be forced to walk back to France."

In the end, they compromised, with personnel from both Allied forces. Major Burke would accompany the Queen, along with Professor Graves and Sergeant Drummond. Captain Morrison, the next senior officer after Burke, would take charge of the rest of the group, setting up an observation post near the entrance to the museum and tasked with defending the perimeter until the Queen and her party returned.

Burke would have preferred to have another rifle or two along with them in the Queen's party, but she was adamant that her group remain as small as possible and Burke wanted Graves there to get a good look at anything of an arcane or scientific nature that the British might clandestinely be cooking up in the secret lab of theirs. Britain and the United States might be allies, but Burke had learned long ago that sometimes it is those you hold close that you know the least.

Instructions were given to those remaining behind and then Burke gathered up his charges, smiled politely at the Queen, and said, "Whenever you're ready, Your Majesty."

A door to the left of the rotunda-like reading room led to the majority of the galleries on this level and it was through there that Veronica took them.

One moment Burke was in modern London and in the next he was transported to ancient Egypt simply by stepping through the doorway into the next gallery. The room they entered was dominated by a massive stone bust of an Egyptian pharaoh that looked out over the collection of artifacts sharing the room with him, including the famed Rosetta stone. Burke would have loved to linger, having always enjoyed stories of ancient civilizations and lost cultures as a boy, but the Queen swept right on through as if she hadn't even noticed the artifacts were there.

From Egypt they moved forward in time nearly a thousand

years to the kingdom of Nimrud in Assyria. Burke caught a glimpse of stone tablets that once adorned the palace walls in 800 B.C. as they rushed through the room, and he marveled at how they looked as if they had been carved just yesterday. He glanced about for the colossal statue of the winged lions he knew was here somewhere and was disappointed to find he must be in the wrong gallery. *Someday when the war is over,* he vowed silently and grinned at the thought.

Assyria was left behind as quickly as Egypt, and Veronica and her companions found themselves entering the world of Alexander the Great and Hellenistic Greece. This gallery held even more wonders than those before, including a gorgeous marble statue of the Greek goddess Demeter and dozens of smaller terra-cotta figurines and gold bowls and dishes.

As they rushed through the gallery, Burke said a silent prayer of thanks that all this accumulated history hadn't been demolished during the German bombing of the city. A few well-placed munitions and all this would have been lost to future generations; it made him cringe just thinking about it.

Of course, it might still be lost, he knew, if they couldn't find a way of dealing with the shredders and whatever else Richthofen had in store for them in the future.

It was not a comforting thought.

Beside him Graves gave a low whistle. The sound pulled Burke out of his musings and back to the present, where he noted that they had finally come to a halt inside a gallery devoted to Greek culture, if the meticulously reconstructed temple they were facing was any indication.

The reconstruction dominated the room, taking up about half the available floor space, and had no doubt been placed just where it was to draw visitors' eyes as they entered the room.

Three exquisitely carved marble statues stood in the spaces between the four columns that held up the triangular entablature leading to the temple's roof. Relief carvings covered the front face of the temple and ran as a frieze around the lintel just below the roof.

A door stood behind the columns, leading into the depths of the temple itself.

Beside him, Graves whispered, "The Mausoleum of Halicarnassus. One of the seven wonders of the ancient world. Every other mausoleum in the world is named after this one."

Burke could see why. Even the ruins were glorious to behold, and he could barely imagine what it must have looked like with all that white marble shining under the hot desert sun.

Graves continued the history lesson as they walked closer. "Built somewhere around 350 B.C. by Queen Artemisia to honor the man who was her husband, brother, and king all at once— Mausolos. It stood on a platform one hundred forty feet high atop a hill overlooking the city. Mausolos was a great admirer of Greek culture and so the tomb was decorated with relief carvings and surrounded by statues of the Greek gods and goddesses, as you can see."

The men slowed as they drew closer to the exhibit, naturally reluctant to disrupt the exhibit, but Veronica stepped over the velvet rope placed to keep the public from coming too close and walked around the side of the structure.

Surprised, the men scurried to follow suit.

A small set of steps was built into the side of the platform and Veronica climbed them without hesitation, stepping into the temple foyer and approaching the doorway that led inside.

With Graves and Drummond on his heels, Burke followed.

He paused in the temple doorway to let his eyes adjust to the dimness inside and saw that the illusion of a room beyond the doorway was just that, an illusion. In reality the space ran for less than a half-dozen feet before ending flush against the rear wall of the gallery. Veronica stood a few feet away, running her hands over a particular section of the interior wall, clearly searching for something.

Burke was about to ask what she was looking for, intending to help, when she let out an audible "Aha!" She twisted her hands once, sharply, and then stepped back.

There was the hiss of releasing steam, the creak of gears getting under way, and then a loud grinding noise as a portion of the rear wall slid backward a foot and then slid to one side, revealing a set of stairs, lit with flickering lightbulbs, leading downward.

The Queen turned and grinned in their direction. "Gentlemen, welcome to the Round Table."

CHAPTER TWENTY-SIX

THE ROUND TABLE
BRITISH MUSEUM

PORTABLE LAMPS WAITED on a shelf just inside the doorway. Veronica took one for herself and handed one to Burke, showing him how to operate it with the switch on the side. Light illuminated the small space they stood in, revealing the long, narrow staircase leading downward just a few feet away.

"Watch yourselves; the steps can be slippery."

Down they went.

Veronica knew that their destination lay nearly one hundred feet below street level, far beneath the two basement levels the British Museum was known to possess. The complex had been carved out of the bedrock underneath the museum during the building's initial construction with the help of the Arcanaum, a secret order of British mystics devoted to the security and sanctity of the Crown. Only a handful of those who had helped create the facility were still alive and there was no doubt of their loyalty; they would protect the secret until their deaths and, in certain instances, even beyond.

Nicknamed the Round Table by those in the know, the facility served as the headquarters for Project Merlin, the British government's answer to the research and development programs being run by both the Germans and the Americans. It was here that the Crown's best and brightest gathered together to discuss advancements that might improve the welfare of the empire, just as Arthur and his knights had once done. Where America had its Tesla and Germany its Eisenberg, Britain had James Damien Highmoore III, or just JD for short. Veronica just hoped he was in a good mood; he could be a cranky old codger when he wanted to be.

A large vaultlike iron door waited for them at the bottom of the stairs. Veronica stepped over to it and spun the hand wheel that secured it, dialing through a sequence of six digits, spinning the tumblers first one way and then the other until the entire combination sequence was locked in.

"That should do it," she said, when she was finished. She spun the massive flywheel in the center of the door to the left until it clicked and then stepped aside. "Sergeant, if you would be so kind?"

Drummond stepped forward, grasped the handles in both hands, and pulled.

The three-foot-thick door opened without a sound, revealing a large room beyond. There were lights on inside the vault, and Veronica could hear music playing faintly somewhere in the background.

Good, she thought. *At least JD is up and active.* She'd been afraid the recent bombing might have sent him into one of his infrequent "sleep" periods. She listened for a moment, recognized the strains of Wagner's *Ride of the Valkyries* and frowned a bit at the choice of selection. The Germanic opera was a bit too prophetic at the moment for her taste.

"Is there a problem?" the American major, Burke, asked suddenly, and she turned to find him watching her closely, clearly reacting to the expression on her face despite how little she'd let show.

He's more perceptive than I expected, Veronica thought.

She smiled and waved away his concern. "Everything's fine. German opera just isn't my taste."

At his puzzled expression, she realized that he hadn't noticed the music at all, that he must have been paying more attention to her than to the room before them.

How interesting, she mused, and turned away to hide the slight heat she felt in her cheeks.

She liked the idea that the American officer found her intriguing and had to admit that she found him just as interesting in turn. He was very different from what she might have expected.

She'd met a few American officers before, the high-ranking types that were often invited to state dinners hosted by her parents, and as a whole she found them to be loudmouthed bores with few social graces and an appalling lack of manners. They were all too often convinced of their own superiority and attractiveness and unfortunately were far more often wrong on both counts than right.

But Burke seemed . . . different. Yes, he was full of the easy self-confidence that she'd seen in other American officers, but it was a confidence that appeared to be tempered by an innate understanding of his own limitations.

He did not make grandiose pronouncements and, in fact, said very little beyond what was actually necessary. That silence did little to hide the intellect she knew was lurking there, though; he appeared to miss very little, as the incident of just moments before had shown.

At first she'd been a bit annoyed that he hadn't simply followed her orders back at Bedlam, but that was before she had reminded herself that he was an American citizen and not a British one. Her orders were not his orders, no matter how much she might like them to be. His stubborn refusal to simply take her to the museum when she'd first stated that would be their destination had definitely been irritating, but in hindsight she had to admire him for both his clear focus as well as his steadfast dedication to saving her life.

This was a man who took his orders seriously, she knew, and

despite barely knowing him she had to admit that she did feel better knowing he was in charge of seeing her clear of this disaster.

Even that mechanical hand of his was more intriguing than anything else. It was impossible to miss, with its brass gears and steel panels clicking and whirring while in use, but it was so intricately designed and exquisitely manufactured that it almost looked natural, rather than artificial.

Veronica found herself idly wondering what it would be like to be touched by that hand.

She shook herself, scattering her thoughts and bringing herself back to the issue at hand. *Enough nonsense about the American,* she scolded herself. *You have a job to do, now get to it!*

The room before her was large and rectangular in shape, running lengthwise away from the staircase. Tables and benches were scattered throughout, taking up much of the available space while still leaving rows to walk between them all. Every visible surface was covered with an experiment of one kind or another, from partially disassembled firearms to partially dissected shamblers. There were strange chemicals boiling away in beakers atop small gas flames and plants in giant terrariums being subjected to the effects of different types of gas. It was a wizard's laboratory, and she was here to find the resident wizard.

It didn't take long to find him, just a few moments, in fact, for JD was right where she expected him to be, bent over a table near the back of the room with his hands inside his latest experiment. If reports were correct, the experiment was a device designed to bend light in such a way as to make things seemingly disappear into thin air. Invisibility, he called it, which sounded bright and fanciful but that, at the moment, had yet to yield any results.

"Good afternoon, James," the Queen said brightly.

The automaton was fashioned of brass and steel, giving its "skin" a decidedly shiny appearance. Overall it was the same size and stature of a man, albeit a short one, and it was even dressed in a blue jumpsuit that covered most of its bodily form. Its face had been molded to give it a male appearance, complete with a reasonable facsimile of a smile, but its eyes were completely mechanical and seemed almost alien in comparison to the other attempts to make the creature fit in with the humans around it.

The automaton didn't look up at the Queen's greeting. It kept fiddling with whatever part had captured its attention, its head bowed, while rudely addressing her in the tone of an annoyed older uncle.

"Good?" he muttered. "What, pray tell, is good about it?" he asked. "Did we win the war and someone forgot to tell me?"

Burke stepped forward, the anger at the way she was being spoken to plain on his face, but Veronica calmly put a hand on his arm and smiled at him, to show him everything was fine.

"Nothing so dramatic, James. I've simply brought company along with me this afternoon. Perhaps you could say hello?"

That, at least, got the automaton to look up.

James Damien Highmoore III had been one of Britain's most promising scientists, perhaps *the* most promising Veronica knew, until a freak lab accident had caused a fire, leaving him with burns over more than ninety percent of his body. Faced with little chance of survival, Highmoore had decided to use himself as a guinea pig to attempt what had never been done before—transplanting a human brain into a mechanical form. He selected a cutting-edge automaton prototype to serve as his physical form and had then meticulously instructed the country's top surgeons through the procedure itself.

No one had known whether or not it had worked until the day, nearly a week after the operation, when the automaton had opened its eyes and asked to be discharged. There was work to be done on behalf of the Crown, after all.

Since that day nearly two years before JD, as he was now known, continued his efforts to increase the knowledge and scientific ability of the British Empire and would no doubt continue to do so until either the world ended or the Empire fell, and no one was taking bets on which would come first.

With his hands still deep inside the gadget in front of him, the automaton could neither shake nor salute, so it settled on nodding its head slowly in a gesture of respect. "Hello, Your Highness," JD said, in his usual rich, baritone voice.

JD dismissed Major Burke with barely a glance; military personnel usually didn't interest him in any way. The same couldn't be said of Burke's companion, however. JD looked over at him and nodded his head several times in excitement.

"Oh. Hello, Graves," the automaton said. "Good to see you again."

Graves, who had been looking around the room with the expression of a boy turned loose in a candy shop, spun around at the sound of his name and focused on the automaton, his eyes growing wide at the sight.

Without taking his gaze off the mechanical man in front of him, but clearly directing his question to the Queen, Graves asked, "What manner of trickery is this? How did you program it to know my name already? Are you doing it remotely somehow?"

Veronica winced, but by then it was too late. The automaton stopped what it was doing and then, very slowly, raised its head to stare at Graves with those unblinking eyes.

"It?" JD asked, in an icy tone. "Did I just hear you call me an 'it'?"

If JD's earlier remark had surprised Graves, this last one practically knocked him off his feet.

"Good God!" he swore, his voice trembling with what sounded to Veronica like excitement. "It's self-aware."

Beside her, Major Burke opened his mouth to say something, but JD beat him to it.

"Of course I'm self-aware, you idiot! How do you Americans ever manage to get anything done when all you do is go around spouting the obvious? It's a wonder Tesla ever took you on as his student. I would have sent you back for remedial lessons in observation!"

Graves took a few steps forward, staring at the automaton closely. Veronica could see the confusion playing across the man's face as he tried, no doubt, to determine just how this was happening.

"Come, come, Graves! I've never known you to be so slow. Surely you remember the time you and Nikola came to visit me at Cambridge?"

Graves jerked in shock. "Highmoore?" he whispered.

The automaton chuckled. "Were you expecting God himself? Of course it's me! Now get over here and lend a hand with this while you tell me why you are in my country."

As Graves hurried over to his friend's side, Veronica turned and looked at Burke. "You didn't tell me Professor Graves knew Dr. Highmoore," she said, with a hint of accusation in her tone.

"Given that I didn't know Dr. Highmoore existed prior to a few seconds ago, I would think you'd have to forgive me for that. What are we doing here, anyway?" he asked, glancing around the place with what seemed to Veronica to be a combination of awe and loathing. Given the clockwork arm he wore, Veronica guessed he'd had some personal experience in someone else's version of this place and the memories weren't all that pleasant.

"Before leaving London, I need to fulfill my father's last command, which was to remove a certain item from this place and keep it safe. It won't take long, I promise."

Veronica headed toward the two scientists, now lost in earnest conversation. Along the way she stopped at a table and picked up a satchel and several lengths of cotton packing material. She would need both to transport the stone.

Reaching the two men, she leaned in and interrupted them, speaking directly to JD. "I need to access the vault," she told him.

It was as if he immediately forgot the conversation he'd just been involved in. He stiffened, nodded, put down his tools, and then waved one brass hand in a "follow me" gesture. He led her over to the blank wall that she knew actually contained the hidden entrance to the vault.

The automaton turned to her and asked for the password.

"Londinium has fallen," she said clearly and distinctly,

knowing that the rules governing the automaton's behavior allowed for only one response. If she was misunderstood, the jig was up, as the Americans liked to say. They wouldn't get another chance.

Thankfully, JD understood her just fine. He nodded, once, and if that brass face could have changed expression, she was certain it would have smiled.

Grasping his left hand with his right, JD gave a sharp twist and removed the entire appendage from his wrist, exposing a strip of iron that looked very much like an old-fashioned skeleton key. The automaton then stepped forward and inserted the iron on the end of his wrist into the slot in the wall.

Electricity sparked and spattered as the connection was made and the smell of ozone filled the air. Veronica waited patiently; she'd seen the vault opened once before and knew what to expect. After a moment, a door appeared in the center of the blank wall in front of her as the electrical current running across its surface countered the magnetic field that kept it concealed.

She turned to Major Burke, said, "I'll be but a moment," and then pushed through the door before he could protest. She wasn't worried about being followed; JD was under orders to prevent anyone but the royal family from entering the vault unless expressly ordered to allow it and she had given no such command.

Inside this vault were some of the most precious secrets of the British Empire. Artifacts, both ancient and modern, lined the shelves. From the ancient yellowed skull of the dragon that had once claimed all Britain as its own to the very table over which the facility itself had been named, the vault and its contents had been watched over and protected by the royal family for as long as Britain had existed as a kingdom.

The object she was looking for stood on a pedestal near the center of the room. It was a smooth red stone about the size of an ostrich egg. It had gone by many names through the years—the lodestone of Merlin, the eye of Solomon, the Prima Materia—but Veronica simply knew it as the philosopher's stone.

The most commonly accepted story of the stone's creation went back to the thirteenth century, to the scientist, philosopher, and mage Albertus Magnus, who is said to have discovered the stone and passed it to his pupil, Thomas Aquinas. Aquinas in turn would pass it on to his closest disciple and so on until it ended up in the hands of the Swiss alchemist Paracelsus, who in turn gifted it to a young prince who would later become King Edward VI. The stone had remained under control of the current British ruler from that point until now.

The stone was rumored to do many things, not the least of which was turn common metals like lead and iron into gold. Veronica put no stock in the old legend, for she was one of the few people alive who understood that the stone did no such thing. If it did, the British Empire would be the wealthiest nation on the face of the planet, war or no war, and that was far from the case. No, the stone's true purpose was far more valuable than the simple ability to convert lead into gold, for it provided its possessor with a certain sense of invulnerability that, under normal circumstances, would keep the bearer from ever being defeated.

These, of course, were not normal circumstances, Veronica noted as she walked over to the pedestal on which the stone was stored. The kaiser had employed a group of powerful mystics to counter the protection provided by the stone and, if recent events were any indication, had found a way of neutralizing that invulnerability, even if only for the short term. Allowing the stone to fall into enemy hands might result in Britain's complete downfall, rather than just the temporary setback it was experiencing, and so it was Veronica's solemn duty to see to it that that did not happen.

She removed the glass lid covering the stone and set it aside. She then gently lifted the stone from the velvet pillow on which it rested. The stone felt slightly warm to the touch, as if someone had been holding it in their hands and only just replaced it before Veronica had entered the room, but she knew that wasn't the case. The last time the stone had been taken from the vault had been in the midst of the Napoleonic War; as Keeper of the Vault, she'd studied the records extensively. The heat was just one of the strange properties of the stone, observed time and time again over the generations that it had been in the care of the British royal family but no more understood than the day it had come into their possession.

No matter, she thought. She wasn't here to solve all the stone's riddles, just to carry it away to safety where it could continue to provide the realm with its arcane protection for as long as possible.

She wrapped the stone in the cloth, put the parcel into the satchel, and slipped the satchel's strap over her head so that the bag hung at her side beneath her right arm. This would give her freedom of movement but also allow her to keep one hand on the bag whenever she felt the need to.

Satisfied, she replaced the glass lid on the now-empty exhibit and returned to the door. A touch of a button, the quick hiss of releasing steam, and the door slid open once more to allow her to leave the vault behind.

Burke was leaning against a nearby wall, waiting for her, when she came through the door. She could tell by the way his eyes widened that he got at least a quick glimpse over her shoulder at some of the objects stored in the room behind her.

He tried to make light of it to cover his reaction.

"I bet you've got Excalibur and the Holy Grail stored in there somewhere, too, don't you?" he asked.

She had no intention of giving him anything.

"No," she quipped. "Those are stored in a different facility."

She kept a straight face until she'd walked past him and then, when he couldn't see her expression anymore, let the smile she'd been holding back break across her face. *Let him wonder,* she thought. *We might be allies but that doesn't mean we have to share all our state secrets.*

After letting him stew in his own juices for a minute or two, she glanced back and caught his eye.

"Come on, the wireless is this way."

Veronica was feeling pretty good; she had the stone in hand and, hopefully soon, would have a plan for getting out of London as well.

She smiled as Burke hustled across the room toward her.

After a rather horrible start, the day was certainly turning around.

CHAPTER TWENTY-SEVEN

Veronica led Burke to an alcove on the far side of the room where a wireless station had been set up. Wireless devices had been in use in the trenches for the last several years, and most officers underwent rudimentary training in their use, Burke among them. This particular model looked a bit more complicated than the basic set he was used to, but he was confident that he could manage it well enough.

He sat down behind the table and spent a few minutes familiarizing himself with the switches and dials on the device in front of him. When he was satisfied he had it all down properly, he flipped the power switch, waited for the device to warm up, and then pulled on the headphones.

He picked up the notepad that was lying on the bench nearby and jotted down the messages he intended to send. Having them in front of him would make it easier to transpose them into Morse when it was time to send them out over the wire.

He dialed in the particular frequency that he knew was being used by the MID this week, pulled the operator's lever closer to him, and, after a quick prayer for luck, typed out his first message.

Eagle One to Nest. Eagle One to Nest. Stop.

Graves was still speaking with the automaton, but Drummond decided to join Burke and the Queen and so the three of them spent a few anxious moments waiting to receive a response. When Burke heard the dots and dashes of the reply begin coming in over his headphones, he snatched up the pencil and began copying down the message.

Nest to Eagle One. The first is the sunshine . . .

Burke answered the pass code query with the next line of the song, the same Dixon and Woods number they'd used during their last communication.

. . . the second is the rain.

Music had never been his thing; he hoped he was remembering the lyrics correctly. There was a short pause and then the answer came through.

Roger. Stand by for Condor. Stop.

"Condor?" Veronica asked, reading over Burke's shoulder.

Burke nodded. "Colonel Nichols, Your Majesty. Head of U.S. Military Intelligence. Otherwise known as my ranking superior."

Whatever response the Queen was going to make was lost when the telegraph started up again.

Condor to Eagle One. How did Goldilocks like the porridge? Stop.

Burke nearly laughed; Veronica was a poor Goldilocks, and he could just picture a German intelligence agent somewhere trying to make sense of this one.

Porridge just right. Stop. Bed rather uncomfortable, however. Stop.

The response was almost immediate.

Understood. Better accommodations await. Stop.

Yeah, Burke thought, *if only it were that easy.*
He quickly tapped out his reply.

Would love to visit. Rowboat sunk. Need alternate transportation.

He could imagine the colonel standing there beside the wireless operator wondering just how the hell he had managed to sink a British submarine. Burke was tempted to follow his request with a note that it wasn't his fault, but resisted the urge, knowing it would only confuse things. It would all end up in his report and there wasn't anything they could do about it while he was stuck in England anyway.

The answer, when it came, wasn't surprising.

Wait one.

The one ended up being closer to ten, but eventually Nichols came back with an answer.

Send Goldilocks via airmail from KG station, dawn tomorrow.

Burke frowned. The airmail reference clearly meant that they were going to try and get Veronica out of London by airplane, but KG station? That he didn't recognize.

He turned to Veronica. "Do the initials KG mean anything to you?"

"Do they reference a person or a place?" she asked.

"A place, I guess."

She answered without hesitation. "Kensington Gardens would be my guess."

Burke had no idea what that was. "Gardens? As in the vegetable kind?"

"No, as in a park. Kensington Gardens is like your Central Park, only smaller."

"Ah. Can you land a plane there somewhere?"

Veronica shrugged. "I don't know. I guess that would depend upon how much room you need. There's a long grassy mall that leads from Long Water to the palace that might be suitable, but I don't know enough about flying to say for certain."

Burke didn't know how much room an aircraft needed to land, either; flying was his brother's specialty, not his. Presumably Colonel Nichols had checked with somebody before issuing his instructions, as the man was a stickler for details, and Burke had learned to follow his direction when given.

He turned back to the wireless and sent a final message.

Instructions received. Package will be ready. Out.

Just knowing they had a plan to get the Queen out of the city made Burke feel better. If worse came to worst, he knew he and his men could attempt to drive themselves to the coast, maybe get picked up by a fishing trawler or patrol boat from there, but he hadn't wanted to take the chance in doing so with the Queen still in his care. There were just too many things that could go wrong with such an attempt, including running into a roaming horde of shredders like that which Calhoun had encountered.

Better to get the Queen on her way and then figure out how we're getting home.

"Are we all set?" Veronica asked.

"Yes."

"Good, then just one more thing to do before leaving." She stepped around Burke and opened a panel in the side of the wireless console. She fiddled around inside the case for a moment and then instructed Burke to pull the front section toward him.

When he did so, the entire apparatus, dials, switches, and all, came free in his hands.

For a second Burke thought he'd exerted too much strength with his artificial hand, but when Veronica didn't appear at all concerned that he was holding the guts of the wireless device in his hands, he relaxed a bit.

The Queen took the device from him, made a few deft movements with it in her hands, and before he could say, "God save the Queen," she had turned it into its own self-contained box about the size of a loaf of bread.

"Turn around," she told him and when he did, she strapped the box to the outside of his rucksack.

"There, that should do it." She gave the straps one last pull to be certain they would hold and then spun him around to face her. "The battery won't last longer than seventy-two hours, so you'll need to find a power source for it if you pass that point. Understood?"

Burke fought the urge to salute.

"Yes, ma'am," he said instead, with a smile.

She dazzled him with one of her own in turn, and then the moment passed as she became all business once more.

"All right, enough playing around," she said loudly, taking in the others in the room at the same time. "We've got work to do. Let's get a move on, people!"

Burke watched Graves say good-bye to his colleague, only realizing at that moment that the Queen intended to leave the automaton behind.

"Don't you think we should bring him with us?" Burke asked quietly, not wanting JD or Graves to overhear. "Given the information he's carrying around in that tin noggin of his?"

"I'd be happy to," the Queen replied, "but unfortunately it's not possible."

"Not possible? Why's that? He seems to move pretty well. If need be, we could have a couple of the guys carry him for short distances . . ."

Veronica was shaking her head. "It's not his mobility that's the issue, it's his power supply. He doesn't have one. Or rather, he doesn't have an independent one; his body is powered by the same energy source that runs the museum. Remove him from the museum and he'll last an hour, maybe two, but no more than that."

"What if one of my guys could rig something up?"

Burke knew Williams was a technical wizard. If he, Graves, and JD put their heads together, he was sure they could come up with something.

The Queen, however, wasn't seeing it the same way.

"Your tenacity is admirable, Major Burke, but I'm afraid that even if you were to solve the power issue, and I have little doubt that you could, the simple truth of the matter is that this is JD's home. He will not abandon it, no matter the risk in staying. Believe me, I've tried; this isn't the first time the issue has been raised."

Burke glanced back across the room, looking for some support from the man (*machine?*) himself, but JD had already gone back to his experiments, the presence of the others either forgotten or filed away as being no longer relevant. *How do you rescue a man who doesn't want to be rescued?* Burke asked himself.

The answer was obvious.

You don't.

Just because it was obvious did not mean Burke was happy about it, however. He made a mental note to pass on the information about Highmoore to whoever showed up to collect the Queen on Colonel Nichols's behalf; at least that way someone higher up the command chain would know the automaton was there. Let them decide what to do about him.

The climb back up the steps seemed twice as long as the journey down, but eventually they reached the top and stepped back through the concealed door into the Mausoleum of Halicarnassus.

They were halfway across the gallery, headed for the door at the other end when it was thrown open suddenly, admitting several of their companions, and one look was all it took for Burke to know something had gone seriously wrong.

Doc was in the lead, helping support a limping Williams, and immediately behind them were Jones and Cohen. The sharpshooter looked disheveled but didn't seem injured. One side of Cohen's face was covered in a cascade of blood that was dripping down from an injury somewhere above his hairline, and he kept reaching up to wipe it away so that he could see. The foursome came rushing down the length of the gallery as fast as they could, unmindful of the display cases and priceless artifacts that they were bumping into, and, in some cases, accidentally destroying, in their haste.

When they reached the others, Jones did his best to gasp out a report while trying to catch his breath.

"German commandos . . . backed by shredders. Morrison ordered us to retreat . . . they've breached the front doors and have . . . taken the Great Court."

Commandos? Here? Burke's thoughts whirled. *What did they want? Were they here for the Queen or for the items in the vault downstairs? How long could Morrison hold out?*

The sound of gunfire drawing closer reached their ears and Burke had his answer.

Not long.

Burke turned to the Queen. "Is there another way out of the lab?"

"Yes, but . . ."

Burke didn't wait to hear the rest. He spun to face Drummond. "Get back to the lab and use that exit to get the Queen to safety. Take Doc, Williams, and Cohen with you. Jones and I will provide cover to help the others pull back. We'll meet you at the rendezvous in the Gardens tomorrow."

"Roger that," Drummond said, but Burke barely heard him, for he was already headed for the door Jones and company had come through moments before, intent on reaching Morrison in time to try and break the German assault.

CHAPTER TWENTY-EIGHT

Burke had barely set foot into the next gallery when the door on the far end opened just wide enough to let Captain Morrison and Private Montagna slip through. Both men were bleeding from a half-dozen minor wounds, and the captain's right arm was hanging limply at his side, the bone broken cleanly in two by the bullet that had passed through it.

No sooner were the two men inside than they turned and threw their weight against the door, trying to force it closed against the hands coming through the opening from the other side. Shredder hands. For a moment Burke thought they would not succeed, that the pressure from the undead on the opposite side would prove too great, but the two men rallied and the door slammed shut.

Intent on helping them keep it closed, Burke rushed forward, Jones at his side, but at the sound of their footfalls, Morrison looked up and waved frantically for them to stop.

"Go back!" he cried. "There are too many! We'll never be able to . . ."

Burke never heard the rest, for it was lost in a thundering explosion that filled that end of the room with smoke and flame and threw him to the ground with concussive force.

For a moment he couldn't hear anything, couldn't see anything, and had no real idea where he was or what was happening. He raised his head off the ground and saw a billowing cloud of smoke and dust where the door should have been and, on the floor beneath that cloud, a man's severed leg clad in a U.S. Army uniform. The rest of the body lay a few feet to the right, but was angled in such a way that he couldn't see the man's face.

Burke struggled to lever himself up onto his hands and knees, knowing from what he was seeing that he was in danger but still not lucid enough to make sense of why or how. Something whipped past his ear with a high-pitched whine and he shook his head, thinking he was hearing things.

Suddenly Jones was there, hauling him to his feet and yelling something Burke couldn't hear while the stink of cordite and burnt flesh washed over them both.

Grenade, Burke thought absently.

That was all it took. The events of the last few minutes came flooding back, and he realized they had to get out of there before they were overrun.

As if on cue a German commando dressed in a black uniform came charging out of the smoke, gun blazing, and Burke reacted without thought, using the Tommy gun hanging at his side to snap off several shots that struck the commando in the chest and sent him to the ground.

Burke didn't wait to see if the soldier lived or died; Jones was pulling at him, trying to get him to follow, and Burke gave in, knowing that the enemy soldier was only the first of many. He knew there was nothing they could do for their comrades at this point but live to avenge their deaths at another time and so, with a final glance at their unmoving forms, he turned and raced after Jones.

Bullets whined past them as they left that gallery and entered the next but Burke didn't look back. He was entirely focused on reaching the mausoleum ahead of them; from there, they'd be able to fire back from a position of cover and, if need be, retreat through the door leading to the laboratory.

The moments felt like hours as they raced ahead, expecting at any moment to take a bullet in the back. It was close, but luck was on their side; they reached the protection of the mausoleum's marble structure just as a trio of hounds surged into the room, their handler mere feet behind. The German commando fired over the heads of his charges, and Burke threw himself behind one of the marble columns as bullets whipped through the space he'd been standing in mere seconds before, ricocheting off the marble to spin away into the shadows with a high-pitched whine.

Burke caught Jones's attention, counted down from three on his fingers. On one, the two men popped up from behind the cover of the mausoleum's front wall and began firing at the enemy, causing hounds and soldiers alike to scatter to the left and right looking for cover of their own.

With Jones laying down cover fire, Burke crawled deeper into the reconstructed temple until he reached the wall that held the controls to the hidden door. The Queen's party had closed it behind them, not wanting to provide access to any German troops that might have managed to flank Burke before he returned to that location, leaving Burke to manipulate the controls on his own. Thankfully, he'd been watching the Queen closely when she'd opened it the first time. He put his hand on the section of the wall she'd manipulated earlier, felt the slight indentations that signaled where he should put his fingers, and then gave a sharp twist.

With the hiss of steam and the clank of metal, the stone slab beside him slid backward and then to one side, revealing the stairs down to the laboratory just as it had before.

"Let's move!" Burke yelled over the din to Jones.

As the younger man began backing toward him, Burke sent a blistering wave of fire into the advancing enemy, cutting down two enemy soldiers who tried to leapfrog from the cover of one display case to the other, leaving them wounded and bleeding in the middle of the floor. Burke hoped concern for their comrades would slow the advancing soldiers down, but he quickly found out just how off base the notion was as the other soldiers completely ignored them. One man was crouched less than a yard away from an injured man and he never even bothered to look in that direction, his attention entirely on the retreating Allies. It brought the inhumanity of the foes he was facing into stark focus for Burke, renewing his resolve to get the Queen to safety.

Burke waited for Corporal Jones to pass him and then he, too, backed through the doorway. Once inside he hit the switch to close the door, then stood facing the opening, ready to gun down anyone who showed themselves as he waited for the door to fully close. When it had, he turned and dashed down the stairs with Jones, their footfalls ringing in the confined space.

Surprisingly, the door at the other end was open. He cautiously approached and peeked into the room only to find himself staring down the muzzles of several rifles and one Webley revolver.

"Bloody hell, Major!" Sergeant Drummond exclaimed, as he recognized Burke and lowered his weapon. Behind him the others did the same. "Are you looking to get shot?"

Burke was just as annoyed as Drummond. "I expected to find an empty lab. What the hell are you still doing here?"

Drummond opened his mouth to reply, but the Queen interrupted, drawing Burke's attention.

"He was ordered to remain, Major," Veronica said, her chin lifted slightly in what Burke was coming to recognize as an expression of stubbornness. "I will not abandon you, or any of my men, to the enemy while we run like frightened rabbits."

Burke felt his blood start to boil, but he did his best to keep a lid on it as he replied, "With all due respect, Your Majesty, Captain Morrison and Private Montagna just gave their lives in order to buy you time to escape! You should be long gone from here!"

The Germans would be on them in moments. They didn't have time to debate things any further. He turned to Jones.

"Get that door shut and barricade it as best you can. Drummond, help him."

As they jumped to do his bidding, Burke turned back to face

the Queen. He did his best to ignore her tears even as the voice in the back of his head was calling him an asshole.

"Where is this exit?" he asked, in a gentler tone.

"This way."

Veronica led him over to a corner of the lab and pointed to a steel plate set into the floor with hinges. Burke bent down, got his fingers under one edge, and hauled it open, revealing an iron ladder bolted to one side, leading downward. A horrible stench wafted up from below.

"Ugh. What's down there?"

Veronica's mouth tightened into a thin line. "Sewers. And before you ask, yes, we have to go down there. It's the only way out, unless you want to fight your way through the German commandos you just left behind."

No, Burke didn't want to do that. He glanced across the room, saw that Jones and Drummond, with Doc's help, had stacked several lab tables and a couple of filing cabinets in front of the door as a barricade. It wouldn't do more than slow the enemy down for a couple of minutes, but that might be enough.

"All right," he called to the others. "Let's get out of here."

The automaton, JD, opened up a nearby cupboard and produced two lanternlike devices, each with a handle jutting from one side. When the handle was wound rapidly, the resulting electrical charge caused the lantern to emit a weak but steady light. JD handed one lantern to Sergeant Drummond and the other to the Queen.

With the light in hand, the Black Watch sergeant nodded once at Burke and started down the ladder. He had only just disappeared from sight when a thunderous boom shook the room. The explosion threw Burke to the ground for the second time that day, but he was farther away from the actual blast this time and didn't suffer the debilitating effects he had earlier. He quickly pulled himself to his feet and aimed his weapon at the door, waiting for the inevitable rush of the enemy.

As the dust and smoke cleared, Burke saw that a large hole had been blown in the lab's iron door. He could see a figure standing on the other side, a large, hulking man dressed in the uniform of a German commando. This didn't surprise Burke, but the fact that he recognized the man, despite the ash-gray skin and feral yellow eyes, did.

Staff Sergeant Charles Moore lifted his head and his gaze met Burke's.

Recognition jumped between them.

Burke couldn't believe what he was seeing. *Charlie? Here? Wearing a German commando's uniform?* The sight was so unexpected that it froze him where he stood, his feet weighed down as if he were wearing cement-filled boots. Fighting was going on around him, the enemy soldiers shooting in their direction as Jones and the others returned fire of their own, but Burke couldn't tear his gaze away from the man across the room.

Charlie raised his hand and Burke found himself staring down the barrel of the pistol the big man was holding.

One shot was all it would take.

Burke's mind was screaming at him to move, but his legs weren't getting the message. They held him in place, a sitting duck should Charlie pull the trigger.

Distantly he heard Veronica scream his name.

"Burke!"

Time stretched . . .

Charlie's finger tightened . . .

Burke's mind yelled at him to *move, move, move,* but all he could manage to do was bring his hand up in front of him, as if warding off a blow . . .

The shot struck the outside of his artificial hand and tore through it, the impact altering the trajectory of the bullet just enough to send it sliding past the side of his head and into the wall behind him.

The near miss broke his paralysis, and he threw himself behind a nearby storage chest for cover, still stunned at the events unfolding around him. His thoughts seemed as thick as molasses, and he struggled to find some clarity, to understand the situation in which he suddenly found himself.

Try as he might, however, he couldn't seem to get his mind around one, simple fact.

Charlie was one of them.

Motion beside him caught his attention. The Queen was kneeling there, her hands already moving over his body, searching for injury.

"Oh, my God! Are you all right?" she was asking, but to Burke it seemed as if her voice was coming from a long way away. He tried to say something, to answer her, but the words just wouldn't come.

Charlie was one of them!

Veronica was still talking, but he couldn't make sense of what she was saying. Something about his hand . . .

He glanced down. The last two fingers on his artificial hand were missing, ripped free from his palm by the impact of Charlie's bullet. Through the hole where they should have been he could see the miniature gears and clockwork mechanisms deep inside his palm and found himself wondering if the hand was repairable or if he would need a whole new one.

Burke didn't have time to think about it for long. His attention was drawn back to what was going on around him as Drummond appeared at his side with the injured Williams, the two men grabbing Veronica and dragging her, protesting, away from him and toward the safety of the escape tunnel as bullets whipped around them like angry hornets.

Burke had one last glimpse of Veronica's anguished face, calling out his name, and then she disappeared down the ladder and was lost to his view.

Another thunderous explosion made him cringe, and when he looked up again, he found JD standing beside him, seemingly oblivious to the gunfire going on around him.

"I'll handle this, Major," the automaton said in a calm, steady tone. "Please take yourself and Corporal Jones to safety." With that he turned and walked into the fray, his arms extended straight ahead.

Peering around the storage chest, Burke watched as JD's hands folded out of the way so that the backs of his hands lay flat against his wrists and the stumps pointed directly at the enemy now trying to climb through the makeshift entrance in the ruined door. Without another word JD began firing the automatic rifles hidden inside his forearms, sending the German troops scurrying for cover as his highly accurate fire tore those in the front line to ribbons.

Burke was still trying to shake off his mental fuzziness and might have sat there indefinitely if Jones hadn't taken advantage of the cover JD was providing and come charging over to squeeze in beside Burke.

"He's not going to be able to hold them for long, Major."

Burke didn't say anything.

"Major?"

Nothing.

"All right, on your feet, sir. Let's go!"

The next thing Burke knew he was climbing down the ladder into the darkness and stink of the sewers beneath the museum, struggling to get his mechanical hand to grasp the rungs properly and only slowly coming to understand as he fumbled about that the last two fingers on that hand had been shot clean off.

The light he was using to see his injured hand was suddenly cut off as Jones hauled the trapdoor closed above them. Seconds later he was at the bottom of the ladder beside Burke.

"This way, Major," he said and pulled Burke along in his wake as he hustled to catch up with the rest of their group.

Above them, the firing continued.

CHAPTER TWENTY-NINE

SOME TIME LATER, Burke stumbled along through the sewer in the midst of the fleeing squad, barely aware of those around him or the passage they were taking. He kept seeing Sergeant Moore's face appear above the heads of the zombie soldiers in the German fighting unit, kept seeing the flare of recognition in the man's eyes as Moore spotted him in turn. Burke had no doubt that Moore had known who he was; he was certain of that down to the depths of his soul.

Burke had been wondering about Moore's fate ever since their previous mission, when the big sergeant volunteered to lead the German pursuit away from the rest of the squad in order to give them time to get Major Freeman to safety. Burke had spent several long nights lost in anguish and regret as the mystery over Moore's fate continued. Time and time again he'd second-guessed his decision to use the sergeant as a decoy during their escape, wondering if they might have managed to break free of the rapidly closing German net even if they hadn't split up at that fateful moment. Moore hadn't been the only man lost from that decision, either; Clayton Manning, the big game hunter, had disappeared with him.

Now, at last, Burke knew the truth.

And the truth was worse than he'd feared.

News of Moore's death would certainly have been upsetting; there was no question of that. But he'd been preparing himself mentally and emotionally for that very thing for weeks now and knew he would have handled it just fine. He would have mourned and then moved on.

Hell, he would have even done the same thing if Moore had died and then risen as a shambler, for there was enough evidence now for Burke to rest assured that nothing of the original personality remained behind in that reanimated husk of flesh. It was a walking corpse and nothing more.

But this?

This was different, so different that it was almost too horrifying to consider.

Charlie clearly retained some memory of who he had been prior to being subjected to the transformation into one of Richthofen's supersoldiers. That knowledge hadn't seemed to stop him from trying to kill Burke or his companions, but at least the slate hadn't been wiped totally clean. Maybe the transformation could be reversed.

But what if Burke's identity wasn't the only thing Charlie retained? What if he remembered everything—all the strategy conferences, the after-action reports, the briefings on new gear coming out of Graves's lab? He'd been Burke's adjutant for several years now and had been privy to everything that had crossed through Burke's hands during that time. Granted, there weren't too many national secrets being bandied about in the trenches where Burke had spent most of his time overseas, but there was enough day-to-day operational information to give Burke pause.

Had Charlie shared it all with his new masters?

There was no way to know, and Burke knew that was the scariest part of all.

His attention elsewhere, Burke stumbled over a piece of detritus on the tunnel floor and would have fallen if a strong hand hadn't caught his arm.

He turned to find Jones off to his left.

"You okay, Major?"

Burke nodded, then realized the other man probably couldn't see him in the dim light.

"Yeah . . . thanks."

"None needed."

Jones was quiet a moment and then . . . "You saw?"

There could be only one thing Jones was referring to.

"I saw."

Jones fell silent, no doubt lost in his own thoughts about their previous teammate, but the conversation was enough to drag Burke out of his reverie and get him focused on the situation at hand.

He had no idea of where they were or of how far they had come since entering the tunnels. He wasn't entirely certain any of the others did either, but he was willing to give them the benefit of the doubt. If it turned out he was correct—that they didn't know where they were—that was okay, too, for anywhere was preferable to being trapped back in the lab with the German troops moments away from gunning them down where they stood.

They were moving through a low tunnel that had them all stooping slightly as they pushed along. Dirty, brackish water—Burke didn't even want to think about what was floating there beneath the surface—rose nearly to their knees and sloshed higher with every step they took. Sergeant Drummond led the way, the lantern in his hands illuminating the cracked and crumbling brick that lined the curved walls of the tunnel on either side of them and giving them minimal light with which to see. Behind Drummond was Doc Bankowski, helping along an injured Corporal Williams. Private Cohen came next, followed by Queen Veronica, Professor Graves, himself, and then Jones bringing up the rear. Burke glanced around, looking for Montagna, then caught himself, remembering how the young private and Captain Morrison both had sacrificed themselves so the rest of them could reach the temporary safety of the lab and hence the tunnels beyond.

Coming to the museum had proven to be a costly detour, even if it had provided them with a way to get the Queen to safety once they reached the Gardens.

If they reached the Gardens.

Don't think like that, he scolded himself. *You'll reach the Gardens and you'll get the Queen out of here even if it's the last thing you do.*

Determination replaced despair, and he physically shook himself as if shaking off the negative thought, standing straighter and refusing to be beaten down by recent events. He hadn't lived this long by giving in to his negative emotions, no matter how bad the situation.

Buck up, Burke.

The whispered command to hold up came back down the line, and he decided it was time to stop letting the others carry him along and to do the job he was here to do. He pushed his way to the front of the group where it was immediately clear why they had stopped. A ladder came down from above right in the middle of the tunnel, the first one they'd seen since entering the tunnels. Drummond was standing beneath it, looking up at the faint light coming in from around the manhole cover above.

"What have we got, Sergeant?" Burke asked, stepping up into the light next to the other man.

Drummond seemed relieved to see him.

Was I that out of it? Burke wondered.

"Ladder to street level, sir. With your permission, I'll check it out."

Burke nodded and then watched as the brawny British sergeant practically swarmed up the ladder. *He doesn't like it down here any more than I do.*

There was a grinding sound from above as Drummond slipped the steel manhole cover to one side and peered out into the street. A few moments passed and then Drummond slid back down the ladder to join them.

"Looks clear. No sign of the enemy, human or otherwise."

"Any idea of where we are?"

Drummond shrugged. "Somewhere near Grosvenor Square, I think. Maybe New Bond Street. I've been trying to keep us traveling in one direction as best as I can, but the tunnels have switched back and forth a few times so I'm not positive. We've come a fair distance from the museum, at least."

That was good enough for Burke. He didn't know London's geography well enough for the location to mean much to him, he just wanted to be certain they wouldn't turn the corner and run into Moore's unit again. They needed some breathing room to deal with their injuries and take stock of how things stood.

He sent Drummond back up the ladder to provide security for the rest of them as they cautiously climbed up the ladder one by one and into the street above. When they were all clear, Burke slipped the manhole cover back into place and then took a look around.

The street was lined with a variety of shops. From where Burke stood he could see several clothing stores, both men's and women's, a stationery store, an antiques store, and even a butcher's shop. The doors and windows on all the buildings were intact, indicating that the area hadn't been hit hard in the recent bombing attacks. It could have been an ordinary day in London, if it weren't for the bodies lying rotting in the street, evidence that the shredders had come through at some earlier point.

A heavy stench wafted over him, and it took Burke a moment to realize it wasn't the corpses but himself and his companions that smelled so bad. All of them were splattered here and there with the muck of the sewers from which they'd just emerged, and it was going to take more water than they were currently carrying for them to get clean.

Look at the bright side, Burke told himself. *There's no way the hounds are going to be able to track you now.*

With the sun disappearing below the horizon, Burke thought it prudent that they find a place to hole up and wait out the night in some semblance of safety rather than stumbling about in the dark risking discovery by shredders and German special ops troops alike. Luckily, it didn't take them long to find someplace suitable.

The bank had been serving the financial needs of British customers since 1822, according to the plaque outside the front door. Burke didn't care about that. He was far more interested in the steel gates that had been pulled down over the windows and across the main entrance. The gate protecting the front door was locked, but they could take care of that easily enough.

"Williams, front and center."

When the corporal limped over and joined him, Burke pointed at the gate. "Can you get us in here?"

"Does a pig smack its lips?" came the young man's reply.

Being a city boy himself, Burke had no idea what pigs did or didn't do, but given that Williams was pulling out his tool kit and having a go at the lock he took the other man's answer in the affirmative.

It took Williams less than three minutes.

Inside, the marble floor, mahogany desks, and hand-painted murals on the ceilings spoke to the wealth of the customers who regularly banked there, but the small group barely noticed. They were exhausted from the day's events and simply wanted a place to lie easy for the night. They quickly checked the main lobby and nearby offices to be certain they were free of shredders.

The restrooms still had running water and a nearby closet held weeks' worth of cleaning supplies, so they took turns cleaning the grime from their boots and clothing as best they could. By the time they were finished their uniforms were a bit damp, but at least they didn't smell so strongly of sewage.

Rations were divided up among them so that everyone had something to eat and canteens were filled at the restroom sinks. Burke posted a sentry at the door and then suggested that the rest of them find space on the floor in front of the long counter of teller windows to try and relax.

He was just settling down himself, intending to take a look at the mangled remains of his hand, when he heard Jones give out a whoop of excitement and saw him emerge from the bank president's office, a slip of paper in his hand.

What now? Burke wondered.

Smiling, Jones waved the paper in his direction but didn't stop his motion across the room toward the massive steel door that governed access to the bank's vault.

Uh, oh.

Burke hurriedly rose. "What are you doing, Jones?"

Ignoring him, the other man glanced at the paper in his hand and then began spinning the small combination dial to the left of the captain's wheel on the vault door.

Visions of being court-martialed for robbing a British bank swam through Burke's thoughts as he hurriedly crossed the room to the other man's side.

"I said, what the hell are you doing, Jones?"

The corporal stepped over to the captain's wheel and grabbed the handles. "Found the combination to the vault in the bank president's office. Guy had it taped to the inside of his desk drawer."

Burke scoffed. "There's no way the bank's president would do something so stupid," he said. "It's probably just a decoy."

"I'm sure you're right, Major," Jones said, even as he spun the massive flywheel to the right. There was a brief whir as the tumblers moved inside the lock mechanism, followed by a very loud click.

Jones hauled back on the handle and the vault door swung open on well-oiled hinges.

The corporal grinned, then stepped inside.

Burke followed.

The walls of the vault were lined with safe deposit boxes, most of which were locked shut. Those few that were open looked like they'd had their contents removed in a hurry, making Burke think they might have been the personal boxes of individuals who worked right there at the bank. Who else would have had time to get to their valuables after the German attack?

"Not the fortune you were looking for?" Burke asked, upon seeing the expression of disgust on Jones's face after he poked his nose into a few of the open boxes.

"Only a fool ignores the sound of opportunity knocking."

"No, only a fool would consider this an opportunity," Burke quipped back at him. "You're in the middle of a war zone, Jones. Do you really want to weigh yourself down with stacks of pound notes?"

This time, Jones's expression made Burke laugh aloud. It was clear the other man hadn't thought much beyond the "get into the vault" part of his plan. A criminal mastermind he was not.

Jones might not be happy with how things turned out, but now that he was inside it, Burke thought the vault could be useful. It was large enough to give them all room to stretch out for the night and could even be opened from the inside, but with only one way in and out it wasn't perfect. Still, it would keep them out of sight of any casual passersby on the street outside, human or otherwise, and would prove an effective bunker as a last resort in the event they were overrun and had to wait it out.

Leaving the sentry at the door, Burke rounded up the rest of his group and moved them into the vault where most of them found space to stretch out and then tried to get some sleep.

Burke settled down just inside the vault's entrance, his back to the wall and his gun nearby. The position gave him a clear line of sight to the sentry by the bank's entrance and let him make use of the last of the lingering sunlight coming in through the bank's windows to examine his injured hand.

Thankfully, the damage wasn't as extensive as he'd first assumed. The last two fingers had been torn completely away and would need to be replaced. His thumb, index, and middle fingers were all still fully operational, however, which would allow him to continue using the hand for most tasks, especially since the mechanism that allowed him to lock his fingers closed was still functioning.

"You knew him, didn't you?"

Burke looked up to find Veronica standing over him, her expression impossible to see in the fading light.

"Sorry?"

"Back at the museum. You knew the . . . man leading the German patrol?"

Her hesitation over the word *man* had been slight, but Burke caught it just the same. He didn't blame her; he didn't know what to call Charlie at this point either.

"Yeah, I knew him."

She bent to sit down, and he automatically scooted over to give her some room. She settled in beside him, her shoulder all but touching his own. He was very aware of her closeness.

He gave a frustrated shrug. "Until a few weeks ago, he was my platoon sergeant."

"What happened?"

Burke explained their earlier mission and how Sergeant Moore had volunteered to lead the German pursuit away from them so that the rest of them could escape.

"Sounds like he was a good man."

"He was," Burke acknowledged and was thankful when Veronica didn't comment on the hitch in his throat as he said it.

They sat in silence for a few moments.

"Perhaps the process can be reversed," she suggested tentatively, giving voice to something that Burke had been thinking but had not yet found the courage to say aloud. "The research we'd been doing at the Round Table prior to the attack had been very encouraging."

"Perhaps," Burke agreed, while privately thinking the chances were pretty minimal. They'd have to capture him and transport him back to the professor's lab in France to even attempt such a thing, and even then there were no guarantees they'd be successful. One wrong calculation and they could end Charlie's life rather than restore it. Then again, would that be so bad?

The ethics of the entire situation was maddening.

Burke needed to get his mind off Charlie and so he asked, "Tell me about these Gardens we're going to in the morning."

"Kensington? What do you want to know?"

Burke shrugged. "Anything. Everything. It's hard to say what will prove to be important. Start with the layout of the land and we'll go from there."

He sensed more than saw her nod, the sun all but set at this point, shrouding them in deep shadow.

"All right. Kensington is one of eight royal parks in the city limits . . ."

CHAPTER THIRTY

THEY LEFT THE safety of the bank behind just as dawn's first light was breaking over the ruined city. There had been no sign of Sergeant Moore or any of the other members of the German commando unit during the night, but that didn't stop Burke from ordering his men to take the bottles of bleach they'd found in the bank's storeroom and pour them all over the roadway leading up to the bank's entrance. The stench of the ammonia would hopefully give them a larger head start than without. Not knowing how far the Germans were behind him made Burke anxious in more ways than one. It was bad enough expecting to find a band of shredders around every corner; having to worry about some German commando putting a bullet in the back of his head when he wasn't looking made things much worse.

There was the Queen's safety to worry about as well.

He looked in her direction, caught her adjusting the straps crisscrossing her chest that held the matched set of Webley revolvers she carried, and found himself captured anew by the combination of beauty, grace, and grit that this woman personified. Most of the women he knew, who admittedly were few and far between since the war began, would have been reduced to crying in the corner when those around them started turning into zombies, but not Veronica. She'd not only taken charge but had met the threat head-on and was still doing so even now. They wouldn't have gotten out of the museum if it hadn't been for her quick thinking.

He was anxious to turn her over to the pilot of the incoming aircraft, whoever that might be, but at the same time he realized that the thought of leaving her side was strangely upsetting. He hadn't felt attracted to a woman since Mae's death and to feel so now, in the midst of all this, was rather surreal and just too much for him to think about.

Never mind the fact that she's the bloody Queen of England!

Burke tore his gaze away from her hands and looked up to find her watching him in turn. She raised one eyebrow questioningly and he blushed, realizing that he'd been staring. He shook his head and waved his hand in an "it's nothing" gesture before turning away lest he embarrass himself further.

His thoughts, however, kept returning to the way those straps emphasized her womanly curves . . .

To get his mind off Veronica, Burke considered what he knew about their destination. Kensington Gardens was one of several royal parks scattered about the city. This particular one was home to Kensington Palace, the birthplace of both Queen Victoria and her second cousin, Queen Mary, who was Veronica's mother. Burke knew that Veronica had spent plenty of time there while growing up; she'd been the one to tell him all this last night. She'd also described the park to him; 275 acres of woodlands, meadows, and riverfront views, all connected by a series of paved paths and gated entrances. It seemed an unlikely place to land an aircraft, but he'd been assured that there was a wide swatch of land in the middle of the park that would do the trick.

Guess we'll find out soon enough, he thought.

They reached the eastern edge of the park without difficulty, but rather than enter at that point they followed Park Lane south until it bisected Kensington Road and then they headed west. They entered the park through the Albert Memorial Gate, near the memorial erected by Queen Victoria to her beloved husband, Albert, who had died of typhoid nearly fifty years before the war. The memorial itself was quite the affair; a statue of a seated Albert stood on a raised dais over which a canopy held up by four columns had been erected, the canopy very much in the style of the ciborium that stands over the altar in many English churches.

Must be close to 175 feet tall, Burke thought as they made their way past it and into the park proper.

Just past the memorial was a long, paved walkway known as Lancaster Walk that ran directly north, deeper into the park, and it was along this pathway that Veronica took them. Trees grew thick on either side of the path and Burke was just starting to wonder how on earth Colonel Nichols thought anyone was going to land a plane here when they emerged into an open area where six different pathways, including the one they were on, intersected. An open mall of green grass stretched out to either side, like a long rectangle with the crossroads at its center. Looking left he could just make out the waters of Round Pond, and beyond that, the grandiose structure of Kensington Palace off in the distance, while to the right the mall extended in the other direction all the way to the banks of the river known in this part of the park as the Long Water. He estimated the distance between the two bodies of water to be a bit over three hundred yards, which seemed like more than enough space for a qualified pilot to land and take off in.

It would have been perfect, if it weren't for the damned statue that was situated smack in the middle of it.

Physical Energy, it was called, and though Burke didn't really see how a naked man on horseback shielding his eyes against the sun represented that particular concept, he did agree that it was a wonderful piece of work. Unfortunately, the massive bronze sculpture and the granite block on which it had been erected stood right on their planned runway.

There simply wasn't enough room for a plane to land on either side of the statue without striking it. At first Burke wondered how the hell someone as meticulous as Nichols could miss something so obvious, but then it dawned on him that it hadn't been missed at all; Nichols simply expected him to find a solution and deal with it.

Looking the sculpture over, it was immediately clear that there was no way they were simply going to drag it out of the way. It had to weigh at least a quarter ton; he doubted they even had the brute manpower to knock it over.

No, their solution was going to have to be of a more permanent nature, no matter how much Burke regretted it.

He slipped off his rucksack and dug around in it until he located the two Mk III concussion grenades he'd stashed there before leaving France. The grenades were cylinders made of black painted cardboard with a crimped metal bottom and top, surrounding a core of TNT. A fuse assembly with a safety pin and pull ring projected out of the upper end. Unlike the Mk IIs, which were standard defensive fragmentation grenades, the Mk IIIs had been specifically designed to be used during trench and bunker assaults without producing fragments that could injure the user or other friendly forces nearby. Burke figured they'd do the trick quite nicely.

He wasn't thrilled with the need to use the grenades for the noise was sure to bring something running, be it shredders or the German commando team. He didn't see any other option, however. He'd have to take the risk and hope the distance and all the nearby buildings diffused the sound enough that Sergeant Moore and his undead commandos would be unable to get a fix on their location.

He stepped over to the base of the statue and began looking for the best place to situate the explosives, knowing he had only the two devices to work with and wanting to get it right the first time.

He decided to place one, ignite it, and then use the second to finish the work if the first didn't do the job.

"What are you doing?" Veronica asked, coming close and eyeing what he was doing with a wary expression.

"The statue's in the landing zone. It needs to go."

"What do you mean 'needs to go'?"

Burke was busy thinking about blast points and explosive yields and so he didn't hear the flat tone of her voice or see the carefully neutral expression that crossed her face.

"We've got to get rid of it. It's too heavy to drag out of the way, so I'm going to have to blow it up."

"Blow it up?"

Burke looked up, finally hearing the tension in her tone.

She didn't give him a chance to respond, just laid into him. "You do understand that this is one of the greatest masterpieces ever sculpted by George Frederic Watts? That it is a one-of-a-kind, priceless piece of art that can't be replaced?"

Burke steeled himself, nodded. "I do."

"And you are still going to blow it up?"

"I am. Unless you have some other solution?"

Veronica put her hands on her hips in irritation. "Well, of course I do! You can just . . . ah . . . well . . . um." She glanced around for help, but no one had any better suggestions it seemed, for they simply stared back at her. Finally, she looked down at Burke again, who hadn't moved from his position at the base of the statue.

"Fine! Blow it up."

Doing everything he could not to let his amusement show on his face, Burke nodded. "Of course, Your Majesty."

The grenades had a five-second fuse, which wasn't very long at all, so he had the others move back to the safety of the trees before he did anything further. When he saw that they were out of the blast zone, he placed the first grenade directly beneath the horse's legs. Satisfied that its position should send the blast up and out, he pulled the pin, turned, and ran like hell for the tree line, counting as he went.

One one thousand . . .

Two one thousand . . .

Three one thousand . . .

Four one thousand . . .

He threw himself to the ground and covered his head with his hands, bracing himself for the blast to come.

The grenade went off with a loud bang, and seconds later pieces of statue began raining down around him. Burke opened his eyes just in time to see the statue's head hit the ground and roll to a stop a few feet away. A cheer went up from the trees, and Burke found himself grinning as he pushed himself up on his hands to see that nothing of the statue remained intact except for a small hunk of the granite base.

His timing couldn't have been more perfect, either, for as Burke climbed to his feet, he heard the drone of an aircraft approaching in the distance. He shrugged apologetically at the Queen's anguished expression over what had been done to the statue and then joined the others in searching for the aircraft overhead.

CHAPTER THIRTY-ONE

KENSINGTON GARDENS
LONDON

AT FIRST, BURKE couldn't see anything—he just heard the drone of the engine—and then gradually he could make out a dark speck moving high against the clouds above. The pilot made a single pass overhead, coming in over the palace to the west and disappearing into the cloud cover to the east. He was too high for Burke to pick out any details, and there was no indication from the pilot that he'd seen them down below.

"Was that him?" Sergeant Drummond asked, but all Burke could do was shake his head.

He turned in place, trying to track the aircraft by sound alone, but didn't have much luck. The combination of the rising sun and intermittent clouds mixing with smoke from fires burning elsewhere in the city made it almost impossible for him to keep his eye on anything above the horizon.

A few minutes passed, and then gradually the sound of the plane grew louder, closer, and then suddenly it was right there, diving out of the rising sun to roar overhead, so close that Burke had to resist the urge to dive to the ground to get out of the way. Only the presence beside him of the Queen, who had shown no inclination to do anything of the sort, kept him on his feet.

As Drummond and several of the others were picking themselves off the ground, Burke and Veronica turned to watch the aircraft make its touchdown on the sward behind them.

The pilot ran out the landing as far as he could to bleed off his remaining speed and then slowly wheeled the aircraft about and taxied back to the end of the mall where Burke and his squad waited. When the aircraft came to a halt about fifty feet away, Burke went out alone to meet it.

As he reached the plane, the pilot shut down the engine and then hefted himself out of the cockpit to drop over the side of the fuselage to greet him. The flier was dressed in drab-colored overalls, boots, and a thick leather jacket to ward off the chill of the higher altitudes, pretty much the uniform of the day for pilots all across the front, but something about the way the man moved seemed familiar to Burke. When the pilot pulled the leather flying cap and flight goggles off his face, Burke understood why.

"As I live and breathe, if it isn't Madman Burke himself," his half brother, Major Jack Freeman, drawled in an exaggerated greeting.

For a moment, all Burke could do was stand there and stare.

"What's the matter? Cat got your tongue?" Freeman teased.

The sudden pulse of irritated anger that swept through Burke restored his capacity for speech. Stifling his urge to curse, he asked, "What the hell are *you* doing here!"

Freeman stiffened with anger of his own. "What do you think I'm doing here, you idiot? The brass wanted the best pilot we have to fly the fairy princess out of monster country and like it or not, that's me!"

Burke stared at his half brother, knowing he was right but unable to stop the memories of the last time he'd entrusted someone he cared about into this man's hands. Mae's death had been ruled an accident—Burke knew that and even accepted it now—but there was no denying the fact that her death had driven a wedge between the two men that had only recently started to heal. Now here he was, being asked to entrust the only woman he'd cared about after Mae to the very man who'd gotten his former fiancée killed. It was as if the universe was out to get him!

But what really made the situation worse was the fact that Freeman was right; he *was* the best pilot on the Allied side of the lines. Short of Richthofen, he might even be the best pilot in the entire war.

Burke really had no choice. He had to trust his brother, if for no other reason than there weren't any other options.

Now he did curse, once, beneath his breath, before getting himself under control and addressing his brother once more. "She's the Queen now, not the princess. Act like an officer and show some respect. And you'd best get her back to headquarters safe and sound or so help me God . . ."

Freeman's eyes narrowed, and he studied Burke carefully for a moment. "Well, I'll be a sonofabitch!" he said at last, with something almost like awe in his voice. "You're smitten, aren't you? You're smitten with the bloody Queen of England!"

Burke couldn't help but glance back to where Veronica was patiently waiting, surrounded by the rest of his men. He knew she couldn't hear them, but for some reason he still felt guilty . . .

He turned back to his brother. "We're wasting time. The two of you need to get out of here before that German patrol we ran into shows up. You just remember what I said!"

"Wouldn't dream of forgetting," Freeman quipped, then got serious. "HQ says they're rerouting an airship for you and your team. They should be here in about two hours, so you're going to have to lie low until then."

Burked nodded. "Understood." He didn't like the idea of having to hang around at all, but he figured they could stay ahead of Charlie's squad for a couple of hours.

"Oh, and they gave me this to pass along," Freeman said as he unstrapped a wooden ammunition box from where it had been stored beneath his seat and handed it over to Burke.

The sight of the box put a smile on Burke's face, a smile that grew wider when he opened it up to discover that it was full of ammunition for both the men's Lee Enfield rifles and his Colt pistol.

"Oh yes, this will definitely come in handy," Burke said.

He turned and waved Veronica and the rest of the men over to them. When they caught up, he handled the introductions.

"Your Majesty, this is Major Jack Freeman," Burke said. "He's going to see you to Allied headquarters safe and sound. Major Freeman, may I present Her Majesty, Queen Veronica."

Freeman snapped off a near-perfect salute and then smiled warmly at the Queen. "It's a lovely day for a jaunt across the Channel, Your Majesty. Trust me, we'll be in France in no time."

"I certainly hope so, Major," she replied, smiling in return. "Let me just say that your exploits precede you and that I'd recognize the name of the Allies' top ace with or without your trademark Jack of Spades painted on the fuselage. I have no doubt I'm in good hands."

"You flatter me, Your Majesty," Freeman replied, casting a mischievous grin over his shoulder at Burke, who had to stifle the sudden urge to punch his brother in the nose.

"Let me help you up into the cockpit," Jack began, but Burke cut him off by stepping in front of him.

"Get the plane ready to go," he said. "I'll help the Queen."

To his surprise, Jack didn't even bother to argue; he just climbed up into the cockpit, leaving Burke to help Veronica into the rear seat all on his own. Not that it bothered him at all; he would have happily helped her in and out of the aircraft a half-dozen times if that was what she wanted. Burke knew himself well enough to know that Jack had been right—he was smitten with her, far more than he should be in fact, but that was how things were and there wasn't much he could do about it now. He made a cradle with his hands and, when she put one booted foot into it, he hefted her up and over the wooden side of the fuselage, then watched as she used the canvas straps to belt herself in.

"All right?" he said.

Veronica nodded, her face tight.

"What's wrong?" Burke asked, upon seeing her expression.

The Queen shook her head. "Nothing. Just never flown before." Her hands came up, one on either side of the fuselage, gripping the leather that rimmed the seating compartment.

Burke smiled, recalling his own reaction to flying. "You'll be fine," he told her. He put his hand over hers and squeezed it once, quickly, then let go.

He took a few steps forward and glanced up at Freeman, who was just settling his goggles back into place. "You're carrying the Queen of England, so no screwing about. Get her to headquarters as quickly as possible."

Freeman grinned down at him. "Yes, sir, Major, sir!" he said, his voice full of mock sincerity. He fired off a salute in Burke's direction, despite the fact that the two of them were the same rank.

Refusing to let Freeman get a rise out of him, Burke ignored the salute. "I'm serious, Jack."

To his surprise, Freeman dropped his usual antics and turned uncharacteristically serious. "I hear you. I'll get her back safe and sound, Burke, you have my word on it."

For once Burke believed him.

"One more thing," Jack said, beckoning his half brother in close. "I saw some strange-looking tunneling equipment in a park just north of the Thames and suspect you aren't the only ones looking for the Queen. Watch your back, all right?"

Burke flashed back on the German tunneling devices that had breached the trenches in the days before his mission behind enemy lines. He wanted to describe them to Freeman, see if they were the same type of vehicles he'd seen as he'd flown over the park, but he knew they didn't have time. So he thanked him instead and then moved around to the front of the aircraft, ready to help get the engine restarted.

At a signal from Freeman, Burke grabbed the edge of the prop and pulled it around in a full revolution, a technique known as hand-propping. He did this seven times, priming the engine, and then waited for Freeman to make some adjustments to the controls. When he was ready, Freeman gave him another thumbs-up and Burke repeated the process one more time, stepping quickly out of the way as soon as he released the propeller. The blades spun around once, twice, and then the engine started with a roar.

Burke waved to Veronica one final time and then backed away to give Freeman room to maneuver.

They'll be fine once they're off the ground, he told himself, doing what he could to quell the nervous tension spreading through his stomach. He watched as Freeman taxied the aircraft to the other end of the mall so they could take off into the wind and fought the growing uneasiness he was feeling.

Freeman was a hell of a pilot and the war zone was no place for a Queen, he reminded himself.

That's when the first of the shredders burst from the trees near the other end of the mall and raced directly at the aircraft.

Burke was still in the process of bringing his gun up when the crack of a rifle shot echoed from behind him and the shredder he was staring at collapsed to the ground. He spun, saw Jones with his rifle to his shoulder, and breathed a sigh of relief.

It was short-lived however, as several more shredders emerged from the trees in the wake of the first. Like the one before them, the new arrivals caught sight of the aircraft and rushed toward it.

By this point, Freeman had turned the plane around and was starting his run back down the length of the mall toward Burke and his squad. The plane was moving, but not very quickly yet, and it was clear to Burke that the shredders would reach it before it gained enough momentum to carry the Queen to safety.

He couldn't allow that to happen. He waved for his men to follow him and rushed forward to engage the shredders at close range.

CHAPTER THIRTY-TWO

Veronica sat stiffly in the rear cockpit as Major Freeman took the plane to the end of the mall and then swung around in a tight circle so that they were facing back the way they had come. She could see Major Burke and his men still standing together near the remains of *Physical Energy* and, behind them, the gleaming surface of the Long Water in the early morning light.

Freeman glanced over his shoulder and shouted something at her, but she couldn't hear him over the sound of the engine. She smiled and gave him a thumbs-up anyway; it seemed the thing to do.

Apparently that was good enough for him, for he gave her the signal in return and turned back to his controls. A moment later the sound of the engine increased and the plane began its run toward the end of the mall and the skies beyond.

Veronica considered herself a brave woman, but the sudden realization that she was going to be thousands of feet up in the air in nothing but a flimsy wood and canvas aircraft caused her to grip the sides of the cockpit in fear.

Saints preserve us, she thought and glanced over at Burke, hoping to see him give another of his reassuring waves.

The look on his face was anything but reassuring, however, as he stared past her for a moment before he suddenly snatched at the pistol on his belt. Behind him, Veronica saw the sharpshooter named Jones bring his rifle up to his shoulder and fire a shot in her direction. Veronica flinched, thinking at first that he was shooting at the plane, and only realized he was aiming at something behind them when he let off a second round.

With her heart hammering in her chest, the Queen twisted around to see what he was shooting at, only to discover shredders charging out of the woods to the right of the mall and racing directly toward the plane.

The lead shredder took a bullet in the forehead from Jones's rifle and was flung to the ground, only to be crushed beneath the feet of its companions as they surged forward. The pop of a pistol, most likely Burke's, joined the crack of Jones's rifle as he continued firing, but for every shredder they cut down, another took its place. If they didn't get out of here soon, they were going to be in deep trouble.

Veronica leaned forward and urgently tapped Freeman on the shoulder. When he glanced back, she shouted "shredders!" and pointed behind them. She doubted that he heard her, but her gesture did the trick as he followed the line of her pointing finger, his eyes widening at the sight of what was headed toward them. He spun back to his controls and a moment later the engine roared even louder than before, the plane picking up speed as he tried to outdistance their pursuers.

An anxious glance back let her know that it wasn't going to be enough; the shredders were going to reach the plane before they got off the ground.

Freeman must have realized the same thing, for he suddenly angled the plane to the right, desperately trying to widen the gap between them and their pursuers. Unfortunately, doing so brought him across the path of Burke and his men, who were charging forward to engage the shredders. As the U.S. commandos scrambled to get out of the way of the oncoming aircraft, Veronica knew they were out of options. If she didn't do something, the shredders would have them!

Without thought to her own safety, she slipped free of her shoulder straps and spun around in her seat, yanking her Webley out of the belt around her waist as she did so.

The nearest shredder was less than two feet from the tail of the plane when she swung her arms up, the pistol gripped securely between both hands. Centering the barrel on the rotting bridge of the creature's nose, she pulled the trigger. At that distance, it would have been hard to miss. Blood, brains, and flesh exploded in every direction as the Webley's bullet tore the shredder's head apart.

She barely had time to smile in satisfaction, however, before another shredder loomed up beside her. She spun, a movement made difficult in the tight confines of the cockpit, and was still trying to bring her weapon to bear when the creature's legs were cut out from under it by a burst of gunfire from one of Burke's men.

A glance showed more of the shredders closing in, but Veronica had bought Freeman the time needed. The plane hit a rut in the grass and bounced, throwing her against the side of the cockpit and bruising her ribs in the process, but the impact she expected as the wheels hit the ground again never came. The plane lifted off the ground instead, transforming in an instant from a bouncing, shuddering contraption of wood and canvas into a graceful flying machine that rose into the sky with silken smoothness.

For a moment she was overwhelmed with wonder as she glanced about and saw the city of London slowly coming into view below her and then the realization that she was a hundred feet off the ground and getting higher by the second suddenly registered. Her heart jumped into her throat and she literally threw herself back into her seat, frantically tugging the straps over her shoulders and securing them as tightly as she could to the underside of the seat, terrified that a sudden turn on Freeman's part would throw her right out of the aircraft.

Closing her eyes, Veronica prayed that the flight would be over soon.

Vizefeldwebel Jaeger and his men had been standing inside the bank the Americans had used as shelter the night before when the American aircraft passed overhead the first time. Their attention had been focused on determining which direction the American commando squad had taken earlier that morning and as a result they were caught unprepared by the plane's sudden arrival, managing only to dash outside and get off a few meager shots in the plane's general direction before it flew out of sight.

Jaeger knew the plane had been sent to carry the Queen to safety and he wasted no time in sending his team after it. If he didn't find it quickly, he knew there was a good chance that their quarry would slip the net before they got close enough to do anything about it. He had no intention of letting that happen.

"Hound master!"

The other man stepped forward quickly. The men hadn't been with Jaeger for long, but they were already wary of his temper.

"Are the hounds ready to be loosed?" Jaeger asked, still staring off in the direction the plane had taken, comparing the plane's path with the map of London he kept in his head as he tried to work out just where it was headed. It couldn't be far; the sound of its engine had already faded.

"No, sir," the hound master said in a trembling voice.

Jaeger glanced over at the handlers and noted that the hounds appeared to be in some sort of distress, bucking and pulling at their leashes.

"What's the problem?"

The hound master pointed at the roadway beneath their feet. "The Americans covered their tracks by pouring something, a chemical of some kind, all over the street in front of the bank. It's playing havoc with the hounds' sense of smell."

Jaeger frowned.

Beside him, the hound master flinched.

Jaeger barely noticed. He didn't care if his subordinates loved him or feared him, as long as they got the job done properly. And right now the hound master was not doing so.

To be honest, Jaeger hadn't realized the Americans had dumped anything in their wake, for the simple reason that he couldn't smell anything. Hadn't been able to, in fact, since his transformation. He doubted any of the other men in the squad could either. To some degree that absolved the hound master from the way his hounds were now acting. It did not, however, absolve him from the fact that he hadn't had the foresight to prevent this mess from happening.

"Tell me, Sergeant, who is your second in command?"

"Unteroffizer Fitz, *Vizefeldwebel*."

"And how would you rate Unteroffizer Fitz's competence?"

The hound master hesitated. "He is . . . competent," he said at last.

Competent was good enough for Jaeger, for it was a description he would not apply to the hound master himself. Without another word he drew his Luger and shot the hound master through the forehead. The body was still twitching when Jaeger called out.

"Unteroffizer Fitz!"

A burly young man handed the reins of a struggling hound to another and hurried over to stand before Jaeger.

"Sir!"

Jaeger looked him over; decided he would do. "You are hound master now, Fitz. I want the Americans' trail found and I want it found quickly. Do you understand?"

Jaeger noted that Fitz did not even glance at the body by his feet as he replied, "I do, sir."

"Then get to it."

Hound Master Fitz wasted no time. He began barking orders immediately, telling the handlers to spread out until they found the edges of the spill and to start looking for the trail at the point. Like Fitz himself, his men needed no further encouragement to do as they'd been instructed. The handlers spread out in a wide circle, waiting until their hounds stopped reacting to whatever it was that the Americans had poured over the pavement before beginning the search in earnest. Jaeger watched for a moment and then turned away. He was about to order the rest of his men into formation when the sound of an engine caught his attention.

It was the airplane. Coming back.

As the sound grew closer and the men around him began looking to the sky above, Jaeger shouted, "A week's leave to the man who shoots that plane down!"

He didn't wait to see if the others were responding but turned instead toward where the machine-gun crew stood around the weapons sled. The Maschinengewehr 08, or MG 08 for short, was a water-cooled heavy machine gun mounted on a sled that was capable of firing four hundred rounds per minute. The weight and bulk of the weapon required that it be mounted on a tripod and made firing it at more than a forty-five-degree angle difficult, which was why the gun crew was currently readying their rifles instead of the MG 08.

Jaeger's transformation had made him stronger than most men and he didn't hesitate to snatch the machine gun off its mount and hold it in his arms. The crew was under standing orders to keep the gun loaded at all times. All Jaeger had to do was cock the weapon and he was ready to go. He held the gun by his waist and pointed the muzzle toward the sky, waiting.

It didn't take long.

The American aircraft arced into view overhead as it gently banked to the right, and for a moment the red, white, and blue rondel on each wing was clearly visible to those on the ground, resembling nothing so much as a colorful bull's-eye that gave them an easy target at which to aim.

Jaeger's men began firing at the plane as soon as it came into view, the sound of their rifles like music to their commander's ears, but the machine gun in Jaeger's hands remained silent. He waited, watching to see what the plane would do in response to the ground fire. As the pilot began to react, Jaeger anticipated his next move and opened fire.

The roar of the machine gun filled the air and, high above, the pilot of the aircraft began to have a bad day.

A very bad day indeed.

It was the *pop, pop, pop pop* of small arms fire that caught Veronica's attention. She'd heard the sound too many times in the last few days not to recognize it for what it was, even at this height. Wondering what was going on, she summoned the willpower to open her eyes and look over the edge of the cockpit toward the ground below.

She could tell right away that they were retracing the route she had taken with Burke and the others not so long ago. Ahead of them she could see Cleopatra's Needle, still pointing finger-like into the sky, and the spires of the Royal Courts. Off to her right was the bombed-out remains of Parliament and beyond that, the dark expanse of the Thames. Directly below them was Grosvenor Square, and it was from there that the firing originated.

Veronica could see at least a dozen soldiers gathered in the street and firing up at them as they passed overhead. Details were hard to make out from this height, but from the dark colors of their uniforms she guessed they were Germans. Perhaps even the unit that had attacked them the day before in the museum.

She reached forward and tapped Freeman on the shoulder. When he glanced back, she pointed at the Germans below them.

Freeman looked in that direction, nodded back at her to show he understood, and then put the plane into a steep, banking climb to get them out of range of the riflemen as quickly as possible.

He'd barely begun the turn, however, when bullets began to tear through the right wing, sending wood, wire, and cloth exploding upward. Almost as an afterthought, the roar of the machine gun reached them a half moment later.

Veronica sat there, too stunned by the ferocity of the machine-gun attack to do anything, but Freeman reacted instantly to the damage to his aircraft, yanking back and pulling sideways on the stick at the same time, throwing the plane into a looping turn in the opposite direction he'd been traveling in an attempt to get out of the line of fire.

Whoever was manning the machine gun on the ground had other plans, however. He readjusted his own stream of fire, correctly anticipating Freeman's move in the bargain, and riddled the fuselage with another barrage. This time Veronica screamed, instinctively drawing her limbs in as tight to her body as she could get them, as bullets crashed through the floor and whipped past her like a swarm of angry hornets.

Freeman threw the plane across the sky in a series of twisting maneuvers designed no doubt to get them out of the mess they were in and it was all Veronica could do to hang on for dear life as the plane tipped and twisted and twirled. When he finally brought the aircraft level again, they had lost nearly half their height but had passed out of range of the gunmen on the ground.

Veronica felt moisture on her face. When she touched it with her hand, her fingers came back wet with blood. She knew she hadn't been hit, which left only one other possibility.

She craned forward, trying to get a good look at her pilot.

Freeman was still strapped into his seat, preventing her from seeing how badly he was injured, but the thin line of blood that was leaking across the narrow piece of fuselage that separated the two cockpits told her it couldn't be good.

She shouted over the wind.

"Are you all right?"

He nodded, but that was all.

Was it her imagination or was he listing a bit to one side?

Before she could say anything more, the engine gave a loud bang and began spewing a thick stream of black smoke.

That's not good, Veronica thought.

She didn't know what scared her more, the fact that her pilot was bleeding from an unseen injury that could incapacitate him at any moment or the flames that crept up over the engine cowling seconds after the smoke.

CHAPTER THIRTY-THREE

★

IMPERIAL PALACE
BERLIN

THE LAST FEW members of the Chinese delegation were just leaving the Throne Room when Eisenberg came hustling down the corridor for his afternoon meeting with Kaiser Richthofen. He looked into their faces, one by one, trying to get a sense of how the meeting had gone, and therefore what mood the kaiser might be in, but the men sent by former general and now self-proclaimed emperor Yuan Shikai were professional politicians and gave nothing away with their carefully blank expressions.

Inscrutable, he would have called them.

Eisenberg watched the delegates move down the hallway until they turned a corner and disappeared from view, then he turned back toward the Throne Room. He cautiously stuck his head in the doorway and, after a quick glance about the room, discovered the kaiser standing over the map table in the far corner, his back to the entrance, seemingly lost in thought.

The doctor had been around Richthofen long enough to know the man was never caught unaware—he had the senses of a large hunting cat it seemed—and so Eisenberg wasn't surprised when the other man spoke before he could announce himself.

"How stable is Shikai's hold on the Chinese imperial throne?"

Eisenberg considered the question as he crossed the room. "I would think that would depend on the next six months, Your Imperial Majesty," he said at last.

"Oh?"

Richthofen's tone gave nothing away as to his state of mind, so Eisenberg had no choice but to blindly plow ahead and hope he didn't say the wrong thing.

"Our agents within the Forbidden City suggest that high-ranking officers in the National Protection Army might be able to gain enough support to challenge his rule and bring back the republic."

"Might?"

Eisenberg shrugged. "Shikai needs to keep the nationalists from undercutting his power base within the army while at the same time preventing the Japanese, and by extension the rest of the Allies, from seizing any more territory on the Shandong Peninsula. That's a hefty task."

"But can he do it?"

The head of Germany's Tottensoldat program frowned; he hadn't missed the faint hint of urgency in the kaiser's voice. *Why was this so important?* he wondered. *Exactly what had that meeting been about?*

He glanced down at the map table in front of him, hoping it might give him a clue. The large-scale map was well over six feet in length and easily four feet wide. It normally showed the conflict currently engulfing western Europe, with carved wooden markers representing the various force elements involved in bringing the rest of the continent under German subjugation. Today, however, the map had been moved to the left, revealing the vast expanse of Mother Russia and its surrounding environs, including China, Japan, and the German-held Marshall Islands. Aside from a few German forces—mainly elements of the Ninth Army—poised along the Russian border to keep Czar Nicholas from attempting to take revenge for the execution of his cousin, former kaiser Wilhelm II, there was very little information about their eastern forces to be seen and next to nothing about the forces available to either the Chinese or Japanese emperors.

Eisenberg didn't know the answer to Richthofen's question. Normally he would have simply said so, but something about the kaiser's tone put him on edge; Richthofen wanted an answer and Eisenberg had the sense that a noncommittal one would be far more trouble than it was worth.

Taking a deep breath, he said, "I think so, yes. Especially if he gives the army something to keep it occupied enough that it doesn't try to oust him, with or without the nationalists' help."

Some of the tension seeped out of the room as Richthofen nodded, either having reached the same conclusion on his own or simply agreeing with Eisenberg's assessment. Given Richthofen's intelligence, Eisenberg had little doubt that it was the former.

"I've just received the most intriguing offer," Richthofen told him.

"Oh?"

"It seems that Emperor Shikai has far grander ambitions than I was aware of. Grand enough, in fact, that he just offered me an alliance."

"An alliance?"

"With the Japanese pressuring him from the south, Shikai is worried that Czar Nicholas will take advantage of the situation and move on him from the north, effectively trapping him in a pincer movement between two forces."

Eisenberg couldn't imagine a country as large as China being trapped by anything, but then again, military science was not his forte. He said nothing as Richthofen continued.

"Shikai has offered to attack Russia from the south, distracting the czar's forces long enough for me to march east while he is otherwise occupied and take Moscow."

Eisenberg frowned. That didn't seem like the brightest move

on Shikai's part, given that it left him vulnerable to attack by the Japanese while he was otherwise engaged with the Russians.

"What about . . ."

He didn't get any further.

" . . . the Japanese?" Richthofen finished for him. "That, my good *Doktor*, is part two of Shikai's grand plan. He has requested that I loan him a few battalions of Tottensoldat shock troops, along with advisers to show him how to control them. In return, he will use those troops to spearhead an attack south, eliminating the threat posed by the Japanese and leaving their British allies farther south in Australia and New Zealand cut off from help."

Now it was Eisenberg's turn to echo the kaiser's question from just moments before. "Can he do it?"

Richthofen grinned like the devil. "There's only one way to find out. Now, what did you want to see me about?"

Eisenberg shook off thoughts of the Chinese situation and focused on what he'd come here to report.

"I received word from Vizefeldwebel Jaeger this morning. He has confirmed that Princess Veronica is alive and in the care of Major Burke's unit. He has them on the run and expects to have the princess in custody before sundown."

Richthofen clapped his hands in satisfaction. "It is settled then, Herr *Doktor*! With Veronica's death we will have eliminated any legitimate claim to the throne to our east and can turn our attention to her upstart cousin on the throne to the west."

"And after that?"

Richthofen's eyes gleamed as he looked out the window into the distance.

"Why, America, of course, *Doktor*. Where else would we go?"

CHAPTER THIRTY-FOUR

ALLIED AIRCRAFT
OVER LONDON

VERONICA FOUND HERSELF mesmerized by the twisting, churning flames as they crept over the edge of the engine cowling and began their inexorable march toward her. The forward motion of the aircraft was fanning the flames with all the oxygen they could ever want, and it wasn't long before the entire front of the aircraft was a blazing pyre.

She knew she was going to die; it was just a question of whether the fire or the fall would get her first. After all the fighting, all the running, it was going to end like this. It didn't seem fair, and yet she just couldn't seem to summon the will to do anything more than stare deep into the fire and wait for the end.

She might have sat there until the end if the plane hadn't suddenly whipped over on its side and plunged straight down toward the ground below.

Thinking her pilot had just lost complete control, Veronica screamed, "Freeman! Do something!," before realizing that the dive hadn't been an accident at all, that Freeman *was* doing something and that was trying to get them down as close to the ground as possible before the fire consumed the entire aircraft.

Their dive was so steep that the plane began to shudder and shake around her, leaving Veronica to think that they were going to break up in midair long before either the fire or the crash killed them. She squeezed her eyes shut and began praying with everything she had, desperate to live and absolutely unable to do anything about it; the helplessness was probably the most infuriating thing about the entire situation in her view. If she was going to die, she at least wanted to go out her way, for heaven's sake!

The plane lurched abruptly upward, rattling and shaking so hard that Veronica thought it must be held together solely by the pilot's sheer force of will, and then it settled down to fly smoothly once more.

She opened her eyes only to find Freeman holding the stick with one hand and beating at the flames, now only inches from the cockpit, with his flight coat. The shoulder of his shirt was stained deep red with blood and she found herself wondering just how he'd managed to get the coat off while wounded.

She was still pondering that question when something swam into view ahead of Freeman. When she focused on it, Veronica could see the five arches and iron expanse that made up Blackfriars Bridge looming ahead of them. Freeman must have seen it at that moment too, for he suddenly tossed the jacket, itself now fully ablaze, into the waters of the Thames less than fifty feet below them and grabbed the stick with both hands. He nudged it forward slightly and the plane responded by lurching for the river below like a whale too long out of water.

Freeman hurriedly corrected the error and Veronica looked on in amazement as he flew the plane right through the rightmost arch of the bridge, mere yards above the water. She knew it would have made a hell of a sight, had anyone been around to see it— an American biplane with its nose ablaze and the Queen sitting rigidly in the backseat roaring beneath the bridge like a wounded raven searching for a home.

As soon as they were clear of the bridge span, Freeman turned and shouted back to her. "Hang on! I'm going to try and put us down!"

Down? Here? In the middle of the Thames?

They were coming in fast, too fast to land, something that was obvious to someone with even her limited knowledge of aeronautics, but that didn't stop Freeman from bouncing the belly of the aircraft off the surface of the river several moments later. There was a loud crash—*Probably the landing gear,* Veronica thought—and then Freeman pulled the plane a few dozen feet back off the water.

It only took Veronica a few seconds to realize that not only had Freeman managed to put out part of the fire that was currently consuming the front of their aircraft, but he'd also slowed them down significantly.

Perhaps even enough for them to land!

For the first time since smoke had begun pouring out of the engine, Veronica allowed herself to hope that she might live through this flight after all.

She'd overheard Freeman boast that he was the best pilot the Allies had. *Looks like he's going to get his chance to prove it.*

The Southwark Bridge came into view ahead of them, or rather, what was left of it. More than one German bomb must have struck it dead on during the barrage several days before for it was little more than a crumbled heap of iron and steel, but given their current height and lack of control that was probably for the best. Freeman steered for an open area and sailed over the top of it with only a few feet to spare.

Ahead of them was a nice wide expanse of the river with nothing on it until the London Bridge a few hundred meters farther downriver.

It seemed the perfect place to try to land.

A good thing, too, for at that moment the plane engine gave up the ghost, seizing with a loud crash.

"God save us," Veronica said as Freeman brought the plane down toward the river for the last time.

There was a loud hiss as the belly of the aircraft bounced off the surface of the Thames for the second time and then fire finally reached Freeman's cockpit and there was nothing more he could do but put the plane into the river and hope for the best.

Veronica had a split second to brace herself, and then the bi-plane struck the water a final time. There was a tremendous crash as the lower wing was shorn away and then the Queen's head slammed against the edge of the cockpit and darkness quickly followed.

IT HADN'T TAKEN Burke and his men long to deal with the dozen or so shredders that had rushed their makeshift runway, giving Freeman time to get his aircraft into the air. They'd watched as Freeman had waggled his wings in farewell and had headed out over the city, only to freeze in horror as the sound of a German heavy machine gun had split the morning air and the plane was forced to take evasive action, carrying it out of sight.

Burke turned for the nearest tree, intent on getting a better vantage point, but Corporal Williams beat him to it, scrambling up the trunk and disappearing into the branches above.

When he came back down, Burke could tell the news wasn't good from the expression on his face.

"Tell me," he said, steeling himself for the worst.

"They're hit but still in the air for now."

Burke kept his face carefully blank, but hope bloomed in his heart. *They were still alive!*

"What do you mean 'for now'?"

Williams winced. "There's a lot of smoke streaming from the engine. No way they can make it back to France like that."

Burke knew he was right; the minute word got out, every German fighter pilot within fifty kilometers would be angling in, trying to get an easy kill off the crippled aircraft.

Williams's next words told Burke he wasn't going to have to worry about anything like that, however.

"Last I saw they were in a steep dive. It looked like Major Freeman was trying to get them down as quickly as possible."

Sergeant Drummond was already unfurling his map. "Show me," he said, spreading it out on the grass.

Williams looked it over for a moment and then pointed to an area northeast of their current position, over the Thames River. "I could see the bridges in the distance so they were around here somewhere."

Drummond and Burke exchanged glances. "Are you thinking what I'm thinking?" the sergeant asked.

Burke nodded. "We don't have any choice. Our mission was to rescue the Queen. If Freeman manages to get the plane on the ground, they're going to need our protection all over again. Especially with the German commando unit still out there somewhere."

He turned to the others. "All right, saddle up and get ready to move out. Williams, get on that wireless and let HQ know what's happened. Tell them to get the airship to hold position above the city until they hear from us. I want the rest of you locked and loaded—that German squad is still out there somewhere, and it sounds like they've brought in some heavy firepower to boot."

Five minutes later they moved out, threading back through the park the same way they had come earlier that morning. The machine-gun fire had clearly come from north of their position, so Burke had decided to head east, following Kensington Road until it reached Grosvenor Place, skirting the grounds of Buckingham Palace until they reached Victoria Street, which would take them back to Westminster Bridge. Hopefully the route would steer them clear of the German patrol and allow them to reach the Thames with a minimum of delay. From there they could follow the river until they located the plane or Freeman and the Queen if circumstances forced them to leave the plane behind.

They stopped for a short break in the shadows of the Westminster Bridge, in sight of the *Reliant*. Burke stared across the water at the hatch that stood open near the boat's conning tower, the same hatch he and the rest of the men had exited less than seventy-two hours before, watching it carefully. When he didn't see any activity after several long minutes he turned, caught Williams's eye, and gestured him over.

Burke pointed across the water at the motionless hulk of the submarine. "If we can get aboard the *Reliant,* can you get the engines started?"

To his credit, Williams didn't rush in with an answer but gave it some serious thought. Once he had, he said, "A diesel engine's a diesel engine, I suspect. I don't see why not."

"What about the controls? Can you handle those?"

"If you're just talkin' about driving it down the river, then yes, sir, I can, with the help of one or two other men up on the bridge, but I don't think I'm capable of getting that thing to dive, at least not if you want her to come back up again."

It was no more and no less than what Burke expected. He had no intention of diving the boat, at least not unless their survival demanded it and then only as a last-ditch Hail Mary sort of move, so he was okay with Williams's response.

Then again, knowing Williams's way with machinery, he had little doubt that the young corporal could figure it out if circumstances required it.

Now all they had to do was retake the boat.

He sent Williams away, called Drummond over, and explained what he wanted to do.

Drummond was frowning by the time Burke finished. "Any of your guys driven a submarine before?"

"Nope."

"Any of them served aboard a submarine before?"

"Nope."

"Any of them have . . ."

Burke cut him off. "Nope."

Drummond sat back. "So let me get this straight. You want us to go over there, clear out any shredders that might still be hiding inside the boat, and then, with a crew that's barely spent any time inside of a submarine before, never mind actually driven one, use it to make our way upriver until we locate the Queen."

"And her pilot," Burke said.

From the look on his face Drummond must have thought he was nuts, so Burke was surprised when the other man's face lit up with a smile.

"Bloody hell, Major, that's just crazy enough that it might work!"

"Let's hope so, because I'm sick of walking back and forth across this city, I'll tell you that."

The idea of fighting shredders in the narrow confines of the submarine didn't thrill either man, but it seemed a better alternative than marching endlessly up and down the streets of central London with the Germans in hot pursuit. Taking to the water might buy them some time and would certainly keep the enemy's hounds from tracking them.

Burke gathered the men together, explained what they were going to do, and had them retrieve the rubber lifeboat they'd used to make landfall what felt like weeks ago.

With the men loaded into the boat, they headed for the *Reliant*.

CHAPTER THIRTY-FIVE

★

VERONICA AWOKE TO water splashing across her face.

She lifted her head, sputtering to get rid of the mouthful of the stuff she involuntarily inhaled, and opened her eyes to find herself sitting waist-deep in water amid a crumpled pile of wood and cloth. Her gaze fell upon the red, blue, and white roundel hanging in front of her and she realized with a start that the water was the Thames and the wreckage was all that was left of Freeman's plane. That's when the whole sorry event came back to her.

They'd apparently survived, if the fierce pain she was feeling where the safety straps were digging into her shoulders was any indication. She shifted position, loosening the pressure enough that she could reach down below the seat to unhook first the left-hand strap and then the right, freeing her from the belts' hold. With the pressure relieved she was able to straighten up a bit in her seat and take a look around.

She could see immediately that the plane had come to rest in the shallow water near the north bank of the Thames. The nose and wings were a crumpled mess, but the main portion of the fuselage had remained reasonably intact. Freeman was in the cockpit in front of her, slumped over the instrument panel, unmoving. From this angle she could see that his face was above water, so he wasn't in any immediate danger of drowning, but she wasn't able to discern the extent of his injuries.

Looking downriver she could see the square face of the Tower of London looming on the edge of the left bank and, just beyond it, the wide bulk of the Tower Bridge spanning the Thames. She knew there were government offices inside the tower, perhaps some with food and water, and she knew that was where they had to go.

But first she had to tend to Freeman and get him out of the aircraft.

The twin cockpits were only separated by a narrow stretch of fuselage no more than a foot in width and Veronica knew she would have no trouble clambering from one to the other, but when she moved to do just that, the wreckage of the plane suddenly lurched sharply to the right, sending her sprawling in a heap against the front cockpit wall.

When she tried to regain her footing, the plane shifted position again, sliding another foot farther into the river.

With dawning horror the truth of the situation finally sank through her still fuzzy thought processes. The whole plane was slowly being pulled by the current out into deeper water. If that happened, they were in serious trouble.

A glance at Freeman showed him still unconscious. If she didn't get him free of his safety straps before the plane went under, he was going to drown before she could do anything about it. She knew she had to act and act fast.

Move, girl!

Ignoring the movement of the aircraft beneath her, Veronica scrambled over the short divider between the two cockpits and hauled Freeman back against his seat from behind. Blood covered the front of his shirt from a wound high on his shoulder. He groaned when she moved him, and she took that as a good sign.

At least he wasn't dead yet, she thought. Being stranded in this place alone was not something she wanted to experience.

The cockpit was already half filled with water, and it was growing deeper by the moment. She reached down beneath the surface and began tugging on the straps that kept Freeman secured to his chair. Her actions caused the tail of the aircraft to start sliding around, away from the bank, and she knew in just a few moments they'd be broadside to the flow of the river. At that point the current would yank them out into deep water where, given the condition of the wreckage, they'd sink pretty darned quickly.

She had to get them out of here!

The straps weren't cooperating, though. She tugged and pulled, but something must have gotten twisted up in the crash because she couldn't get them to move at all, never mind slip off the hooks that held them in place. A closer look showed they were pulled taut across Freeman's chest as well, so much so that she would have had trouble trying to slide her fingers beneath either strap.

The wreckage chose that moment to lurch several more inches into deeper water.

You're running out of time!

Her hand bumped up against something attached to the outside of Freeman's boot, and when she drew it out of the water, she found herself holding a wide-bladed combat knife. The moment she recognized it she went to work, using the blade to cut through the straps that held Freeman in his seat.

It was tough; the material was reinforced to withstand the heavy shocks of flying, never mind being waterlogged from sitting in the river, but she kept at it, sawing furiously. When the first strap parted with an audible snap, she turned and started on the second one.

That's when she noted that they were adrift.

The current was slowly pulling them simultaneously away from the bank and downriver. At the same time the front of the aircraft was sinking below the surface, the weight of the engine dragging it down toward the bottom.

She had a few seconds, at most, to get them out of here.

"Come on! You bloody stupid sonofa—"

The knife cut through the final section of the belt. Without hesitation Veronica grabbed Freeman by the jacket and pulled him with her over the side of the cockpit, into the water.

When she surfaced seconds later, one arm wrapped around Freeman's chest from behind to help keep his head out of the water, Veronica saw that she'd been just in time. As she watched, the tail of the plane tipped upward and then quickly sank beneath the waves as the weight of the engine dragged the rest of the wreckage to the bottom of the Thames.

Not that Veronica was immune to the current; far from it, in fact. Even as she watched the plane sink she was being carried steadily downriver, Freeman still held tight against her upper body, and she knew that if she wasn't careful, she'd be carried right down the Thames estuary and out into the sea. Drowning in the English Channel was slightly more attractive than getting eaten alive by shredders, but only slightly. She wasn't going to go out that way if she could help it.

Her only option was the tower.

Long used as both a prison and a place of execution, the Tower of London was infamous for its long and bloody history but it had the one thing she needed right now above anything else—a way out of the river.

Traitors' Gate, the only water gate entrance to the tower, had originally been built by Edward I in 1275 as his own private entrance to the castle when St. Thomas's Tower was being used as accommodations for the royal family. When the Tower of London became a prison, the gate earned its more infamous nickname because it was through here that prisoners were brought in by barge off the Thames, passing under the Tower Bridge where the heads of those recently executed were displayed on pikes. The prisoners were then turned over to prison officials inside the safety of the tower walls.

Veronica knew that an arched tunnel led beneath the Tower

Wharf to a set of stone steps that led up from the river directly in front of St. Thomas's Tower, one of the smaller buildings in the tower complex. If she could get them close enough to the wharf, she should have time to maneuver them into the tunnel before the current pushed them past.

Already tired from her fight with the safety belts and the after-effect of all the adrenaline coursing through her system from the crash, Veronica nevertheless began to swim against the current, kicking her legs as hard as she could, hoping to get in closer to shore before the cold water leached the last of the strength from her weary muscles. She kept her arm clamped tight around Free-man's chest and did her best to keep his head out of the water as she went. For every foot she managed toward shore, though, the current carried her a half-dozen more downstream, and she was soon stroking with her free arm, Freeman's combat knife still gripped securely in hand, as well as kicking with her feet to get her out of the flow of the current and over to the bank.

Just as she thought she couldn't do any more, her outstretched hand smacked against the stone wall that held up the Tower Wharf and she breathed a sigh of relief. The current was weaker here along the base of the wall and she was able to hug the wall for the last several yards as the archway leading to Traitors' Gate loomed closer. When they were parallel with the opening, she kicked out with her legs and forced them out of the current en-tirely, putting them in the calm waters of the narrow estuary that led beneath the wharf and under Traitors' Gate. From there it was a simple matter to dog-paddle the length of the tunnel, slip under the half-raised portcullis that was used to block off the entrance every evening, and then stagger a short way up the staircase at the far end, dragging Freeman behind her as she went. Once they were both out of the water, she collapsed on the stone steps and tried to catch her breath, letting the knife slip from her fingers to the ground beside her.

She didn't know the shredder was there until it was almost upon her.

Some long-buried instinct for self-preservation caused her to lift her weary head and she caught sight of the shredder while it was still a couple of yards away. Adrenaline dumped into her system, sending her heart hammering into overdrive, and she snatched at her belt, clawing for her pistols, only to find it wasn't there. She must have lost them in the crash!

She still had Freeman's knife, though, and as the shredder rushed down the steps toward her, she grabbed the knife from the step beside her, gripped it tightly, and stood to meet the shredder's charge . . .

CHAPTER THIRTY-SIX

ON THE THAMES
LONDON

THE MEN WERE tense as they rowed cautiously toward the *Reliant*. Burke didn't blame them; he was tense, too. He kept waiting for a mob of shredders to come pouring out of the hatch, and every second that passed in eerie silence only served to tighten his nerves.

Sergeant Drummond stood in the bow, having volunteered to be the first aboard. Burke had served with his fair share of men over the years and had to admit that the Black Watch sergeant had certainly proved his worth on this mission. Behind Drummond was Jones, another man with nerves of steel, and then Burke himself. The three of them had volunteered to be the ones to clear the boat, which seemed fair to Burke given that it had been his idea in the first place.

While the three of them handled the dirty work below, Corporal Williams and Private Cohen would guard the hatch. Both men were under strict orders to seal the hatch if it looked like any of the shredders were going to escape the confines of the boat. Neither of them had looked happy, but they'd accepted the orders and Burke knew they'd carry them out if it became necessary.

Let's just hope it doesn't.

Last but not least, Doc Bankowski and Professor Graves would remain aboard the lifeboat, oars in hand, ready to get them out of there at a moment's notice.

To everyone's surprise they reached the boat without any shredders pouring up from below.

As Bankowski and Graves brought them up alongside the hull, Sergeant Drummond deftly jumped up onto the deck, Jones at his heels. Burke followed suit, only to have his lead foot hit a patch of decking slick with river water and go right out from under him. His reflexes took over, putting out a hand to catch his fall.

Unfortunately for all concerned, it was his mechanical one.

The resulting bong that echoed through the hull when his metal fist made contact with the outer deck felt like the loudest sound in the entire world at that moment.

Everyone froze, Burke included.

For a long moment no one even dared to breathe. All eyes were on the hatch.

Waiting.

Watching.

Expecting a horde of ravenous zombies to come swarming out of the belly of the boat and fall on them at any moment.

But nothing happened.

The only thing coming out of the boat beneath their feet was silence.

Drummond looked back at Burke and when the other man nodded his head, he stepped quietly over to the hatch. He hesitated the barest fraction of a second and then poked his head quickly over the opening before ducking back again.

He gave it a heartbeat and then did it again, this time more slowly.

A hand signal told the others he wasn't seeing anything significant.

Jones helped Burke to his feet, and the two men joined Drummond by the hatch. The ship's battery was still good, for there were lights on in the bridge compartment at the bottom of the ladder. Cautiously, one after another, they started down.

This is it, Burke thought, as Drummond made his way down the ladder. *We're trapped in the narrowest of tubes without room to maneuver or even bring a weapon to bear. If they have any sense at all, this is where they'll jump us.*

Drummond stepped off the ladder, no worse for wear than he'd been seconds before. Burke watched him glance both ways, fore and aft. Then came the signal for the others to join him.

His heart hammering in his throat, Burke followed.

The first thing he saw as he stepped off the ladder was the eviscerated body of Captain Wattley. His flesh had been eaten right off his bones, but it was clear from the uniform he wore just who it was. Burke felt a pang of regret; differences about the mission aside, the gruff sailor had been a good man.

A few other bodies lay where they had fallen, most of them unrecognizable thanks to the way the shredders had torn at the exposed flesh.

Under cover of the guns carried by his two companions, Drummond stepped to the far end of the compartment and gently pulled the bulkhead door shut, spinning the handle to seal it closed for the time being.

The plan was for the trio to move aft, clearing the rear of the boat before moving forward and doing the same to the bow. Sealing off the forward compartments would keep any shredders from sneaking up on them from behind.

They waited a moment by the bulkhead door to see if anything responded to their presence. When all remained quiet, they turned and headed aft.

Compartment after compartment, they found the same thing; a few bodies here and there, but no sign of any shredders. Damage to the interior of the vessel appeared to be minimal as well for it seemed the shredders' initial attack had been so overwhelming that word hadn't had time to spread through the boat fast enough to allow any of the sailors to mount a coordinated response. With the aft section of the boat cleared, the trio turned their attention to the forward compartments, only to find the same results.

Once the all clear was given, the squad set about making the boat seaworthy. Williams disappeared into the engine room, after shanghaiing the wounded Cohen to help him. Doc and Graves were given the task of trying to identify the bodies, then wrapping them in blankets weighted down with whatever they could find and giving them a quick burial at sea. A few of the men, Drummond in particular, pressed for the bodies to be taken to France with them, but they had already started to decompose and without adequate refrigeration equipment it just wasn't possible. Regretfully, Drummond at last agreed.

Drummond and Burke spent some time familiarizing themselves with the boat's controls so that when the time came, they'd be able to manage the vessel while under way. Both men were quick learners and the fact that all the control systems were clearly marked in English certainly made their task easier.

An hour after boarding, they were ready to give it a go.

There was another moment of tension as they waited for Williams to fire up the engines. He'd been right though—a diesel was a diesel—and the big engine came alive with a grumble that vibrated through the whole boat.

Once the cheering stopped, Burke gave the order to haul up the anchors and get under way. They started out with the engines at less than one-eighth speed, moving out from under the shadow of the bridge and giving them time to get used to how the boat handled. They had one scary moment when they scraped hard against something submerged in the water, but the bulkheads all held and the inexperienced crew breathed a sigh of relief.

Since they weren't familiar with all the complexities of the boat, they kept things simple. Burke stood over the open hatch in the conning tower, shouting commands down to Cohen, who stood at the base of the ladder and relayed them to Drummond, who was sitting in the driver's seat. Next to the sergeant, in the planesman's chair, sat Graves. While Drummond kept them on the straight and narrow, it was Graves's job to keep them on the surface and running level. Jones and Doc Bankowski were out on deck with Burke, scouring both banks for signs of the downed aircraft. Jones was using the spotting scope off his rifle while Doc had a pair of binoculars they'd found in the captain's cabin.

Yard by yard, they made their way down the river.

Burke hadn't forgotten about Charlie and his team of German commandos, so he made it his mission to watch for signs of the enemy as well as for the missing aircraft. It wasn't an easy task; much of the city around them was in ruins thanks to the German bombing campaign that had coincided with the release of the gas, and shadows loomed everywhere amid the rubble. Between that and the shredders wandering the streets, it made Burke's job a tough one.

They had moved about a half mile downstream and were just passing beneath Waterloo Bridge when Doc gave a shout.

"I think I see something! Over there!"

He was pointing to something on the south bank of the river, behind the remains of the National Theatre, so Burke shouted down orders to hold their position so they could investigate. Williams was quick to respond and the boat came to a halt in the shadow of the bridge above.

Burke and Jones quickly moved to Doc's side.

"What have you got?" the major asked.

"Over there," Doc said, pointing. "Behind that building with the slate roof; is that the tail of an aircraft?"

Burke didn't see it until Jones handed him the spotting scope, at which point the round curve of the airplane's rudder came into view. But their initial excitement was quite squelched when Jones spotted a section of the wing nearby with the German cross boldly emblazoned upon it.

It was an aircraft, all right, just not the one they were looking for.

"Must have been playing escort for the airships that conducted the bombing raid," Burke said.

"One less pilot to be shooting at our boys at least," Jones replied, "and good riddance to him."

Burke nodded; it was a sentiment with which he could easily agree.

The trio turned around, intent on returning to their respective positions, when something dropped onto the deck of the boat from the bridge above. It rolled for a moment then came to rest against the deck gun about ten feet in front of them.

Burke recognized it immediately.

He'd spent years in the trenches and knew a German stick grenade when he saw one. The wooden handle made them easy to throw and the bulbous head contained the explosives that made them so deadly. His gaze immediately traveled to the handle of the device, looking for the cord that would be there if the thrower had forgotten to arm the grenade, hoping against hope that it was still there, but of course they couldn't get that lucky.

Time slowed to an imperceptible crawl, every second feeling like an eternity as they ticked by in Burke's mind.

One.

Burke started forward, his mouth opening to shout a warning.

Two.

Someone shoved past him, kicking him aside, as a voice shouted in his ear.

"Grenade!" Jones cried, as he pushed past Burke and threw himself atop the explosive, smothering it with his body.

Three . . .

CHAPTER THIRTY-SEVEN

TRAITORS' GATE
LONDON

QUEEN VERONICA MET the shredder's charge head-on, letting it get close enough for it to lunge toward her, arms outstretched, before she stepped nimbly to one side, bringing Freeman's knife up in a vicious side-arm blow that struck the creature in the hollow of the throat and tore upward through the roof of its mouth and into its brain.

It was dead before it hit the ground at her feet.

Heart pounding in her chest, Veronica bent over, wiped the knife blade clean on the thing's ragged clothes, and then kicked the shredder down the steps past Freeman into the water where it quickly sank from view.

She bent over, trying to catch her breath, when she suddenly remembered the philosopher's stone. She'd forgotten all about it in the excitement of the crash and their escape from the river. She was relieved when, quickly checking her satchel, she could found it still safely inside.

Noise to her right caused her to look up in time to spot five more shredders headed in her direction. They were still a long way off, but there was no doubt that they had seen her and weren't inclined to give her a free pass through their territory. She estimated she had ten minutes, maybe less, to find somewhere secure or she was going to be facing several of them at once.

She moved back down the staircase until she stood a few steps below Freeman, then used the leverage the position gave her to get him up over her shoulder. He was still unconscious, which kept him from struggling against her but made him feel fifty pounds heavier than he really was, and she staggered for the first few steps before she found her footing. Climbing the remaining steps to the walkway above, she glanced about hurriedly, desperate for a solution.

The shredders on her left were definitely closer, and now there were a few coming toward her from the opposite side as well. That left her with only one valid option.

She spun around and moved quickly for the entrance to St. Thomas's Tower.

The door was wooden and heavy and for a moment she thought it might be locked, but she backed up and kicked it once, twice, and then the door popped open, the wood having swelled a bit in the heat.

Until recently, St. Thomas's Tower held the Irish spy Robert Casement; Veronica knew because it had been part of her duties to occasionally visit the man. Her father had hoped that Casement might let some important detail of his activities slip in the hope of impressing a beautiful girl like the Crown princess, but Veronica knew within seconds of meeting the man that he had no interest in women, pretty or otherwise. Still, a duty was a duty and she'd faithfully visited the man until six months ago, when he'd been executed for treason against the Crown. In Veronica's eyes he'd been a nasty, bitter man and she hadn't been sorry to see him go, though the circumstances of his departure weren't something she was all that comfortable with even now.

The benefit of having spent time in the tower was that she

knew the layout of the place with a fair degree of accuracy, which was why she knew that the great room she entered after coming through the door wasn't good enough for what was to come. It had once served as Edward I's audience chamber, a place where he would receive visiting nobles or spend time with the poor he governed. There were too many windows with nothing but blown glass and flimsy wooden shutters to protect them, never mind a fireplace with a chimney wide enough to allow two men to come down it at the same time.

No, she needed something smaller and more defensible.

Thankfully, she knew just such a place.

At the back of the audience chamber was a small room that had seen use as everything from a wine cellar to a meditation chamber. What made it so attractive was the fact that it had no windows to speak of, just four stone walls, plus a very thick door that could be barred to prevent entry. It was just the kind of place they could hunker down and wait for Burke to rescue them.

If Burke even comes to get you, her conscience replied.

Shut up! she argued with herself. *Of course he's coming.*

This time that voice in the back of her head was silent.

She moved across the audience chamber, kicked open the door to the storeroom, placed Major Freeman on the floor, and hurriedly turned back toward the door.

On the far side of the audience chamber, directly opposite the storeroom, she saw a shadow darken the doorway.

The shredders had caught up with her!

Stifling a cry of desperation, Veronica flung herself across the room to the doorway and desperately began to push the heavy oak door shut again.

She had it halfway closed when the shredder on the far side of the room spotted her.

Their gazes met.

The shredder suddenly gave a weird, howling shriek and then rushed toward her, moving so quickly that it might have caught her if she hadn't chosen that moment to throw her full weight against the door and slam the heavy crossbeam into place the second the door clicked shut.

On the other side of the barrier, the shredder howled in frustration. It was not a pleasant sound.

To take her mind off it, Veronica went back over to Freeman's side, determined to take a look at his shoulder.

She rolled him on his side and then used his knife to cut his shirt away. She'd been right; the bullet had entered in the front but seemed to have gotten caught up on something as it came through his body, for there was no exit wound. How he'd managed to get the plane down safely with a bullet lodged in him she didn't know, but that didn't make her any less thankful. Blood was still trickling out of the wound, which wasn't a good sign. Veronica knew she was going to have to do something about it if Freeman was going to survive.

She hunted around the odds and ends stored in the room until she came up with some cloth to use as a bandage and a bottle of brandy to clean the wound. Freeman was still out of it, which was probably for the best. She had to dig the bullet out of his shoulder and didn't know how squeamish he might be.

Better an unconscious patient than one fighting your every move, she thought.

She doused her hands and his knife with the brandy, then she did the same for the entry wound in the front of his shoulder.

He didn't even flinch, which was not a good sign.

She felt around in the wound with fingers until she'd located the edge of the bullet and then used the tip of the knife to pry it out. She poured more brandy into the wound, washing it out as thoroughly as she could, then created a compress and secured it in place with some makeshift bandages.

As she was finishing she noticed a rhythmic thumping in the background. It had been too faint to hear while she'd been concentrating so intently, but now that the hard part was over she heard it quite clearly.

Thump, thump, thump.

She got up from where she'd been working and walked over to the door.

The closer she got, the more the door seemed to radiate a palpable sense of evil. By the time she stood right next to it, the hair on her arms and the back of her neck was standing on end and she was almost overwhelmed with the malevolence that exuded from the other side.

She could imagine them out there, the shredders that had been chasing her, pressed up against the door, waiting for her to make a mistake.

What was it the Americans said? So far they were shit out of luck!

She couldn't agree more.

Veronica checked the brace one more time, reassuring herself there was no way for the shredders to get into the room, and she then went back to worrying about when Burke was going to show up.

It had better be soon, she thought.

CHAPTER THIRTY-EIGHT

BURKE WOULD NEVER forget that last second, never forget that look on Jones's face.

The corporal's dive put him on his stomach, with his head turned in Burke's direction, and in that last second the sharpshooter flashed his trademark grin at his commanding officer.

What's a guy gonna do? that grin seemed to say.

Burke methodically identified that dull crump that sounded from beneath Jones's body as the detonator cap going off, a cruel, ugly sound followed by a larger blast milliseconds later that flung Jones away like a rag doll and knocked Burke off his feet and sent him sliding down the deck of the *Reliant,* where he bowled over Bankowski, who was shielded the most from the blast by his position at the rear of the group. The two men tumbled to a halt, smoke and the stench of burnt flesh in the air, their thoughts dazed and confused.

It might have ended right there had the riflemen on the bridge above them been better shots.

The two of them were caught dead to rights, and once they were taken out it should have been a simple matter for the sharp-shooters to pick off anyone charging up to the deck from the interior of the submarine. But whether it was due to the angle they were shooting from or some unexpected jittering in their undead flesh, the shots were all too high or fell short of Bankowski and Burke, giving them time to gather their wits about them.

Bullets whipped and whined through the air as first Doc Bankowski and then Burke began to return fire. From where he knelt on the deck Burke could see at least a dozen commandos on the bridge above, their dark uniforms stark against the sky. Several leaned over the side of the bridge, firing at them, while others readied something in the background. Burke wasn't certain exactly what that something was, but it didn't take too much imagination to presume it was a heavy support weapon of some kind. A machine gun like that which had been used against the Queen's plane or perhaps something more man-portable like a mortar. Either way they were going to be in serious trouble if they were still sitting here on the deck when the enemy got whatever it was up and working.

Another potato masher grenade came tumbling through the air, but this one skipped off the decking and disappeared beneath the surface of the Thames before detonating, leaving the two men on the deck unscathed.

"We need to get below!" Burke shouted, only realizing how badly his hearing had been disrupted by the earlier blast when his voice sounded to him like it was coming through a bucket of cotton. He couldn't imagine how it must have sounded to Bankowski.

Whether he heard him or not, the Doc had apparently come to the same conclusion as Burke, however, for he pointed at the open hatchway then looked at the major, a questioning look on his face.

Burke nodded a very emphatic yes.

Ropes suddenly came whistling down from above and Burke understood that there was only one reason for them being there. They weren't going to be alone for much longer; if they were going, now was the time.

As if on cue the two men broke into a run, firing as they went. There was no room on the narrow deck for them to dodge without falling over the sides so the best they could do was charge straight ahead and hope that they made it to the hatch before an enemy bullet found them.

By some miracle, they reached the hatch uninjured and practically fell down the ladder together, Burke making sure to haul the hatch closed in their wake.

From their tangled heap at the bottom of the ladder, he shouted, "Dive the boat!"

Drummond stared at them from his position in the pilot's chair, the grease and dust smeared across his cheek now bisected by a slowly dribbling trail of blood where he'd apparently banged his head.

"Wh . . . wh . . . what?" he stammered, his ears no doubt ringing as loudly as Burke's from the echo of the explosions against the boat's hull.

Burke stared him dead in the eye, said it again, slower this time in case Drummond needed to read his lips, and used his hand to simulate a diving motion.

"Dive the boat!"

That must have done it, for Drummond's eyes got wide as recognition dawned. He dove for the controls as the sound of boots ringing out against the deck above their heads sang through the hull.

The German commandos were aboard the boat!

The sound galvanized the rest of the men into action. Orders were shouted through the talk box to Williams in the engine room while Graves began dumping ballast out of the tanks in preparation for the dive. Urgency gripped them in an iron fist; if the Germans blew open the hatch before they could get beneath the surface, they would be left fighting hand to hand inside the narrow confines of the sub's hull.

The engine spun up and the plane of the boat began to dip downward as Graves worked to get them below the surface as quickly as possible. Not being submariners, it didn't occur to anyone to think about the depth of the river until the bow of the boat began dredging its way along the river bottom. A sliding, grinding sound filled the boat and more than one pair of eyes frantically sought out the seams in the hull around them, praying that they would hold against the pressure of both the impact and the water.

"Level off!" Burke shouted, as he finally managed to extract himself from the tangled heap in which he'd fallen and rushed to Graves's side. Between the two of them they hauled back on the control levers that controlled the plane of the boat, fighting the momentum the boat had built up, and there were several long anxious moments before the noise stopped and the boat leveled out.

Their relief was short-lived, however. No sooner had the sound of the hull grinding against the river bottom stopped than another sound could be heard.

A rhythmic knocking on the hatch.

Knocking that was coming from outside of the boat.

"Bloody hell!" Drummond said into the stunned silence, and every living man aboard that boat agreed with him.

The dead didn't need to breathe.

The Germans were still out there.

And they wanted in.

A sudden image of several of the zombielike commandos clinging to the hatch, unaffected by the cold or the environment, as the sub dove for the bottom came to mind and Burke shivered in his boots.

How the hell do you fight an enemy like that? he thought.

When the answer came to him, it was in a voice that sounded suspiciously like Jones. *Relentlessly, that's how.*

Right. If there was anything that Burke was good at, not giving up until the fight was over was certainly it. And they had a long way to go in this one.

The reminder snapped him back into action.

He put on a confidence he didn't feel and faced the others.

"Graves, get us on the surface. Drummond, I want you and"—he almost said Jones, stopping himself only at the last moment—"Cohen with me by the hatch. If we don't knock them free as we surface, we'll open the hatch and give them a blast from the Tommys to force them back and then finish them as necessary. Everyone with me?"

Cohen looked a little green, though that might have been from the head wound he'd sustained back at the museum. Burke tried not to think about it too much. Drummond would hold up his end of things, and that would have to be enough.

Moments later Graves signaled that they'd broken through the surface and Burke ordered the engines to idle. The men moved into position as instructed, with Doc standing nearby to serve as backup if needed.

If those things get down in here, we're going to need a lot more than just Doc to stop them, Burke thought, but he kept the determined expression on his face and his thoughts to himself.

With Burke standing a few steps up the ladder, Tommy gun at the ready, Drummond climbed up beside him and spun the hatch locking mechanism to open.

There was no sound from outside; nothing tried to grab the hatch and haul it open.

Doesn't mean they're not out there waiting for dinner, Burke thought.

Drummond counted down—three—two—one—and then threw the hatch upward and open.

Burke stepped up, spinning in a circle with his gun ready.

A shredder's face thrust between the bottom of the hatch and the lip of the opening, practically right on top of Burke.

His finger tightened automatically, bullets from the Tommy tearing the undead thing apart before it, or anyone else, could react.

That was it; they were alone.

Burke climbed out on deck, Drummond on his heels, and took a look around.

London Bridge sprawled across the Thames in front of him while to his left stood the imposing bulk of the Tower of London.

He might have stood there, staring at the landmarks, both strange and oddly familiar, for quite some time if Drummond hadn't tapped him on the shoulder and pointed.

"What's going on over there?" the sergeant asked.

Shredders were streaming in through the water gate to the building on the other side of the walls as if someone over there had just rung the dinner bell.

Maybe they had.

Burke turned and shouted down the hatch.

"Port bank, as quickly as you can, boys!"

CHAPTER THIRTY-NINE

THE STORAGE ROOM
ST. THOMAS'S TOWER

QUEEN VERONICA WAS eyeing the door nervously when Freeman spoke for the first time since she'd pulled him out of the wreckage following the crash.

"Don't worry; he's coming."

She started in surprise and spun around to find the major watching her from where he sat propped against the rear wall. His skin had a gray, shallow cast, indicative of all the blood he'd lost, and there were dark circles under his eyes, but at least he was conscious and making sense.

Maybe.

"Who's coming?" she asked, as she crossed the room to crouch beside him and check that he hadn't loosened his bandages when he'd awoken.

He sat patiently through her ministrations—grunting in pain as she tightened a bandage here and there—and then said through gritted teeth, "My brother. He won't let us just rot away in here.

All we need to do is hold out long enough and he'll find us. That's what he does."

Veronica watched him, looking for any telltale signs of a head injury. His eyes seemed to be reacting properly to the light and there didn't appear to be any knots or swelling along his skull . . .

"I'm sorry, Major. You have me at a loss. I don't know who you are talking about."

For a moment he just stared, then broke out into a weak chuckle that turned into a coughing fit. When he finally settled down again, he gave her a short grin.

"My apologies, Your Majesty. I thought you knew. Madman Burke—*Major* Burke—is my brother."

Veronica sat back on her haunches, taken completely by surprise. She'd heard the two men arguing—had known they had a history of some sort together by the way they were acting—but she had no idea that they were related.

Her thoughts were on her own family, lost to the bombings and their aftermath, when she said, "It must be reassuring to know you've family who would risk so much for you."

This time Freeman's laughter was heartier and went on for several minutes, which just confused her even more. She sat staring at him, seriously considering examining him again for a concussion or similar injury, anything that might explain his strange behavior, when he waved a hand as if to dismiss her unvoiced thoughts.

"I'm sorry, Your Majesty, truly I am. You have no idea how ironic your comment is to me. Burke may be many things, but a loving brother he is not."

"But you just said . . ."

"Who I am doesn't matter a lick in this situation," Freeman said, reining in his amusement. "No, I could be the son of his worst enemy and he'd still come after me if that's what his orders said. The man's a stickler for orders."

That's not such a bad vice to have, Veronica thought.

But Freeman wasn't finished. "Besides, it's got nothing to do with me," he said, glancing away with what seemed to be some hidden disappointment of his own. "I saw the way he looked at you."

Veronica was so surprised by his revelation that she didn't bother to try to hide the flush that washed over her at the thought of Burke's possible affection. With death looming outside the door, she'd be a fool not to admit it to herself at this point.

Hurry, Burke, she thought.

Freeman was overcome by a coughing fit at that point, chasing away any other thoughts Veronica might have had beyond their immediate survival. When he was finished, she noted flakes of blood on his lips.

That wasn't a good sign.

The bullet wound in his shoulder was obvious, but now she found herself wondering what other unseen injuries he might have sustained in the crash.

He must have caught the worried expression on her face, for he tried to smile. "Don't worry about me, Your Majesty. I've survived being held prisoner in a German POW camp after being shot down by the Red Baron, and growing up as the illegitimate son of our illustrious president. No way I'm going to let a couple of rotters take me out."

Son of the president . . . ?

Before she could ask, Freeman's so-called rotters began pounding on the door in earnest, as if to remind them that they weren't safe yet. The door creaked and groaned, but still held.

Heaven only knew for how much longer, though.

Freeman must have had a similar thought, for abruptly he asked, "Can you shoot, Your Majesty?"

Veronica nodded. "Yes. Quite well, in fact. My father believed in making certain his children, male and female, were ready for whatever life might throw at them."

"Sounds like a wise man," Freeman said, as he choked back

another round of coughing. He stuck a hand inside his flight boot. "Here, take this."

It was a standard service pistol for the American troops, a Colt Model 1911. Veronica had fired one several times in the past, and although she might not be proficient, she was certainly familiar with one. To illustrate that fact she triggered the magazine release, checked to see if it was fully loaded, and then slotted it back into place with smooth easy motions.

When she looked up, Freeman was holding out another magazine to her.

"With my shoulder messed up the way that it is," he said, "I won't be able to shoot so well. It's best that you have everything you need."

Taking it, she slipped it into her belt.

"Let's hope we don't need to use it."

He eyed her carefully for a moment, then said, "Do I need to tell you to keep two in reserve?"

Veronica shook her head. Captain Morrison had impressed on her the undesirability of being caught by the shredders what felt like weeks ago but she hadn't forgotten that lesson. She'd count her shots and, if worse came to worst, use the last two on first Freeman and then herself to be certain that they both went out with a bit of grace and dignity.

Preparations made, they settled in to wait.

The shredders had been gathering outside the door for some time now, their strange calls and odd cries an unsettling counterpoint to the constant banging they made against the door. The shredders at Bedlam hadn't been intelligent enough to make use of the tools around them; all it had taken was the sheer weight of their numbers for them to break into just about every room in the hospital until Captain Morrison and the others had managed to get the barricade system into place. These were no different; she could imagine them piling against the barrier, pushing forward continually, kicking and shoving and pounding against it, until, at some point, it would finally give way beneath their weight. It didn't matter how many of them were destroyed in the process, just as long as they reached their quarry on the other side.

Veronica knew it was just a question of time.

Trouble was, she didn't have any verifiable means of telling how much time had passed, never mind how much they had left.

At first, it wasn't too bad. When they grew nervous or the constant noise of the shredders became too much for either of them, there was always the other person to talk to.

But as time passed it became more and more apparent that Freeman was suffering from some serious internal injury. His color grew worse and his energy levels faded at a fair clip, until she was left sitting beside his near-unconscious form just as she'd done when they'd first arrived.

Except that by this point, the shredders were making serious progress toward reaching them.

A corner of the thick, oaken door suddenly splintered and buckled, leaving a small gap that the creatures tried to exploit to their advantage, ripping and tearing at it with their hands and teeth.

Veronica rushed over and fired several shots through the gap, killing the shredders dumb enough or hungry enough to show their faces on the other side of the hole. But by the time she'd gone through most of the first magazine, she was ever the more uncomfortably aware that there were dozens behind the ones she'd already killed. She would run out of ammunition long before they ran out of undead bodies.

So as the minutes passed and the gap in the door widened, Veronica surrendered to the inevitable and returned to her place by Freeman's side, putting an arm around him and holding him close. She didn't know if he was aware enough to recognize that she was there with him, but if there was even a chance that he was, then she didn't want him thinking that he was going to have to face the end alone.

And, truth be told, it helped give her the strength she needed to face what she had to do next.

Another crash echoed through the room, another splintering piece of wood tore away from the door, and the shredder at the front of the pack began trying to work its body through the gap. It got one leg through and was trying to squirm its way forward when it was crushed from behind by the others, all wanting to do the same thing.

For a moment, there was an impasse at the door.

Do it now, while you still can, Veronica thought.

She glanced at the gun in her hand and then at the man by her side.

What was the best way of doing this?

She wanted to be certain, but at the same time didn't want to make it more difficult than necessary as she would still need time to take care of herself.

One shot to his temple and then a second to her own?

Yes, that would do.

She checked to be sure the safety was off and then laid Freeman gently down on the stone floor beside her.

Quickly now, before you lose your nerve . . .

The sound of bullets ripped through the hallway outside. Veronica recognized the unmistakable *rat a tat tat* of an American Tommy gun accompanied by the sharp crack of several rifles, and she nearly pulled the trigger of the gun in her own hand in surprised shock.

The very notion appalled her—to have come so far only to be lost at the last moment through her own negligence—and she hurriedly made the weapon safe and pushed it away as she climbed to her feet.

She heard more gunfire, the shredders at the door turning away to face something behind them, and she heard a voice raised above the howl of the undead mob.

"Veronica! Veronica!"

It was Burke, of course; he'd found them.

She bent next to Freeman, whispered, "You were right. Your brother came for you. For us. Now just hold on!"

"Veronica!"

She turned to see Burke shoving his way through the all-but-destroyed door and the joy on his face at finding her alive matched that on her own.

She ran to meet him.

CHAPTER FORTY

WHITE TOWER
TOWER OF LONDON

AFTER A MOMENT, Burke tore himself away from Veronica to deal with matters at hand. He might have found the Queen, but he still needed to get her out of London and there was, of course, his brother to see to as well.

Doc Bankowski quickly confirmed Veronica's less learned diagnosis.

"He's bleeding internally," he said, after looking Freeman over for a couple of minutes. "Probably cracked a rib and punctured a lung when the plane came down. He needs surgery and he needs it quickly."

"Something you can do here?" Burke asked.

Bankowski shook his head. "Not unless you intend to remain behind for the next several weeks while he recovers. Once we operate, he's not going to be able to be moved or we'll risk a greater chance of infection. I wouldn't want to operate, only to kill him by dragging him through the ruins of London."

Burke had to agree that that would be a less than optimal resolution.

"All right then. Guess the scenic route is out. It's back to France as quickly as we can go."

Which, in this case, was going to be by airship.

Burke pulled off his pack and removed the wireless unit that Veronica had strapped there after their visit to the Round Table. Watchful of any lingering shredders, Burke stepped outside and contacted the pilot of the airship that had been circling the city waiting to pick them up since they'd passed on reports of the Queen's plane going down.

A plan was quickly devised between them. Mindful that the Germans were still in hot pursuit, it was decided that Burke and his team would immediately escort the Queen to the roof of the White Tower, the highest point in their immediate vicinity, at which point they would all board the airship by means of rope ladders lowered from the gondola above. Once the Queen was aboard, the airship would transport her and the commando team back to headquarters in France, where she would already have been had things gone well the first time around.

A makeshift gurney was made for Freeman and carried by Cohen and Williams, with Doc and Veronica hustling along on either side, ready to tend to the patient if need be. Drummond led the way, with Burke and Graves bringing up the rear. With everyone in position, they crossed the inner ward as a group and quickly made their way into the White Tower.

Over the course of its eight-hundred-year history, the Tower of London had been many things, palace, fortress, prison, arsenal, mint, and zoo, among others. Originally built by William the Conqueror after his invasion in 1066, the tower was largely unused at the moment, the armory and barracks having been moved elsewhere at the start of the war. It was a small bastion of peace and quiet in the thick of the city, and today Burke was especially thankful for that fact for it kept their shredder encounters to a minimum.

Built on the location of the original donjon established by William himself, the White Tower was a four-story stone building with narrow defensive towers in each corner and an interior consisting of three rooms per floor. Burke wasn't interested in any of them; all he wanted to do was get the group up the narrow staircase to the roof above.

The stairs spiraled upward in the far corner of the building. The lighting was poor and the passage narrow, which Burke took as a good sign. It would be easily defensible if they needed to keep the enemy from closing in on them.

Not five minutes after thinking them, Burke's thoughts turned prophetic. While passing a window on the third floor, Graves stopped and then pointed across the quad to where a group of German soldiers were just emerging into view.

"Company, Major," he said quietly.

Burke watched them for a moment, his gaze seeking out one form in particular . . .

There!

Charlie's large bulk rose amid the smaller members of his squad. It seemed the two of them would have another chance at a reunion.

Let's hope this one goes a bit more in my favor.

As if on cue, the newly made German pointed in the direction of the tower. *Go get them*, the gesture seemed to say, and Burke had no trouble imagining that Charlie's orders had been something right along those lines.

"Let's move, people," Burke shouted, and the group hurried its pace to the top.

It was colder up here and the clear weather of the last few days had passed that morning, leaving low-cast clouds of sickly gray in its wake. Contact with the airship told them that the pilot was still five minutes out, which meant Burke and his men were going to have to hold their position against the German troops until the pilot could arrive on-site. This presented a bit of a tactical problem, as Burke only had a handful of men and four staircases, one in each corner of the tower, to defend.

Knowing he had minutes, at best, to come up with a solution,

Burke chose the brute-force method, just as he'd done with the statue in Kensington Gardens. Pooling the team's resources got him several Mills bombs; he used them to render three of the four staircases impassable. Shouts from the courtyard below told him that he'd made their position quite clear to the enemy by doing so, but he didn't see that he'd had any other option. The Germans would know where they were when the big shiny airship descended out of the sky overhead anyway, and at least this way they had to defend only one direction.

"Why not destroy them all?" Veronica asked, no doubt not seeing the wisdom in leaving one stairwell intact.

Burke shrugged. "If something happens to the airship, we're going to need a way down."

Uncomfortable but true.

Please don't let anything happen to that airship, he breathed, though whether to himself or some higher power he wasn't sure.

"Drummond, Williams, you're with me," he announced to the group, picking the two best marksmen he had now that he'd lost Jones.

"Doc, I want you to help Freeman. Graves, you and Private Cohen escort the Queen, please."

"Where are you going?" Veronica asked, and Burke was pleased to see she was genuinely worried that he was leaving.

"Someone's got to keep these bastards off your back while you get aboard, Your Majesty. Turns out it's my lucky day."

She stepped closer, so the others couldn't hear.

"Don't put me on another aircraft by myself, Burke. I don't think I can deal with two aerial disasters in the same day."

He nodded, hearing the fear and insecurity beneath her lighthearted tone. "I'll be along right after you, Your Majesty. You have my word."

"I will hold you to it, Major Burke."

They stared at each other a moment longer, then Veronica turned away and rejoined the others waiting in the center of the roof while Burke hustled over to the top of the staircase.

Drummond and Williams were already at work, building a makeshift barricade at the top of the stairs, with decent fields of fire downward in the direction the enemy would be coming. With enough ammo, they could hold out here for a while.

Hopefully they wouldn't need to.

The sound of an approaching engine split the air, and Burke almost missed the arrival of the enemy, so intent was he on locating the sound. Williams's shout of "Contact!" was followed almost immediately by gunfire coming up at them from the landing below.

Shooting up and at an angle was difficult; doing so when your enemy was shooting down at you from behind a well-constructed barricade even more so. Burke, Williams, and Drummond took advantage of that fact, pouring firepower down on the enemies' heads without exposing themselves to much of the enemies' counterfire in response.

A shadow passed over them, and when Burke looked up, the airship was there, hanging over the tower. It wasn't nearly as large as the one he and the team had taken into Germany on their last rescue mission, but it was big enough to dwarf everything below it. Ropes unfurled from the gondola above, followed almost immediately by a long rope ladder. Two airman scurried down the ladder as Burke watched, weighting it down and providing some much needed stability for the others who weren't used to running about outside a ship when it was hundreds of feet in the air. One of the airmen jumped off and rushed over to the Queen, prepared to help her board. He also quickly maneuvered Freeman over his shoulder to take him up the ladder right behind the Queen.

Gunfire from below intensified as the enemy realized their quarry's salvation was near at hand. Burke could hear a commander—*Charlie, maybe?*—shouting at the men to rush their position, and he had just enough time to warn the others before several soldiers in dark, Tottensoldat uniforms came charging up the narrow staircase.

It was a slaughterhouse.

There was no room for the enemy to maneuver, and as one man fell, he caused more difficulty for his comrades on either side. The assault didn't make it more than a few steps up the staircase before it was thrown back.

Another glance showed the Queen ascending the ladder, an airman above her and the other behind her with Freeman. This was the part where she was most vulnerable, and Burke rained fire down on the enemy as quickly as he could to make certain she had the chance to make her destination without interference.

To his surprise, Graves and Doc didn't bother waiting for the ladder to be free, but had each grabbed one of the guide ropes and were pulling themselves upward, hand over hand. They were only saving seconds, but those seconds might mean life or death to Burke and his companions still on the roof of the tower.

Burke smiled, proud of his men.

He turned and slapped Williams on the back. "Go!" he shouted.

The other man didn't hesitate. He turned and ran pell-mell for the rope ladder hanging there several feet above the rooftop as Burke and Drummond poured a fresh round of gunfire down on their enemies pinned in the stairwell below them. The longer they could hold them there, Burke knew, the better chance they all had of getting out of here alive.

Not all, he thought, as the faces of the dead—Morrison, Montagna, Jones—flashed before him. The price had been high, and he vowed that it would go no higher; he would get his people out of here if it was the last thing he did.

He glanced back across the roof and saw that Williams had reached the ladder and was already clambering upward. That left only the two of them.

"You're next, Sergeant," Burke said, as he slapped another magazine into his Tommy gun.

"Age before beauty, sir," the other man quipped, even as he popped up from behind the barricade they were using as cover and put a bullet through the throat of a German commando who had stuck his head out just a little too far.

"I don't think so, Drummond. You're getting on that ladder next. That's an order."

The Black Watch sergeant grinned. "And if I refuse?"

Several of the undead suddenly burst from cover in an attempt to charge up the steps and Burke had to wait a moment before replying as he emptied nearly half his magazine into the lead soldiers, knocking them back down onto the others.

When he ducked back down, he said, "You won't. Refuse, that is. Your Queen needs you more than I do."

Burke glanced over and nearly laughed at the flummoxed look on Drummond's face. The sergeant couldn't argue with him, for Burke had said just the right thing and knew it, too.

A horn blared out somewhere above them, the prearranged signal that the Queen had safely reached the airship's gondola. It was time to go.

"They'll be coming now," Burke said in all seriousness. "Best get moving; I'll hold them off. Besides, I've still got one last present for them."

He held up the final Mills bomb that he'd been saving for just this occasion.

"See you topside then, Major," Drummond said and headed for safety.

Burke stepped in front of the stairwell and held down the trigger of his weapon, sending shot after shot down the shaft in front of him, the bullets whipping and whining as they ricocheted in the narrow space. When the magazine ran dry he tossed the Tommy aside, pulled the pin on the Mills bomb, and tossed it down the stairwell.

Burke turned and ran like hell for the ladder behind him.

CHAPTER FORTY-ONE

VIZEFELDWEBEL JAEGER WAS many things, but a tactical idiot was not one of them. Within moments of arriving inside the White Tower he knew assaulting the American position via the last remaining staircase was tantamount to suicide. He didn't have the numbers needed to force his way up that bottleneck while taking heavy fire from above. Those in front would be cut down almost immediately, their bodies making the already narrow passage even more difficult to navigate.

No, there had to be another way.

He sent a squad of troops up the staircase anyway, just to keep the Americans occupied, and then turned his attention to the opposite side of the building. *If he could come up behind the Americans...*

Five minutes of searching the other staircase left him convinced that the Americans had done their job well; he would have a hard time getting his men up any of them without ropes and hooks, neither of which he had with him. Lack of such equipment meant he also couldn't scale the outside of the tower...

... Or could he?

He smashed out a window with the butt of his rifle and stuck his head outside, staring at the building's exterior. The stone was rough, its surface cracked and uneven, which might give him the hand- and footholds he needed to make the climb. It was worth a try.

Jaeger slung his rifle over his shoulder and selected two men from the group with him, sending the others to join their comrades trying to take the staircase. The Tottensoldat had no fear of dying, so they accepted the order without concern for the consequences. He explained to the remaining two what he intended to do, just so there wasn't any confusion, and then started upward.

It was all about the rhythm, he discovered. First find a niche to place the tip of his boot, either in a crack or on the edge of a small protuberance jutting out from the wall, then search upward for a spot where he could crimp down with his fingers to hold him steady while he lifted the other leg and searched for a foothold. Once that foothold was found, he pushed upward with his leg, taking the weight off his fingers for a moment and allowing him to search for the next handhold.

Step by step, handhold after handhold and foothold after foothold, he moved up the face of the building.

About halfway up he heard a commotion behind him. When he paused and looked down, he discovered that one of his men had fallen and, in the process, taken the other with him. Both lay on the ground, unmoving.

Jaeger shrugged and continued on. He could handle the Americans on his own.

Just beneath the lip of the roof he paused, considering. Did he move forward slowly, peering over the top and assessing the situation before sliding over the edge or did he just commit right from the start, hoping the element of surprise was in his favor?

The old Charlie would have chosen the smarter option, but that Charlie had all but ceased to exist the moment the green gas had been released into Dr. Eisenberg's chamber of horrors. Jaeger didn't consider the danger, just the potential outcome of the mission. Why run the risk of letting them discover he was there when he wasn't yet in a position to do anything about it?

He chose to commit.

Jaeger reached up, gripped the edge of the roof with both hands, and then powered his body up and over the side with one deft movement.

He stood to find Burke racing across the rooftop toward a ladder that was hanging from the underside of an airship mostly concealed in the low-lying clouds overhead.

Burke's head came up even as Jaeger reached for his rifle.

As Burke raced for the ladder, he saw a dark-clad figure slip over the rooftop directly opposite him and climb to his feet.

Even from here, Burke had no trouble recognizing his former staff sergeant, and his eyes widened in surprise as he realized there was no sign of any climbing equipment; the man had just climbed the outside of the building unaided!

Charlie was going for his rifle, and Burke knew he was a sitting duck. At this range it would almost be impossible to miss. There was nothing for him to hide behind. Nowhere for him to go.

That's when the grenade went off behind him.

Confined by the narrow passage of the stairwell, the blast seemed overly powerful, shaking the rooftop beneath his feet and sending Burke crashing to the ground. As he fell he saw Charlie, already unbalanced as he tried to get his rifle off his shoulder, stumble backward a few steps. His ankles hit the low edge of the roof and he teetered on the edge.

For a moment Burke was torn between wanting to save him and hoping he'd fall over backward.

Charlie's luck went a little bit both ways.

As Burke watched, the big soldier shifted his weight, saving himself from toppling over the edge, but he lost his rifle in the bargain as it slipped from his grasp and plunged over the side of the roof.

When the shaking stopped, the two men stared at each other.

Then they both ran for the ladder.

Burke reached it first and began clambering upward as quickly as he could go. But Burke was exhausted; it had been a grueling mission and he'd been running on adrenaline for what felt like days. His body hurt all over and even his artificial hand, a little extra advantage he'd come to rely on when things got tight, had been damaged in the assault at the museum.

The ladder was swaying back and forth beneath his weight while rising at the same time; someone above had been watching and the airship had taken off the minute his hands had touched the ropes.

Still, that effort wasn't enough to stop Charlie. He grasped the rungs of the ladder before they rose completely out of reach and began climbing after Burke. As one of the new breed of German supersoldiers, Charlie was no longer hindered by fatigue or fear. He could go on relentlessly, day after day, night after night, with little to no difference in his physical capabilities. He had only a minimal need for sleep—a few hours every few days—and was only truly motivated by his need to fulfill the mission.

As a result, even with the ladder swaying dangerously back and forth beneath their weight, it didn't take him long to catch up to Burke.

Burke was all but out of weapons. He'd lost his knife some time ago; he didn't even remember where. He'd just thrown down his Tommy gun, and his pistol was out of ammunition. All he had left were his hands and feet, and he needed the former to hold on to the ladder.

Still, that didn't keep him from trying.

He waited until Charlie was almost directly beneath him, just inches from his leg, and then raised his knee and brought the heel of his boot down on the other man's head as hard as he could. He didn't wait to see the result, just brought it up and did it again.

And again.

Each blow struck solidly, and within seconds Charlie's face was streaming with black blood from the savage tears Burke's boots had inflicted in his flesh.

But he hung resolutely to the ladder and for all Burke's effort it didn't seem like he could dislodge him.

Burke wasn't ready to give up, though.

He raised his leg and brought it powering downward . . . only to miss his target as Charlie slipped deftly around to the other side of the ladder.

The missed strike nearly caused Burke to lose his grip, and as his concentration faltered for a second Charlie made his move.

As Burke began to pull his leg back up after his strike, Charlie reached out, caught it in his iron grasp, and yanked downward.

Burke gasped in surprise as his hands were torn from the rungs. He fell.

As he shot past a blood-smeared but grinning Charlie, arms and legs flailing, he felt something brush his fingers.

PleaseGodplease!

He snatched at whatever it was.

Burke felt it burn through his fingers for a moment and then a horrible tearing pain shot through his shoulder as his body came to a sudden, jarring stop.

He hung from the second-to-last rung on the ladder, his body twisting in the wind a hundred feet above the Thames.

It was all he could do to hang on.

A dozen or so feet above him, Charlie drew a pistol from the belt at his waist and looked down.

And so it ends, Burke thought, fully expecting the other man to shoot him where he hung.

But apparently his former sergeant had other ideas. Rather than wasting a bullet on Burke, he climbed a few rungs higher, wrapped an arm around the rope ladder, and then began firing at the aft section of the airship, no doubt hoping to bring it down.

DRUMMOND DISCOVERED THAT the airship was the HMS *Dover*, a British observation vessel that had been stationed at York prior to the fall of London. By the time Drummond was pulled into the cargo bay, the Queen had already been hustled off to the safety of an interior cabin and the other Americans, especially Freeman, were hustled off to sick bay. That left only Drummond and a few British airmen in the cargo area to wait for Burke.

"Sergeant!"

Drummond turned at the urgent tone in the airman's voice and hurried over to where he stood by the winch controls. Without a word the other man pointed down through the hatch at the ladder the sergeant had just ascended.

Looking down, Drummond saw the problem.

Burke was hanging off the end of the ladder, barely holding on with one hand, while a German soldier stood several rungs above him, firing at the rear of the airship!

"If he hits the rudder controls, or God help us the aether converter, we're going to be sitting ducks for whatever German aircraft we run into between here and France," the airman said. "If we don't blow up first!"

They'd come too far, lost too much, to fail at this point—so close to success. Drummond brought up his rifle, intending to shoot the bastard off the ladder, but couldn't manage to line up the shot without fear of hitting Burke. Jones might have been able to pull it off, but they'd lost him to the grenade back on the *Reliant*, and no one else in the squad was as talented with a rifle as he'd been.

The dull crack of another gunshot reached his ears and this time Drummond thought he heard an answering *spang* as the bullet struck something along the hull of the airship.

"Do something!" the airman urged.

Drummond glanced down, saw the dark waters of the Thames some hundred feet below them as they slowly climbed. Burke had regained the ladder and was climbing upward toward the German soldier, even as the other man lifted his weapon to fire again.

The airman was right, something had to be done.

The Yank was a good man; Drummond had enjoyed serving with him. He was the kind of commander who could inspire men to selfless acts, the kind that drove them forward against all odds and somehow managed to come out on top time and time again. He'd done the impossible, locating the Queen not once but twice in this shattered wasteland of a city, had managed to fight his way out of a half-dozen confrontations and deliver her as he'd promised to the safety of her countrymen. Even now he was still fighting, refusing to go down until he'd done everything that he could.

He was a good man; he didn't deserve to go out like this.

But then Burke's own words from the barricade earlier came back to him. "Your Queen needs you."

Drummond couldn't escape the truth of those words now any more than he could earlier.

Burke was right; this had all been to rescue the Queen and to fail in that endeavor now would make all their sacrifices useless.

That decided it.

The ladder was attached to a winch that was normally used to haul cargo up into the airship's bay. It came with a quick release lever—there for use if the cargo got away from the cargo master and threatened to damage the ship in the midst of a delivery. The lever was easily identified by its bright red handle.

Steeling himself against the consequences of what he was about to do, Drummond stepped over and without hesitation pulled the lever.

A sudden whine filled the bay as the line holding the ladder ran itself back through the machine and then zipped away through the opening.

Drummond caught a glimpse of the ladder, and the two men it carried, falling away from the airship toward the water below before turning away, his heart heavy in his chest.

CHAPTER FORTY-TWO

★

MID HEADQUARTERS
FRANCE

COLONEL NICHOLS WAS seated behind his desk, trying to make heads or tails of the latest German intelligence intercepts, when the door to his office was thrown open and a woman, with long auburn hair and dressed in a men's styled white shirt and pants, stalked into the room, flanked on either side by a pair of British army officers wearing the emblem of the Queen's guard.

It didn't take much intelligence on Nichols's part to recognize that he was in the presence of Her Royal Majesty, Queen Veronica.

Behind her was the Black Watch sergeant he'd sent along with Burke—Drummond he thought the man's name was—and Professor Graves.

Surprised by the interruption, Nichols rose to his feet and found himself pinned beneath the angry glare of the Queen's deep green eyes.

"Colonel Nichols?" she asked, in a tone that Nichols hadn't heard since his childhood days, and then usually only after he'd stolen a piece of his mother's pie from the kitchen counter. To his amusement, he felt just as guilty now as he'd felt then and he didn't even know what he'd done.

Nichols was never one to let his emotions get the best of him, however. He returned her gaze without rancor and bowed, deeply, at the waist.

"Your Majesty," he said.

"Don't give me any of that crap, Colonel. I'm not in the mood."

Nichols spent his days dealing with everyone from the American president to the senior brass of all the Allied forces. He knew how to move with the tide when the situation demanded it.

"As you wish, ma'am."

She glared at him over the ma'am remark, but let it go. "Tell me what's being done," she said.

Somehow he knew she wasn't asking about their response to Richthofen's latest advance along the front or China's recent declaration of war against the Allies. No, it was something else, otherwise Drummond and Graves wouldn't be here.

Drummond and Graves . . .

Ah, I see.

Still, he'd wait for her to say it. "I'm sorry, ma'am, but you have me at a loss."

She kept him pinned with her gaze.

"What's being done to rescue Major Burke?"

Nichols let the question hang in the air for a moment. Over the Queen's shoulder he caught the disappointment that washed over Graves's face; he, at least, knew the answer before it needed to be said.

Then, calmly, Nichols put the papers he was holding down on his desk and said, "Major Burke is dead, Your Majesty."

"We don't know that."

Her response was said as calmly as his own, but Nichols could hear the emotion underneath it. He chose his next words carefully.

"Major Burke perished when Sergeant Drummond released the rope ladder from beneath the HMS *Dover,* Your Majesty." He glanced over the Queen's shoulder, caught the now-angry glare of the Black Watch sergeant and held it. "And for the record, Sergeant, it was the right call. Not easy, I'm sure, but the right call nonetheless."

Drummond nodded, one professional to another. His eyes betrayed his pain, however.

"I don't believe that," the Queen replied.

Nichols focused on her once more. "That it was the right call?"

"No. That Burke is dead."

Nichols nodded, acknowledging her point. "I'm sorry for that, but there isn't anything I can do at this point."

"You can send someone after him."

Nichols's tone turned to that of a schoolteacher dealing with a recalcitrant child. "Your Majesty, in the last twenty-four hours Richthofen has moved three divisions of armor and four of infantry to the center of the front line and has been charging forward ever since. We've been pushed back nearly five kilometers already and expect to lose twice that, and possibly more, before we can stop him. *If we can stop him.*

"At the same time, China has declared war on Japan, your sovereign ally, need I remind you, and is rumored to be about to do the same to the United States, a move that is sure to pull troops from the front in anticipation of an attack on the Pacific Coast of the Americas, further weakening our position here. With all that going on, I do not have time or resources to spend on a search for a man that, by all logical reason, is already dead, no matter how much I liked him."

He didn't mention the fact that she, of all people, should have known that was going to be his answer before she'd even walked in the door. Then again, he didn't have to. He could see it in her eyes, eyes that no longer shone with anger but were filled with such an aching sense of loss that Nichols literally took a step back. He had no idea what had happened between Burke and Queen Veronica, but whatever it was, the loss of the man had struck her to the bone.

She stared at him, not saying anything for what seemed the longest moment, and then nodded, once.

"You are right, of course, Colonel," she said at last, her voice steady and calm and yet somehow full of heartbreak and despair at the same time. "I am sorry for barging in so rudely. I hope you will forgive me."

Nichols tried a gentle smile. "There is nothing to forgive, Your Majesty. I miss him, too. He was an extraordinary soldier."

"He was far more than just a soldier, sir," she said, but this time there was no anger, just weariness.

Nichols nodded, accepting the rebuke without comment. It was the least he could do.

"Good day, Colonel," the Queen said, then turned and swept out of his office as abruptly as she'd entered it.

Her visit had forced Nichols to face something that he hadn't yet wanted to face, however, and the day now seemed darker and more dreary because of it.

He sat back down. Opening the bottom drawer of his desk, he pulled out a bottle of scotch and poured a generous portion into a tumbler on his desk. He carefully recapped the bottle and put it away in the drawer; as much as he wanted to, now was not the time to get rip-roaring drunk.

Raising the glass, he said softly, "Here's to you, Burke. I hope you're still giving 'em hell, wherever you are."

CHAPTER FORTY-THREE

AT THAT VERY moment, the man that Nichols was toasting was being led from the dark depths of a train car into the cold night air. He suspected he was in Germany somewhere, but he couldn't be certain. All he knew for sure was that he was alive and in the hands of the enemy.

Burke had vague recollections of being dragged half drowned out of the waters of the Thames, of being loaded aboard some kind of metal contraption that stank of sweat and oil and dead flesh. He'd been shackled to a bulkhead and left alone for what felt like days, his wounds slowly bleeding and his thirst growing worse by the hour. Finally, when he thought he couldn't take any more, they'd come for him, dragging him out into the sunlight and feeding him some kind of cold porridge and a hunk of stale bread. He'd recognized his captors then as the squad that had been hunting them in the ruins of London, though he didn't see his former sergeant among them. He wondered if it had been Charlie who had broken his fall into the river.

After a brief rest, he'd been loaded aboard a train with half a dozen other prisoners and the journey had continued. They had traveled for a day, maybe more, before coming to a halt at their present location.

Burke found himself standing in a clearing. At his back was a pine forest, the trees tall and foreboding in the moonlight. There was a light dusting of snow on the ground, and the air was crisp and cold. Far too cold for the ragged remains of his uniform in which he was dressed.

What appeared to be a walled town of some sort filled the clearing ahead of them. Portable lights had been erected, running off a steam generator that could be heard but not seen. The lights all shone on the thick metal wall that surrounded the town and rose to a height of about twenty feet. Barbed wire surrounded the walls at the top.

Guards in German uniforms milled about, some watching the prisoners but most keeping their attention on the structure in front of them.

Almost as if they were afraid of what might come out if those gates opened.

Not if, Burke thought. *When.*

A German officer stepped out of a squad car parked nearby and tossed a cigarette away into the darkness. Pulling on his gloves and raising the collar of his coat against the cold, he walked along the line of prisoners, looking them over. He stopped in front of a hardy-looking fellow a few men before Burke, looking him over carefully.

The prisoner stared back defiantly.

"Oh, yes," said the officer. "He'll do."

Guards came over, grabbed him about the arms, and hustled over to the gate guarding the entrance into the structure. A whistle was blown, and the gates were pulled open with the help of large winches on either side.

Must be heavy, Burke thought, making note of it for later just in case he needed the information for his escape.

There was no way he was staying here, that was for sure.

As soon as the gates were opened wide enough, the man the German soldiers had taken out of line was forced through the opening and the gates were closed behind him.

The guards turned away and resumed what they were doing.

The screams didn't start for a moment or two. Once they did, however, they spiraled upward and outward, enveloping the newcomers in their deathly embrace.

Another moment passed, and then two.

The screams abruptly stopped.

Into the sudden silence, the officer spoke up.

"My name is Berhard Emmerich; I am the warden here. The facility you see before you, my facility, is officially identified as Stalag 91, but most of us here have a simpler name for it. The Hunting Ground. You will see why in just a few moments."

Burke hated the man's smug exterior the minute he laid eyes on him. Emmerich just oozed fake sincerity.

"There is only one rule here at Stalag 91."

The man paused for dramatic effect.

"Survive."

One by one the prisoners were led toward the gate and forced inside. Most times, the screams were cut mercilessly short. Other times, they went on for long unbearable minutes. One of the men in line tried to make a run for it, only to be shot down before he'd taken half a dozen steps toward the trees behind them.

Burke watched as one of the men tried to fight his captors when they came for him. They beat him unconscious, dragged him through the snow, and threw him through the gate anyway.

There were no screams that time.

Burke waited, biding his time, saving his strength. He knew there was no way he could escape out here, but maybe, once inside, another situation might present itself. He passed the moments memorizing the warden's features, determined to be able to identify him in the future no matter what the circumstance.

He made a vow then and there; he was going to kill Warden Emmerich.

When it was his turn, the guards came with their batons raised as if expecting resistance, but he went along with them docilely enough and only got a jab in the back a time or two for his trouble.

They stopped in front of the gates and waited for them to open.

When they had, the guards stepped forward, intending to force him inside the opening like they'd had to do with all the others.

But there was no need.

As soon as the gates were open sufficiently, Burke stepped between them without hesitation.

He had every intention of meeting this threat, whatever it was, the same way he did everything else.

Head-on.

Behind him, the gates slammed shut with a clang.

ABOUT THE AUTHOR

JOSEPH NASSISE is the author of more than twenty novels, including the internationally bestselling Templar Chronicles series, the Jeremiah Hunt series, and several books in the Rogue Angel action/adventure series from Gold Eagle. He's a former president of the Horror Writers Association, the world's largest organization of professional horror writers, and a multiple Bram Stoker Award and International Horror Guild Award nominee.

Visit him on the web at www.josephnassise.com or Facebook at www.facebook.com/JosephNassise